The Lost Diary

of

Snow White

Trilogy

By Boyd Brent

Contact: boyd.brent1@gmail.com

The Lost Diary of Snow White

The Found Diary of Orange Orange

The Return of Snow

Bonus content

I Am Pan:

The Fabled Journal of Peter Pan

3

This diary is the property of Snow White.

Strictly speaking, I'm not supposed to keep a diary. No fairytale characters are. It's *the* unwritten rule of the land. And now I know why: because life here is so unlike anything people in the real world have been led to believe. Once it's finished, I'll have to find a hiding place for it. But if you're holding it now, it means it's been found, and the truth about my life can *finally* be revealed…

Monday

"Mirror, mirror on the wall, who's the fairest of them all?"

"You are Snow White." I've never much cared for this mirror. It's not even supposed to have an opinion – not according to the fairy tale upon which my life is based. It's only my evil stepmother's mirror that's supposed to say what an unrivalled beaut I am. Well, it simply isn't true. I mean, there's pale and then there's PALE. And I'm the kind of PALE that makes me visible from space most nights.

I can't *tell* you what a relief it is to share this secret: you can't believe everything you read in fairy tales. The truth is that all the mirrors in the land (not to mention all the reflective surfaces) are wrong about my fairest-of-them-all status. I caught my reflection in Not Particularly Hopeful's eyes the other day, and his eyes said (you heard me correctly, welcome to my fairytale paradise), "You are without doubt the fairest of them all, Snow White." At this point you may be wondering who Not Particularly Hopeful is. You know there are seven dwarves, and even though you can't name them all, you're pretty certain that none of them are called Not Particularly Hopeful. Yet another misunderstanding about my life. There are *five* dwarves, and contrary to popular belief, none are even remotely Happy. How could they be, with names like Not Particularly Hopeful, Insecure, Meddlesome, Inconsolable and Awkward? According to the little lamb that skips past my kitchen window every morning, the dwarves represent facets of my own personality. Cripes. That's deep. Particularly for a constantly-on-the-go lamb of such tiny proportions.

Then there's Prince Charming. He wasn't supposed to arrive until *after* my stepmother poisons me, and I've been in a coma for a hundred years. As the story goes, that's when he wakes me with a kiss, and after that we live happily ever after. No pressure, then. But the other day, when the little lamb hopped, skipped and jumped past my kitchen window, it bleated something about a hunky prince on a white stallion coming into my life. "Really?" I replied. "Stop the press. We're talking in a hundred years' time, once I'm fully rested and up to the challenge of living happily ever after."

"No," replied the little lamb. "His arrival is imminent."

"Imminent?"

"Any second now."

"Did you swallow a dictionary? Imminent? I don't think…" And there he was, a hunky prince riding a white stallion. He looked me up and down, smiled and said, "Reports of your beauty have not been exaggerated. You are indeed the fairest in the land." Prince Charming isn't the only one who can look a person up and down. And once I'd made a point of doing just that – minus the smile, of course – I said, "What are you *doing* here? You're over a century early. Please. Leave me alone. I'm not ready to live happily ever after yet."

"Nonsense!" said he. "One so perfect on the outside must also be perfect on the inside. And ready for any challenge. What have you to say to that?"

"That you should never judge a book by its cover," said I firmly.

As Prince Charming rode away on his horse, he called out, "I intend to win you over, Snow."

"But why ever would you want to?"

"So we can live happily ever after."

"Really? No pressure, then!"

The next day as I swept the porch, the little lamb saw me crying. It hopped about in a circle and bleated, "Whatever is your problem?" I rested my chin on the broom handle, and my eyes went up and down as they followed its cute bounce. "My problem? At least I can do stationary. What's with all the bouncing, anyway?"

"I was just written this way: always on the move, and quite unable to slow down."

"Really? Well, I was just written this way."

"What way?" asked the little lamb.

"I suppose I'm insecure. And at times such as these, quite inconsolable."

"Anything else?"

"Well, now you come to mention it, I'm awkward and not particularly hopeful."

"About what?"

"About living happily ever after with the prince."

"Why? Is the prince not charming by name *and* by nature?"

"I presume so. But he doesn't understand me at all."

"Then introduce the prince to your dwarves. The clues are in their names," said the wise little lamb.

I began sweeping the porch again and said, "First of all, they aren't *my* dwarves, and secondly the prince is already well acquainted with them."

"Then he's been blinded by your beauty?"

I nodded mournfully, then shook my head. "He must need his eyes tested. I have seen a three-headed toad fairer than I."

Saturday

Today my evil stepmother invited me to tea. Yes, that's right, the same evil stepmother who has hated me ever since she asked her mirror, "Who's the fairest in the land?" and it lied and told her that I was. And ever since that day, she's been trying to poison me with apples. She's quite the one-trick pony in that way: apples, apples, always apples. My friend Cinderella said I should count my blessings.

"*Blessings*?" said I.

"Yes. That your stepmother has absolutely no imagination when it comes to poisoning you." Cinders also pointed out that I'm related to my stepmother. And that when it comes to our relatives, we must make allowances, even if they do hate us enough to poison us with fruit. Then she reminded me of what she has to put up with with her sisters. Poor Cinders. They give her a dreadful time.

My stepmother sent a sparrow with a message this morning. In between tweets, the sparrow read the following to me: 'I'm so excited about your early engagement! You must come for tea! And a slice of apple pie! I baked it myself only this morning! Especially for you!" As you can see, my stepmother is fond of exclamation marks. In my experience, the more exclamation marks a person uses, the crazier they are. It's really no different from someone shouting all the time for no apparent reason.

I stepped onto the porch, and whistled for Barry the boar. Barry runs a taxi service, and is the fastest boar in the land (ask any mirror). He also has the longest tusks, and they're perfect to hang on to. "Mind that hanging branch, Barry!" said I, lowering my head.

"I see it."

"Appreciate the ride, Baz."

"No problem, Snow. Happy to help out. How are the dwarves? Still whistling while they work?"

"Oh, yes. Of course. It helps to keep their spirits up. It's hard work down that mine."

"If I could, I'd whistle while I worked too."

"Then why don't you?"

"I can't on account of my piggy lips. Whenever I try, I blow raspberries instead."

Barry dropped me off outside the palace, and then trotted off, blowing raspberries (at least, I assume he was trying to whistle). And so it was with a heavy heart that I turned and knocked on the door. The palace is very large and the butler very small. The sun had gone down by the time he let me in... and had risen again by the time we reached the parlour, where my stepmother stood over an apple pie, pastry knife in hand. "Pie?" she asked.

"I'll take a rain check on the pie, thank you."

"Nonsense," said she, cutting an ample slice. "You're such a waif of a thing. You need fattening up."

"Oh," I said, looking at my reflection in one of the parlour's many mirrors. "I'm quite fat enough already, thank you."

My stepmother slammed the knife down on the table. "Fat, are you? If you're *fat,* then what does that make me?" She turned yellow and green with envy (she does that a lot around me), then she remembered her charm offensive and assumed a more plausible colour. "No matter," said she. "How lovely it is to see you! I so look forward to your visits. Come and sit beside me. Tell me all about Prince Charming. He must be awfully keen. Why else would he turn up so early?"

I sat down, and she placed a piece of pie before me on a plate. I watched as apple oozed from its sides.

"What*ever* is the matter? It won't bite," she said.

I pushed the plate away. "I'm too bloated for pie. And what's more, I don't want to marry Prince Charming. Not yet."

"Why ever not?"

"Because I'm not ready to live happily ever after."

My stepmother rang a little bell on the table to summon a servant. "We'll skip the apple pie," she told her servant, "and have apple strudel instead."

I rolled my eyes.

My stepmother did the same, then she lowered her voice to a whisper and said, "Trust me. If you have a slice of my apple strudel, you won't have to marry the prince."

"Oh? And why is that?"

"Because it's an enchanted strudel," she whispered, like she was confiding a secret. *You mean because it's a poisoned strudel,* I thought. I straightened my back and said, "I'm in no need of enchantment at the moment, thank you very much."

"Ungrateful girl!"

"Is my father home?"

"The king is away on state business."

"Will he be back soon?"

"Just as soon as you eat some strudel."

"I won't do it," said I.

"How about a nice bowl of fruit salad?"

"Are there apples in it?"

"Just the one."

"No, thank you."

"Toffee apple?"

"No."

"Apple fritter?"

"No."

"Tart, then."

"Ex*cuse* me?"

"Apple tart?"

"No way."

"Perhaps I can tempt you with a delicious glass of apple

cider? Seventy percent proof. Promise I won't tell your father."

I couldn't take any more apple offers, I simply couldn't. So I left.

It was cold and dark, and a long walk back to my cottage. I felt a pang of guilt at not being home to make the dwarves their supper. After all, they had taken me in and befriended me in my hour of need. It seems like only yesterday when my stepmother asked her mirror *that* question, and it lied to her. She told the woodcutter to take me into the woods and make sure that I *never* came back. I promised the woodcutter that if he let me go, I would leave the land for good. And that way, my stepmother's mirror would tell her that *she* was the fairest in all the land. The woodcutter must have been a kindly fellow, for he let me go. I walked for many days looking everywhere for the exit to the land, but the land seemed to go on forever. I grew downcast, and that's when I came upon the dwarves. They were on their way home after a hard day down the mine. "Excuse me," I said. "I have been walking for days, and I'm very tired. I'm looking for an exit to the land. Is it close by?"

Not Particularly Hopeful shook his head (I've since discovered that Not Particularly Hopeful shakes his head a lot), then Inconsolable began to cry. I put my arm around the little fellow, doing my best to console him, but it was quite useless. Awkward went bright red and snorted... awkwardly. He looked at Insecure, who said not to ask him *anything* because he didn't know anything. Not Particularly Hopeful spoke up again, and he said that as far he knew, there was no exit to the land. Not anywhere. That everywhere you went, you found more land. And there you had it. Or didn't. Not if you were looking for an exit, anyway.

13

I sat down on a tree stump and rested my heavy head in my hands. "Do you mean to say that I've spent all this time looking for something that doesn't exist?"

Inconsolable blew his nose, and said it wasn't like it had stopped anybody before. So why should it stop me? Then he pointed in no direction in particular and said the exit was probably that way.

"It can't be. Not if it doesn't exist. Oh, whatever I shall I do! I promised the woodcutter."

"Can you cook?" asked Meddlesome. "Only, Insecure makes all our meals and he's a terrible cook."

Insecure nodded his head in agreement.

"I suppose I can cook. I won't really know until I try," I said.

"What about housework?" asked Meddlesome. "Only, Insecure does all our housework too, and he's terrible at it."

Again, Insecure nodded.

"I suppose I could do housework. I won't really know until I try."

The dwarves went into a huddle, and they decided that in return for cooking and cleaning, I would be given a roof over my head. Apparently, I was almost exactly what they'd been looking for.

The early hours of Sunday morning…

So anyway, back to the present. As you may recall, I'd just left my stepmother's, and had begun my walk home in the dark through the woods. I was just feeling peckish (for just about anything other than apple) when I saw a trail of breadcrumbs. The trail was long and winding, and once I'd eaten it, I found myself on my hands and knees outside a cottage – not my own cottage, but one made entirely from gingerbread. I said to myself, "*Dessert*? I like gingerbread, but don't think I could eat a whole abode."

I peered in through a kitchen window. Inside, I saw a small boy sitting beside a sweet old lady. The old lady was feeding him marshmallows by hand. *How lovely,* I thought. I heard someone chopping wood close by, and hoped it might be the woodcutter. I felt guilty about breaking my promise to him, and wanted to explain why I hadn't left the land. *The land is absolutely everywhere,* I would say. *And therefore quite impossible to leave. And if you did, you'd end up precisely nowhere. And how dreadful would that be*? Having rehearsed my explanation in my mind, and being happy with it, I was disappointed to see not the woodcutter, but a little girl chopping wood. She had long brown hair and big brown eyes, and said her name was Gretel. As it turned out, Gretel and I had a lot in common: she had a stepmother of questionable character too. Her stepmother had left her in the woods with her brother Hansel, where she hoped they would starve to death.

"That's pretty grim," I said.

She nodded and asked, "Did your stepmother abandon you to starve in the woods as well?"

15

"Oh, no. She told the woodcutter to flat-out murder me." I glanced over my shoulder at the gingerbread house. "Thank goodness," I said.

"What do you mean?" she asked.

"That you and your brother found a happy ending after all."

"How so?"

"You came upon a lovely gingerbread house. And a kind old lady who feeds children marshmallows by hand."

Gretel shook her head. "She's not a kind old lady. She's a witch. And she's fattening my brother up."

"But why?"

"So there'll be ample meat on his bones when she eats him. Or so she said."

I tutted.

Gretel echoed my tut and said, "The old witch plans to fatten me up too, and then she's going to eat me. But not before she's worked my fingers to the bone." I reached out and squeezed Gretel's shoulder. "Sorry. That's pretty rough. Whatever does a person have to do to get a break in this land?"

"It beats me," said she.

"I won't have it."

Gretel shrugged her shoulders. "What can you do? What can anybody do? It's just the way our story was written."

"I used to think that way too. And then my prince arrived early, and said he couldn't wait to marry me."

"You must have been so happy," sighed Gretel.

I cast my gaze upon the ground and shook my head. "I'm not ready to live happily ever after. Tell me, is there any mention of me in your story?"

"Who are you?"

"Snow White."

"The fairest in the land?"

I shook my head.

"Well, no," said Gretel. "I don't believe there's any mention of Snow White."

I folded my arms and said, "My own story has been changed. And my being here only goes to prove one thing."

"And that is?" asked Gretel.

I raised an arm and brought my thumb and forefinger together. "That we might change it a *teensy weensy* bit more."

"How so?"

My gaze fell upon the axe in her hands, then I looked over my shoulder at the cottage where the witch was fattening up her brother.

"Oh!" said Gretel. "Why ever didn't I think of that?"

Monday

I'm back at home now, and you'll be pleased to know that
Hansel and Gretel's story ended happily after all. The same
could not be said for the witch. I imagine she had quite a
shock when Gretel burst into her kitchen, axe raised above
her head, and said the story was about to be altered 'a *teensy
weensy* bit more.'

Today Prince Charming invited me to the enchanted lake for
a picnic. He seems quite convinced that he can change my
mind about marrying him early. His invite said that when it
came to wooing the ladies his record was flawless. And that
even if he had to make an effort to understand my feelings,
that's precisely what he would do. His message said I should
fear not and *brace myself for falling hopelessly in love*, and
that if all else fails, *I should get a grip for once in my life.*

I handed the dwarves their lunch boxes and kissed them
goodbye at the garden gate – all except Insecure, who was
even more worried than usual about hitting the wrong part of
the mine and causing a cave-in. "I'll stay with you today,
Snow, that's if you don't mind?" Of all my dwarves, I feel
closest to Insecure. "Of course I don't mind. I'm going to
meet Prince Charming down at the enchanted lake later."

"Do you mind if I tag along?" he asked.

"You know, I somehow thought you might."

Insecure and I walked up a steep hill, on the other side of
which the sun glistened upon an enchanted lake and leaves
rustled upon enchanted tress. At the top of the hill, we

stopped and looked down upon the scene as just described. The only difference was Prince Charming. He lay on a blanket beneath the shade of a tall tree, his perfect head placed in a perfect palm, a blade of grass turning slowly between his perfect lips. Placed upon his blanket were all manner of tasty treats to tempt me.

Insecure looked up at me and I looked down at Insecure. "The prince will not be at all happy to see me," said he. "Of that I'm quite sure."

"What makes you say that?" asked I.

Insecure sat down and hugged his knees to his chest. "Because nobody is ever happy to see me. I'll keep watch over you from up here."

"If you're sure?"

Insecure nodded.

"Okay then."

As I approached the prince, he got up and told me I grew fairer with each visit. "Come and sit beside me," said he, "and share this delightful picnic."

Prince Charming and I sat cross-legged opposite each another. He took an apple from a bowl of fruit and handed it to me. "The apple's ruddiness is intense, is it not?" said he. I glanced down at the apple in my hand. Indeed, it was the ruddiest apple I had ever seen. The prince smiled and said, "I chose that apple for you especially."

"Why?"

"Because it matches perfectly the colour of your cheeks

when you blush."

"Really? Thanks. I think."

"Tell me," said he, leaning closer, "what good and charitable deeds have you performed lately?"

I rubbed the apple against my sleeve to bring out its shine. "What makes you think I've performed any good and charitable deeds?"

"One as fair as you must have charity in her heart."

"Really? Well..."

"Come now, my love, there's no need to be coy about your charitable deeds."

I took a bite out of the apple. As I chewed I said, "I presume my stepmother didn't provide the fruit for this picnic?"

Prince Charming's eyes opened wide, and they filled with wonder. "Not only are you the fairest in the land, you also possess the wisdom of kings."

With a mouthful of apple it wasn't easy to talk, but I did my best. "Are you 'elling me that eye step-um gave 'ou this apple?"

"Yes, my darling. She insisted on supplying all the fruit for our picnic."

I spat out the apple. As I picked bits of it out of his hair and lap, I said, "In the future, if my stepmother offers you fruit... say no."

"But why, my love?"

"She's been trying to poison me with it for years."

"With *fruit*?"

"Apples, to be precise."

"I can't believe *anyone* would wish to harm even a hair on your fair head."

"Believe it."

"I don't want to believe it."

"You must believe it."

"But what if I can't believe it?"

"Then you must try harder."

"But why apples, my darling?"

I shrugged up my heavy shoulders. "Maybe she's just written that way." Prince Charming stood up and hurled the fruit bowl into the enchanted lake. Moments later, a great many fish floated to its surface, all in deep comas from which they would never awaken – well, not unless kissed by a prince who wanted to live happily ever after with a fish. I thought about how unlikely this was, and sighed.

Prince Charming sat down again. "Now," said he, "you were about to tell me of your charitable deeds?"

"But why should I?"

Prince Charming leaned back on the palms of his hands. "I have been led to believe that talking of your charitable deeds will fill you with pride, and make you feel less insecure."

I leaned back on my own palms. "Fat to no chance of that," said I.

"All the same, please indulge me."

"Alright. I helped a brother and sister in the woods yesterday. Does that count?"

"I knew it! One so fair must carry out at least *one* charitable deed every single day."

"If you say so."

"Tell me of these fortunate siblings whose paths crossed your own, my dearest, most charitable darling."

"I simply had to help them."

"Oh, my darling!"

"We had such a lot in common."

"How so?"

"They have a stepmother of questionable character too."

"So how did you come upon the unfortunate brother and sister?"

"Their names were Hansel and Gretel. I came upon Gretel chopping wood. She told me how a witch was fattening her brother for her cooking pot."

The prince looked suitably concerned and said, "Whatever does a person have to do to get a break in this land?"

"Tell me about it."

"So what did you do?" asked the prince.

"Well, I knew I had to change their story, as mine had been changed."

"And?"

"And I considered the options available to me."

"Very wise, my love, very wise indeed. And these options were?"

"Pretty scarce, actually. There was a barn filled to bursting with marshmallows, a well filled with chocolate syrup, and a young girl with a grudge... and armed with an axe."

The prince twirled his moustache and looked very pleased with himself. "Say no more," said he. "It's clear that your plan involved marshmallows and chocolate syrup."

Tuesday

Yesterday, when I described the crime scene that Gretel had created in the witch's kitchen, the prince turned quite pale. I imagined he'd quite fallen out of love with me, but alas, when I asked him if this were true, he looked once again like a love-sick puppy and said, "When faced with evil witches who eat children, charitable solutions are not always possible."

"You're not wrong, and…"

The prince held up a palm. I'm no palm reader, but even I could read that palm. *Pipe down and let me speak*, it said. The prince smiled, and then finished what he was saying using words, "If there had been a way to escape using only chocolate syrup and marshmallows, then you would have found one. Of this I am convinced, my love."

I thought about that for a moment and nodded. "I suppose we *could* have thrown the witch down her well and drowned her in chocolate syrup. Oh! Or we could have locked her up in her barn with *nothing* to eat but marshmallows. She'd have grown fatter and fatter and eventually burst. A proper taste of her own medicine. Or…" The prince raised his other palm, and with both palms now raised, I imagined he wanted to play pat-a-cake. While we played, he told me that while he appreciated my ingenuity, he'd quite heard enough alternative endings for the witch.

Anyway, today I'm going to visit my friend Cinderella. I

expect you've heard of Cinders. Her story is as well-known as my own, and like me she is supposed to go through a terrible time before her Prince Charming rescues her. I rode over to her palace on Barry the boar. As Barry trotted through the forest, I said, "Is everything okay, Barry?"

"I mustn't grumble," said he.

"Only you seem slower than usual."

"I never was the brightest boar in the land."

"That's not what I meant. The spring has quite gone out of your trot. It's my fault, isn't it? I've grown fat."

Barry shook his head. "Is Cinderella expecting you?"

"Oh, yes."

"Only she generally has a lot of palace-work to get through," said Barry.

"Don't I know it."

Barry snorted. "I can't imagine Cinderella complaining much if her Prince Charming arrived early and wanted to live happily ever after."

"*What* did you just say, Barry?"

"I said I can't imagine Cinderella complaining if her Prince Charming turned up early. Not with her working her fingers to the bone every day."

"Barry! You've just given me a brilliant idea! The solution to both mine and Cinderella's woes."

"How so?"

"All I need do is get my Prince Charming to fall in love with Cinderella. That way, I'll have time to sort out my issues, and Cinders can live happily ever after right away. Do you think my plan might work?"

"It might. I hear that Cinderella scrubs up pretty well. And one Prince Charming is just like any other. There's a factory that makes them. And I hear they're pretty easy to put together."

"And why is that?"

"Because they're only one-dimensional characters. Gallant and charming."

I yawned. "That sums up my own Prince Charming to a tee, Barry."

"There you have it, then."

"There I have it."

Barry dropped me off at a side entrance to the palace, and I slipped inside unnoticed. I expect you've heard about Cinderella's sisters: ugly by name and ugly by nature. They don't allow Cinderella to have a social life. What's more, the palace is huge, which means there's always a room in need of scrubbing. But in many ways that's quite handy, as all I have to do to find her is follow the smell of bleach. Today I came upon her in the ballroom. The ballroom is very grand, and Cinders looked out of place in her sackcloth and rags. She was halfway along the ballroom's floor on her hands and knees, scrubbing for all she was worth. I took off my shoes and tiptoed up behind her. "Surprise!" I said.

"Argh!" she cried, and fell flat on her face.

"Do not be alarmed," I whispered. "It's only me. Your good friend, Snow."

She sat for a minute with birds circling her head, and slowly her senses returned. "*Snow*?" said she.

"Hello, Cinders."

She glanced about fretfully. "Do my sisters know you're here? Only, if they find out I have a visitor they will punish me."

"Fear not, good friend of mine. Your sisters' carriage was not on the palace forecourt."

This news cheered Cinders no end. She stood up and extended a hand for me to shake. "Why the formal greeting?" I asked.

"I'm just so pleased to see a friendly face. How are you, Snow?"

"Not so good."

"Is it your evil stepmother? Is she *still* intent on poisoning you?"

I shrugged up my hulky shoulders. "You know how it is. And you? Do your sisters still think of you as a horrid blot on their family tree?"

Cinders shrugged up her beautiful shoulders. "Just look at me. So what's new?"

"Glad you asked me that. My own Prince Charming has

turned up early, and seems keen as mustard to live happily ever after."

"Oh, you lucky thing! Then why the face like you've spent the morning sucking on a rotten lemon?"

"Think about it, Cinders," said I, looking at my reflection in one of the ballroom's many mirrors. While we waited for the mirror to make its predictable pronouncement, I rolled my eyes. "Without doubt you are the fairest in the land," said the mirror.

"Still don't believe the mirrors?" asked Cinders, scraping some dirt from beneath her thumb nail.

"Not just the mirrors," said I. "It seems to me that all the reflective surfaces in the land need their eyes tested."

"But they don't *have* eyes, Snow."

"That explains a lot. Had they eyes, perhaps they wouldn't talk such nonsense. And that's especially true with you standing beside me."

Cinderella looked at her own reflection: her long blonde hair was dirty and matted, and her face smeared with dirt. "Truly, I am a dreadful mess," said she.

"And still more beautiful than I."

Cinderella began to chew a nail. "How'd you work that one out?"

"You just are. And what's more, you're so patient with your sisters. And so accepting of all the awful things in your life."

"What choice do I have, Snow? It's just the way things are

written."

"That's what I used to think, but then my Prince Charming turned up early. And I met Hansel and Gretel in the woods. And neither of these things were in the book."

"What does that prove?"

"That we can change things."

"Not me. But in a year and a bit, give or take, my own Prince Charming will rescue me. And then we're going to live happily ever after."

"What if you don't have to wait a year and a bit for your Prince Charming?"

"But I do."

"But what if you don't? What if my Prince Charming falls for you?"

Cinders cast her gaze the length and breadth of the ballroom. "Is he here?"

"I hope not."

"But why would he fall for me? I'm not the fairest in the land."

"That's just the thing. Barry the boar said there's a big demand for Prince Charmings in stories such as these, and that there's a factory that makes them on demand. One Prince Charming is just like any other, apparently."

Cinders nodded. "Gallant and charming."

"You know, I sometimes think that if my prince was a bit less charming, I'd find him more interesting. I may even think myself more worthy of his attention."

"You mean if he was a bad boy?"

"Whatever is a *bad boy*?"

Cinders lowered her voice. "I sometimes hear my sisters giggling about them. They say they're not in the least bit charming."

"But they are gallant, surely?"

Cinders shook her head. "They are perfectly horrid. I don't understand what my sisters see in them. The worst of all is the Big Bad Wolf. My sisters say he only has eyes for Little Red Riding Hood. I sometimes think they hate her almost as much as they hate me."

"I'm going to arrange a meeting."

"With the Big Bad Wolf?"

"No, silly. Not for me. For you with my Prince Charming."

Cinders looked in a mirror and toyed with her filthy locks. "Do you really think he might prefer me to you?"

"Oh, yes. I'm quite convinced of it."

Wednesday

This morning, I asked Barry the boar about the Big Bad Wolf. "Stay away from that wolf," said Barry. "That wolf is bad by name *and* by nature. Besides, he only has eyes for Little Red Riding Hood."

"So I hear. I believe I've heard of her. Although I can't quite place her. Tell me, what ghastly things must *she* endure before she can live happily ever after?"

Barry shook his head. "There is no happily ever after. Not for Little Red Riding Hood."

"*What*? Not ever?"

"That's right. The Big Bad Wolf gobbles her up."

"Fair enough. We all have our problems. But *then* she gets to live happily ever after?"

"Not a bit of it. That's where her story ends."

"That's pretty grim. I mean, that's grim even by fairytale standards."

"Don't I know it."

"I won't allow it, Barry."

"Not a lot you can do about it. It's the way her story was written."

"We'll see about that. Any idea where I might find her?"

"Little Red Riding Hood?"

"No. The good angel who keeps watch over all good children. Of *course* Little Red Riding Hood. She's clearly in great peril."

"Funny you should ask. I spotted her on my way over here."

"Where was she going?"

"In the direction of her grandmother's cottage."

"What a relief," said I. My relief was short-lived, for Barry shook his head and then explained his reason for doing so. "The Big Bad Wolf has already gobbled up Little Red's grandmother. And now he's dressed in her grandmother's dress and bonnet, and waiting for Little Red in her bed."

"And when Little Red arrives at the cottage?"

"That's when the Big Bad Wolf is going to gobble her up."

I leaped onto Barry's back. "Go! For we must reach Little Red before she gets to her grandmother's cottage!"

"I'm uncomfortable with all this meddling, Snow. If anyone asks, you walked. Alright?"

"Alright. Now we really must get going."

Not long after, we came upon Little Red in the woods. She looked as cute as a button in her red cape and bonnet – way more attractive than me. "Hello, Little Red!" I called. Little Red turned and waved. Then she squinted and asked, "Do I know you?"

"I expect you've heard about me," I said, climbing off Barry's back. "I'm the one that mirrors take a delight in lying to."

"The fairest of them all? But you *can't* be Snow White."

"At last. Someone with exceptional eyesight."

Little Red fiddled with the strap of her bonnet under her chin. "That's not what I meant. You can't be Snow White. She isn't a part of my story."

"Well, she is now. Speaking of your story, do... ah, do you know how it ends?"

"Well, no. Not exactly. I presume I'm going to live happily ever after."

"I'm sorry to be the bearer of dreadful news, but the Big Bad Wolf is waiting for you at your grandmother's cottage... and when you arrive, he's going to gobble you up."

Little Red nodded bravely. "Maybe so," she said, "but after *that,* I'm going to live happily ever after."

I shook my head.

"Really? Then whatever is to become of me?"

I shrugged. "You're to be digested, presumably."

"You mean that's *it* for me*?* Digestion!"

I nodded politely. "That's why I'm here."

"To tell me happily ever after was never an option. And that I'm to be digested. You're supposed to be the fairest of them all, not the cruellest."

33

"I'm neither the fairest nor the cruellest. My only claim to fame may be that I'm the most average."

"Then what *are* you doing here?"

"I've come to help."

"Help? If that's how my story has been written, then what can you do?"

I glanced left and right to check that nobody was around. Nobody was. Even Barry was gone. I lowered my voice anyway. "The thing is, Little Red, I've already made one or two *tiny* changes to other stories."

"To minor stories perhaps. Look," said she, taking off her bonnet and shaking out her red curls. "I have no wish to blow my own trumpet, but my story is one of the most famous."

"And the story of Hansel and Gretel isn't?"

Little Red looked suddenly downcast. "Oh, don't. Those poor siblings."

"Not anymore," said I, proudly.

"You mean to say they're okay?"

"Oh, yes."

"And what of the witch?"

I held the back of my hand to my face and looked at my fingernails. "The same could not be said for the witch."

"Dead?"

"Very much so."

"Oh! So what are you saying?" Little Red lowered her voice. "That you're going to *kill* the Big Bad Wolf?"

"Oh my, no. I hear he's a bad boy. And apparently a bad boy is the complete opposite of a Prince Charming."

"And?" said Little Red.

"And I thought I might go on a date with him."

"Are you *crazy*? What if he decides to gobble you up?"

"Then Prince Charming is *bound* to rescue me." At the very mention of Prince Charming, I yawned. "I expect he's very reliable that way."

Little Red smiled.

"My disappointment amuses you?" I said.

"Not particularly. It's just that, if I'm to be spared digestion, and you don't want your Prince Charming, might you introduce him to me?"

"I'm afraid I can't do that."

"Why ever not?"

"I've already promised him to Cinderella."

"How greedy. Isn't one Prince Charming enough for her?"

I rolled my eyes. "More than enough, I should imagine. But if my Prince Charming falls for her, she needn't work her fingers to the bone while she waits for her own to show up."

"When is he supposed to do that?"

"In about a year. Give or take."

"That's not so long to wait. Not for happily ever after. If her Prince Charming is going spare, perhaps I can have him?"

"I don't see why not." I glanced down at Little Red's wooden shoes. "We'll have to get you a pair of glass slippers fit for a ball."

Little Red bounced a little on the spot and clapped her hands silently. "This is just getting better and better!" She handed me a few pages torn from *the book* – the ones she's permitted to read – and said I should bone up on her story. "It's only the last page that's been torn out of my copy," said she. "And now I know why."

And so it was that Little Red waved goodbye, and I went off down the path that lead to her grandmother's cottage.

It was a pretty little cottage with a thatched roof and hanging boxes filled with flowers, and a little red door with a welcome mat that said *No cold callers*.

Inside, the Big Bad Wolf had already gobbled up Little Red's grandmother, and now he was looking forward to having his main course: Little Red. But Little Red had other ideas, as did I. And mine involved the Big Bad Wolf taking me out on a date. "For the first time in my life, my fairest-in-the-land status is going to come in handy," whispered I, as I turned the door knob and went in. I found myself in a little hallway with a mirror. I stood before the mirror and waited for it to pronounce me the fairest in the land. "*Well?*" said I, expectantly.

"Well what?" replied the mirror.

I sighed and said, "Mirror, mirror on the wall, who's the fairest of them all?"

"Your stepmother the queen is the fairest. No question," said the mirror. Of that it sounded quite certain.

"Just my luck," said I. "A mirror with a sense of humour. No really, who is the fairest in the land?"

"Your stepmother is. And by a country mile."

"Are you *kidding* me?"

"Do I look like I'm kidding?"

"You *look* like a mirror."

"That's good to hear."

"Thanks for nothing," said I. "Is the big Bad Wolf here?"

"Of course he is. He's *supposed* to be here. What have you done with Little Red?"

"I don't appreciate your tone."

"You're in the wrong story. So I'll ask you again: what have you done with Little Red?"

"I've done her a big favour. She's in the woods. And thanks to me, she's looking forward to living happily ever after."

"Oh, but she can't be," said the mirror.

"Oh, but she is," said I. "Just as soon as her Prince Charming shows up."

"Can you read?"

"Of course I can read. How rude."

"Then you must know there is no Prince Charming for Little Red. There's only digestion. And indigestion for the Big Bad Wolf."

"That's where you're wrong. I'm going to provide Little Red with a Prince Charming all of her own."

"Yours?"

I shook my head. "I've promised mine to Cinderella, but I've promised Cinderella's to Little Red. Do try and keep up."

"It's quite the tangled web of Charmings you've weaved. So whose Prince Charming are *you* waiting for?"

"No one's. I've decided to date the Big Bad Wolf instead. I suppose he's waiting for me in Little Red's grandmother's bedroom?"

"You are exceptionally meddlesome."

"It has been said."

"He's in there, all right," said the mirror. "But he's not waiting for *you*. He's waiting for Little Red Riding Hood. Do you really think you're going to fool him by wearing her cloak and bonnet?"

"It matters not, for I intend to whip them off at the appropriate moment. I presume the bedroom's through there?" said I, heading in that direction.

You may have heard what they say about first impressions.

And if you haven't, they say they count. That was certainly true in the case of the Big Bad Wolf, who was lying on the bed wearing Little Red's grandmother's dress and bonnet, with the entire contents of her make-up box plastered on his face. I have never seen such red lips and rosy cheeks. As I watched the Big Bad Wolf paint the last of his toe nails, it occurred to me that he enjoyed dressing like a granny. I crept into the room and announced myself thus: "And I thought *I* had issues."

The Big Bad Wolf pulled the blankets up to his eyes and placed a copper ear trumpet to his ear. All the better to hear me with, I should imagine. "What did you say, dearie? Come closer where I can hear you." His voice sounded rather peculiar, and I supposed he was trying impersonate the old woman whose make-up and clothes he was wearing.

I folded my arms and said, "Just *look* at you."

He dropped the blanket from his face and sat up straighter. "Can you read?" he asked.

"Of course I can," said I, taking a step closer to the bed.

"Then you'd do well to stick to the script. That's right, come closer, so your old granny can get a better look at you."

I stood beside the bed and felt rather tiny next to the Big Bad Wolf. I was about to point out that he'd applied too much blusher when he raised a hairy finger and warned, "Stick to the script."

I sighed and decided to prove that I can actually read. "What large eyes you have, Granny."

"All the better to see you with, dearie."

"And what a large nose you have."

"All the better to smell you with."

"And what large lips you have."

"All the better to kiss you with."

I looked at the Big Bad Wolf's puckered lips, all smudged with purple lipstick. "No kissing. Not until you've learned how to apply your lipstick properly," said I.

The Big Bad Wolf looked down his long nose at me, raised an eyebrow, and pulled out his well-thumbed copy of *the book* from under the covers. He flicked through its pages until he came upon the story we were in. The Big Bad Wolf read quietly to himself for a minute or two. He looked so studious, I thought it rude to interrupt him. At last he put down the book and peered closely at me. "Who are you?" he asked.

It was then that I whipped off Little Red's cloak and bonnet. "It is none other than I, the fairest in the land!"

"And who told you that?" said he.

"I am Snow White, and every reflective surface in the land tells me that – well, every reflective surface except that mirror out in the hallway. So what have got to say about that?"

"That I'm in agreement with that mirror out in the hallway."

I decided I liked the Big Bad Wolf. "Your eyesight is first-rate. And you're nothing at all like Prince Charming," I said.

The Big Bad Wolf narrowed his eyes. "You're in the wrong

fairy tale, *Snow White*."

"I know. I'm not stupid."

"I beg to differ."

"How rude."

"Really? Who else but a stupid person would come here… knowing they were going to be gobbled up?"

I smiled sweetly. "I didn't come here to be gobbled up, Mr Big Bad Wolf."

"You may call me Mr Big Bad."

"Too kind, I'm sure."

"So why did you come here?"

"I came because I heard you're a bad boy. And I thought it might be fun if you took me out on a date."

"A *date*?"

"Yes. Perhaps on a picnic. With sandwiches and cakes."

"You mean sandwiches with Snow White filling? Ditto the cake?"

I shook my head. "Cucumber sandwiches. And a Victoria sponge cake. It's my favourite."

"And what about your beau Prince Charming?"

"What about him? He's much too keen. Not to mention charming. I imagined you'd be neither, and you're actually worse than I imagined."

"I am worse. Much worse. And now I'm going to gobble you up."

"No, you aren't."

"And what makes you say that?"

I placed my hands on my hips, and said in my most commanding tone, "Because it is my intention to change you. That's why not."

"Make me more charming, you mean?"

"No. Just more to my liking. So, from now on, you must think of yourself as my pet project. Understand?"

All of a sudden it went dark, and I imagined it must be a solar eclipse. Then I heard a muffled, "What have you done with my love? Where is Snow White?" *It's Prince Charming,* thought I. The Big Bad Wolf began to impersonate Little Red's grandmother's voice again, and as he spoke I could see Prince Charming, and then I couldn't see him, and then I could see him again and…

"You're in the wrong story," the Big Bad Wolf informed Prince Charming.

"A tactical necessity," Prince Charming informed the Big Bad Wolf. "I had to come."

"Why? Are you stupid and meddlesome as well?"

"To the contrary: I am charming and gallant, and have come to rescue my one true love."

"I haven't seen her," said the Big Bad Wolf, yawning like he didn't have a care in this world.

I waved to Prince Charming from the Big Bad Wolf's stomach. "So, you haven't seen my one true love …" said he, drawing his sword.

"You had better not kill me," pointed out the Big Bad Wolf.

"And why ever not?" said Prince Charming, cutting a figure of eight from the air.

"Because you aren't even supposed to *be* in this story, and I still have to pursue the three little pigs. I expect you've heard of them?"

Prince Charming paced up and down, and thought about that for a while. He stopped pacing and said, "Ah, ha!" Then he reached into the Big Bad Wolf's stomach and pulled me out by the scruff of my dress. He threw me over his shoulder and made for the door. Which was quite gallant, I suppose. If you like that sort of thing.

"Just what do you think you're doing?" said I.

"I'm rescuing you, my petal."

"Who asked you? Put me down this instant!"

"No can do. You're coming with me."

"But where are we going?"

"To live happily ever after. Where else?"

"But I'm not ready! Big Bad Wolf, help! Oh, that reminds me, there's someone I want you to meet. And if you think I'm fair, just wait till you meet Cinderella!"

Thursday

My plan was afoot. That's to say, everything was arranged. I'd told Prince Charming to meet me and my friend Cinderella at the lake, at the most romantic spot you can imagine. I'd discussed my plan with the dwarves, and Meddlesome thought it quite the best plan he'd heard in ages. Not Particularly Hopeful and Insecure said they had their doubts about it, while Awkward hopped around nibbling on a toe nail until he tripped over and fell in a heap on the carpet.

My favourite songbirds – the ones that sing while I do the housework – were to hide in the trees and serenade Prince Charming and Cinders during their date. What's more, Meddlesome had agreed to hide below some lilies on the lake's surface, and proclaim Cinders the new fairest in the land. I had told Prince Charming I would meet him there with Cinders, but I planned to hide in a hollowed-out tree close by.

I met Cinders early and made sure everything was in place. The picnic looked scrummy, and was laid out inside the tumbling branches of a weeping willow tree. Up in the tree's branches, my songbirds rehearsed and sounded enchanting. Just beyond the willow tree the sun glistened on the lake, and upon the lake's surface floated some pink lilies. And submerged below the lilies, with a bamboo cane for breath, Meddlesome rehearsed his line. I leaned over the water and studied my reflection in the water beside the lilies. "Let's rehearse one more time, Meddlesome," said I.

"Want to cue me in?" said he, through his bamboo cane.

"Right you are. Lilies, lilies of the lake, who has by far the sweetest face?"

"You do," said Meddlesome.

"You do, *Cinderella*. Make sure you mention her by name. It's very important." I heard Cinders behind me. "Did someone call me?"

I turned to see Cinders making her way into the little clearing. "Oh, dear," I said.

"Something the matter?" asked Cinders.

"Whatever are you wearing?"

"Don't you like it? It belongs to one of my sisters. I borrowed it, and must return it before six, otherwise she'll discover it missing and have my guts for garters." I shuddered. For in a fairytale land such as this one, when someone has your guts for garters, they make underwear out of your guts. "The dress is designer, you know," said Cinders. "A Panocci. From his spring collection."

I nodded mournfully. "That's why it looks as though a snot dragon has sneezed P's all over it."

"And I have a Panocci handbag to match," said she, pointing out the big green *P* on each side. "What's the matter? Don't you think Prince Charming will like my ensemble?"

I shook my head. "He'll think it vulgar. He imagines the fairest in the land has simpler tastes. And just *think* of all the charitable deeds that might have been done with the money that ensemble cost."

"Oh, dear. Whatever is to be done?" said she.

From below the lilies, Meddlesome made a suggestion through his bamboo cane. "I know of a tailor not far from here. His name is Rumpelstiltskin."

"I've heard of him," said I. "He has a loom, and he uses it to weave gold from straw."

"Yes," said Meddlesome. "But he also makes clothes on the side to make ends meet. I hear he's very talented, and that he doesn't charge an arm and a leg." This was music to my ears, as in an enchanted land such as this, an arm and a leg wouldn't just mean expensive, it would mean an actual arm and a leg.

Cinders looked worried. "I'd prefer to keep my arms and legs if possible, Snow," said she.

"And keep them you shall." I stuck two fingers in my mouth and whistled for Barry.

Barry trotted into the clearing as though he'd been waiting to do so. "Someone need a ride?"

I leapt onto his back and Cinders climbed on behind me. "We need to get to Rumpelstiltskin's, pronto. Thank you, Barry."

Barry the boar kicked up some dirt with his back hooves but remained on the spot. "You sure that's wise? Only, Rumpelstiltskin has a bad reputation."

"How so?"

"Word is he expects the earth in payment for his services."

"Not according to Meddlesome. Anyway, we'll cross that bridge when we come to it. Cinders must have a new dress."

"What's wrong with the one she has on?"

"Have you no taste?"

"I like to think so. It's a Panocci, isn't it?"

"Exactly."

"The bag alone must have cost a small fortune," said Barry.

"*Exactly*. Which is why you must take us to Rumpelstiltskin *now*."

"Alright, but I hear he's a wicked little imp."

I yawned. "Maybe so, but if he becomes troublesome, then my Prince Charming will appear and save me. We'd better make sure it doesn't come to that."

"*Your* Prince Charming?" said Cinders. "Don't you mean *my* Prince Charming?" I stood corrected. Or more accurately, I sat corrected.

Not long after, we came upon a little tower with a single room at its top, from which came the sound of laughter. If I'm honest, the laughter didn't sound particularly good-natured. Indeed, so wicked and mocking was it, that it sent shivers down my spine.

"His laughter is just too horrible," said Cinders.

I climbed off Barry and looked up at the window. "I'll have to climb up there and see what has so amused him."

"Do you think that wise?" asked Cinders.

"Do you still want my Prince Charming to fall in love with

you?"

"Yes. Of course."

"Then I have no choice." Cinders climbed off Barry and offered me a leg-up. Barry began to trot off. "Where are you going?" I asked.

"To get Prince Charming. Something tells me you're going to need rescuing."

"You'll do no such thing. It's important *we* handle this. Otherwise he'll start to ask questions."

I clung to the green vines that grew all over the tower and made my way up to its top. It was a warm day and the window was wide open. I peered over the top of its frame, into a small room with a single chair and loom. Upon the loom was thread of the brightest gold. Rumpelstiltskin was dancing in circles around it – well, I say dancing, but he looked more like someone being savaged by a swarm of bees. As he danced, he laughed his horrid laugh. I was about to enquire what had so amused him, when I heard the sound of a toilet being flushed. A little door opened and a young woman, known in her story as the miller's daughter, stooped to get through it. The miller's daughter had long brown hair that curled at the bottom, and big brown eyes all awash with tears. "I'll give you anything you ask for!" said she. "Anything but my baby! I can get you all the jewels and money you desire!"

Rumpel danced about his loom and replied, "That's only because the king married you! If I hadn't spun all that straw into gold, he was going to kill you instead." Rumpel stopped dancing and took three short steps to the miller's. daughter, whose tiny waist he barely reached. "You made me a promise," he growled. "You promised that in return for spinning the straw into gold, I could have your first-born child. And now you must be off and fetch the little tyke."

"I have forgotten nothing," said the miller's daughter, sobbing.

It was then that I climbed through the window and made myself known. "Talk about grim," said I. "Whatever has a person to do to get a break in this land?" Rumpel and the miller's daughter looked at me in a way to which I have grown accustomed: like I didn't belong in their story. And to be fair, they had a point. Rumpel was about to say something, but I held up a palm and silenced him. "Don't bother. I know. I've heard it all before. I'm not supposed to be here."

"Well, you aren't, and…" I silenced Rumpel by raising my other palm, and with both palms raised, I paused to see if he wanted to play pat-a-cake. The expression on his face led me to believe he did not.

The miller's daughter wiped away her tears with her sleeve. "I recognise you from your illustrations. You're *Snow White,* the fairest in the land," said she.

"Well, yes and no," I replied.

Rumpel narrowed his left eye and peered up at me. "What do you mean, yes *and* no? Either you're Snow White or you aren't."

"It is true that I am she. But even this poor woman, who has never even been given a name, and is known only as the miller's daughter, is fairer than I."

"I think you'll find that I do have a name," said the miller's daughter.

"What is it?" I asked.

The miller's daughter thought for a moment, and then began to sob quietly to herself. Rumpel folded his arms. "Now look what you've done. You've upset her."

"Oh, that's rich. Coming from you. How could you even *think* of taking her baby away from her?" I gave the miller's daughter a hanky so she could blow her nose. "At least you have initials," said I.

My words must have comforted her, for she perked up a little and said, "I do? What are they?"

"T.M.D."

"T.M.D? What do they stand for?"

"The Miller's Daughter. What else?" She began to cry again, so I added, "By the powers invested in me to make *teensy weensy* changes to stories, I hereby take those initials and christen you Thelma Mavis Doodlebug."

"Thank you," said Thelma, blowing her nose again.

"It's the least I can do."

Thelma looked down at Rumpelstiltskin and grimaced. "While you're here, Snow White, might you make another *teensy weensy* change to my story?"

"Call me Snow. All my friends do." I too cast my gaze down at Rumpelstiltskin, and beheld his horrid little face. "I don't see why not," said I.

Rumpel didn't much like being tied up with thread from his own loom, not even when I explained just how lucky he was compared to what had happened to the witch in Gretel's story. Indeed, so appalling was the din he made that I was forced to fill his mouth with golden thread. The very last thing Rumpel said before he was silenced completely was, "Just what are you doing here anyway!" His question was a timely reminder. I looked again at the loom, and down at the tied-up Rumpelstiltskin. "Oh dear," said I.

"What's the matter?" asked Thelma.

"How is Rumpel to make Cinders a new dress?" Rumpel smiled and, despite being cocooned in his own gold thread, and his cheeks BULGING with thread, he somehow managed to look rather pleased with himself.

"You can have *my* dress if you wish," said Thelma.

Thelma's dress was perfect! Cream-coloured and made from silk, and although fit for a queen, it was unfussy and tasteful. "It's perfect!" said I.

"But what am I to wear home?" asked Thelma.

"Have a look out of the window. Cinders is waiting below in one of her sister's dresses. You can swap." As Thelma Mavis Doodlebug moved towards the window, I apologised to her.

"By why are you apologising?" she asked.

"It's a Panocci original."

Thelma Doodlebug was clearly a young woman of taste, for she sighed with resignation and said that as soon as she got home, she'd have it torn up and made into nappies. I spared a

51

thought for Cinders's guts, for her sisters would surely have them for garters now. But as Little Red is to point out later on in this diary, you can't make an omelette without breaking some eggs.

When Cinders and I returned to the lake, I told her to lie down on the blanket and prop her head in her palm. "How's this?" she asked, assuming that very pose.

"It's perfect. You look as pretty as a picture."

"Do you think Prince Charming will find me so?"

"He's not completely blind. How could he not?" I stepped over Cinders and opened a secret door in the trunk of the willow tree. I climbed in, and placed my eye against a little peep hole. Arranged thus, I saw Prince Charming arrive on his white stallion. "What do you think of him?" I whispered through the hole.

"I think him divine!"

"If you like that sort of thing."

"Tall, dark and handsome. And a prince! What's not to like?"

The prince climbed off his horse not ten feet from the weeping willow tree. Its branches were so plentiful, however, that Cinders was completely hidden from view. Prince Charming placed his hands on his hips and cast his gaze over the lake. "I presume this is the correct location," he murmured.

"Say something," I whispered to Cinders.

"Like what?"

"Something like *Here I am! Your princess! And I'm quite ready to live happily ever after!*"

"But I'm not."

"Of *course* you're ready to live happily ever after."

"That isn't what I meant. I'm not *his* princess. You are."

"Not any more. I've given him to you."

"But what if he isn't yours to give?"

"If not mine then whose?"

The prince was about to climb back onto his horse when Meddlesome spoke up from below the lilies. Through his bamboo cane he said, "Where do you think you're going?"

The prince spun about and drew his sword. "Show yourself!" said he. He sounded so gallant that Cinders swooned, and her head fell off her palm and onto the blanket. She lay so still that I imagined her unconscious, then she sighed and placed her head back on her palm. The prince cut a figure of eight from the air with his sword (I've since learned that Prince Charmings are only able to count to eight). "Who are you?" he asked the invisible owner of the voice. "Show yourself this instant! Or forever hold your tongue."

"Hold my tongue? Then how would I speak?" replied Meddlesome from below the lilies.

Prince Charming rolled his eyes. "*Hold your tongue* is an expression. It means to remain silent."

"For how long?" asked Meddlesome.

"I think you'll find the clue in the word *forever*."

"Forever is a long time to remain silent."

"I suspect not so in your case."

"But I need to tell you something, something you're going to find of interest," said Meddlesome.

Prince Charming walked to the edge of the enchanted lake and gazed down at the lily pad. He slid his sword back inside its scabbard. "What possible information could a floating *plant* have that I might find of interest?"

"Only the name of the fairest in the land," said Meddlesome.

The prince placed his hands on his hips and chuckled quietly to himself. "I already know her name. In fact, I've come here to picnic with her."

"You think you know her name but you do not. The truth is you've never even met her," said Meddlesome.

"It's lucky for you you're a floating plant, otherwise…"

"Otherwise what?"

"Otherwise I would challenge you to a duel for casting doubts upon the beauty of my one true love. Let's face it, only a floating plant of questionable intelligence would *not* think Snow White the fairest in the land."

"She might have been, once upon a time. But now there is a new fairest in the land."

"*What* was that?" asked the prince.

"Her name is Cinderella."

"I suspected as much," spat the prince. "And now my suspicions have been proved correct."

"Really?" said Meddlesome. "You suspected that Cinderella was the fairest in the land?"

"No. Don't be ridiculous. I suspected you to be a moronic floater. It is *that* suspicion that has been proved correct."

"Have you ever met Cinderella?"

"I have no need to, for I have met her sisters. And they tell me she is quite the *opposite* of the fairest in the land."

"Is that what they say?"

"That and more."

"More?"

"Yes. Much more. They say that Cinderella's face resembles the face of a constipated warthog."

"Is that what they say?"

"They do. And that her skin is as coarse as a crocodile's. That her eyes – and she has three of them, mind – are as green and putrid as a snot dragon's."

"Is that *all* her sisters say about her?"

"Not all, no. They say her breath smells like a rabid dog's, and that the rest of her smells worse still."

"Is... ah, is that *all* they say?"

"No. They say that when she walks she shuffles like a zombie, and that when she sneezes she sneezes acid that could burn a hole through steel."

"Her sisters have not painted a very pretty picture," said Meddlesome.

"Maybe not. But it's a true picture. Enough of this talking to a floating plant of very little intellect. I have arranged to meet the fairest in the land at this very spot." Bubbles came to the surface about the lilies, a sign that Meddlesome was about to speak. At their appearance, Prince Charming held up a palm. "Say nothing, floating plant. Unless it is to tell me where I might find my one true love."

"She awaits you inside the weeping willow tree yonder."

Prince Charming turned towards the weeping willow, beyond whose falling branches of white blossom Cinders swooned, her head falling out of her palm and onto the blanket again. "Pick it up!" whispered I.

Cinders sighed. "Pick what up?"

"Your head! Otherwise the prince might think you lazy. Or worse still, drunk!"

But it was too late. Prince Charming brushed aside the willow's branches and beheld Cinders. "What is this?" said he, moving swiftly to her aid. "A fair maiden has fallen foul of some dreadful sleeping sickness!" Prince Charming lifted Cinders into a sitting position, removed his hat, and began to fan her.

Cinders opened her eyes and beheld her prince. That's to say, *my* prince. "Oh, Charming!" said she, fluttering her eyelids.

Don't flutter, I thought. *Prince Charming isn't so soppy as to fall for fluttering.*

"Oh, how your eyelids flutter, fair maiden," said he, falling for their flutter. "And what beautiful eyes are revealed... hidden... revealed... hidden... revealed." Cinders parted her cupid-bow lips. "Do you really think my eyes beautiful?"

"I do," swooned *my* prince.

"You are very kind," said Cinders, "but are you not already betrothed to another?"

"To another what?"

"To another *girl*. The fairest in the land, no less."

"The fairest in the what land, my love?"

"*This* land."

"Oh, her." The prince brushed his hand past his nose as though shooing away a fly – a fly called Snow White. Inside the trunk of the weeping willow, my own hands balled into fists.

Cinders fluttered her eyelids again. "Do you really prefer me to Snow White, then? After all, she is far more beautiful than I. Is she not?" said Cinders, fishing for a compliment.

Prince Charming shook his head. "No, she is not. The fact is," said he, solemnly, "that she is so pale that she can be seen from space most nights."

"That isn't very charming," Cinders pointed out, quite correctly.

"They are her own words, not mine. I read them in her diary," said the prince.

"You've been reading her diary?" said a shocked Cinderella.

You've been reading my diary? thought an angry Snow White.

Prince Charming nodded. "I thought her diary might contain clues on how to make her less… peculiar."

"And did it?"

"It did not."

"And what conclusions have you reached?"
"That she's meddlesome, insecure and not particularly hopeful about living happily ever after. But enough about her. You have stolen my heart, and yet I do not even know your name."

"I am Cinderella."

"But you can't be."

"Yet I am."

"No, really. Tell me your name!"

At that moment, the confusion was shattered by the sound of an alarm clock. Cinders jumped up and pulled the ringing clock from her pocket. "Oh, my! Is that the time? I must prepare tea for my sisters, otherwise they will have my guts for garters!"

"You cannot be thinking of leaving now, my love."

"But I must! For I need my guts."

"But I have only just found you!"

With that, Cinders was gone. And a faster runner I have never seen. Prince Charming stood up, then he leaned down and picked something up. It was one of her slippers.

Friday

When I woke up this morning, it occurred to me that things in the land had become a little tangled. My own Prince Charming had fallen for Cinderella, and had since been seen wandering forlornly with her slipper, mumbling about how he must find her. Meanwhile, Little Red Riding Hood's heart was set on Cinderella's original Prince Charming (when he finally shows up in a year and a bit), and Rumpelstiltskin was tied up in his tower, but for how long? He must have spat out the gold thread, because he had been heard shouting about how he's going to make me pay for my meddling – and we know how harsh he can be when it comes to payment. The Big Bad Wolf had been denied his Little Red supper, and he too was out for revenge. I sighed and thought, *at least Hansel and Gretel are happy.*

The dwarves had left for work, and I was about to begin my housework when someone knocked on the door. It was a messenger sent by my stepmother. He handed me a note that read: *You are invited to a cider tasting at the palace today at 12pm.* The invitation reminded me of my most pressing problem: the evil stepmother who is determined to poison me. I say the most pressing problem, because in my story she actually succeeds. And the idea of being poisoned with a sleeping sickness and then waking up to find that two-timing prince *kissing* me was worse than ever. I needed to come up with a plan to stop her. I paced up and down for a time. Then I sat on Not Particularly Hopeful's chair, and did not feel particularly hopeful about finding a solution. So I skipped across to Awkward's chair and fell straight off onto the carpet. Red-faced, I sat on Insecure's chair and felt that any solution would be beyond my feeble little mind. I was quite determined to stop my meddling when I sat on Meddlesome's chair. But it was upon that very chair that the solution came to me! I jumped up, went into my room and stood before my mirror. I placed my hands on my hips and listened to its pronouncement. "Welcome back," it said. "You are still, and without any shadow of a doubt, the fairest in the land."

"You are so predictable," I replied.

"Then why did you ask?" said the mirror.

"Ask? Did you see my lips move?"

"Well, no, but–"

"Well but nothing. And that's just the kind of mirror talk that's got me into so much trouble with my stepmother." The mirror made no reply, and I supposed that had it shoulders, it would have shrugged them. I tried Cinderella's trick, and fluttered my eyelids. "Mirror, mirror on the wall, if I take you to see my evil stepmother, would you tell her *she* is the fairest in the land?"

"Go off message, you mean? No can do."

"Would that be the opinion of all the mirrors in the land?"

"It would."

"That's where you're wrong! I know of a mirror that's of the opinion that my stepmother is the fairest in the land. It belongs to Little Red's grandmother – or it did until the Big Bad Wolf ate her. And I don't suppose she really needs a mirror now that she's been digested."

"What are getting at?" asked the mirror.

"It seems to me that all I have to do is swap Little Red's grandmother's mirror with my evil stepmother's mirror."

"And what will that achieve?"

I didn't much like the tone of my mirror's voice. I placed my hands on my hips. "When Little Red's grandmother's mirror tells my stepmother that *she* is the fairest in the land, and not I, she will no longer want to poison me."

"That's supposing she doesn't find you as annoying as ever. Which is supposing a lot."

"She might," said I, "but not *so* annoying that her every waking moment is spent trying to poison me."

"I have known you a long time," said the mirror, "and speaking from experience, I wouldn't be so sure."

I'd had quite enough aggravation from a reflective surface for one morning, and set off to find Little Red. I wanted to ask her if I could borrow her grandmother's mirror, indefinitely.

It was a nice day, so I decided that rather than whistle for Barry, I would look for Little Red under my own steam (that's to say, I would walk perfectly normally, not impersonate a train). And so off I went in the general direction of her fairytale story, and her grandmother's cottage, and the mirror I sought therein. I hadn't gone far when I came upon a pile of straw that had once been a house. A set of trotter prints led away from it, and close to these I discovered the paw prints of a large wolf. *Oh my*, thought I. *I hope the little pig got away*. I followed the trotter and wolf prints, and soon came upon an enormous pile of sticks. It too had been a house once, before someone had knocked it down. The pig prints went through where once a front door might have been, and so too did the wolf's. I feared the worst for the poor pig, who must have imagined itself safe inside its house of sticks. But then I spotted more trotter prints! It appeared that *two* little pigs had been chased into the woods by one wolf. *Oh my*, thought I. *I hope the two little pigs got away.* I followed the prints, and not long after came upon a pile of bricks that had once been a house. And beside the pile of bricks was a crane with a wrecking ball attached. I'm no Sherlock Holmes, but a pattern was emerging. I was about to look for the prints of two little pigs and a wolf, when I heard Little Red's voice above me. "The Big Bad Wolf has taken them," said she, mournfully. I looked up and saw Little Red sitting on a branch. She was holding her own copy of *the book*.

"The Big Bad Wolf has them?" said I. "The very same Big Bad Wolf who wanted to gobble you up?"

"The very same," said she.

"The very same Big Bad Wolf who I wanted to take me on a date?"

"That would be him, yes."

"And he has *both* little pigs?"

Little Red shook her head. "I'm afraid he has all three of them."

"*Three*? Are you sure?"

Little Red tapped *the book* with her fingers. "It even says as much in their story."

"What's their story called?"

"The *Three Little Pigs*."

"I see. And the story doesn't end well for them?"

"It did end well, once upon a time. The three little pigs were supposed to be safe inside their house of brick." Little Red opened the book and read the following: "And the wolf came upon the house of bricks and said, *By the hair on my chinny-chin-chin, I'll huff and I'll puff and I'll blow your house in!*" Little Red stopped reading. She peered down at me and said, "According to the story, the wolf's huff and puff wasn't strong enough to knock this house down."

I looked at the crane and wrecking ball. "And there's no mention of the wolf using a wrecking ball?"

Little Red closed the book. "None whatsoever. And as I said, the three little pigs were supposed to be safe inside there."

"So what changed?"

Little Red shuffled a little on her branch, and made herself more comfortable. "I watched the Big Bad Wolf erect his crane and wrecking ball in secret. And as he did so, I heard him say the following to himself, 'What is good for the goose, is also good for the gander.'" Little Red pointed a finger at me. "I think *you* are the goose he was talking about."

"*I'm* the goose?" said I, looking over my shoulder and half expecting to see a goose. "What does that mean?"

"That the Big Bad Wolf is of the opinion that if *you* can change stories willy-nilly, then so can *he*."

"Willy-*nilly*? I take exception to that. I haven't changed a single story willy-nilly. I've considered all my changes very carefully."

"That's not the way the Big Bad Wolf sees it."

"So what's to become of the three little pigs now?"

"The Big Bad Wolf is going to have them for supper."

"All of them?"

"Yes. As he carried the little pigs off, he explained to them how erecting this crane had left him famished."

"It's just too horrible! And it's all my fault."

Little Red nodded. "Look on the bright side: at least you saved me. And you know what they say: you can't make an omelette without breaking some eggs."

"You don't suppose that the Big Bad Wolf will change his mind, and make an omelette for his supper instead?" said I, grasping at straws.

"I'm afraid not. His heart is set on sausages. Of the pork variety."

"I won't allow it!" I looked up at Little Red, and she was pointing somewhere. "I somehow thought you wouldn't allow it," said she. "You should know that he's taken the little pigs to my grandmother's cottage. And it's that way."

"How very convenient," said I.

"It is?"

"Yes. And it reminds me: would you have any objections to my taking your grandmother's mirror?"

"Her mirror?"

"The one in the hallway of her cottage."

"You have saved my bacon. *And* promised me Cinderella's Prince Charming. So by all means take it. But what do you want with that old mirror?"

"It is the only one that does not think me the fairest in the land. In fact, it's very rude about my appearance every time I look in it. And that's why I must have it."

"And I thought *I* had issues," said Little Red, swinging her legs.

"It seems that everyone has them," said I. Little Red agreed, and I walked off in the direction of her grandmother's cottage.

I approached the cottage with caution, and tiptoed up to the kitchen window. Inside, the three little pigs were sitting at a table. They might have been waiting for their mother to serve them supper, but for these clues to the contrary: an apple had been stuffed in each of their mouths, they were tied up with string, and wrapped in baking foil. I thought, *What does a little pig have to do to get a break in this land?*

The front door to the cottage was open, and I crept into the hallway. As I tiptoed past the mirror I'd come to find, it said, "You're even uglier than I remember. And stupider."

"I am not stupider," whispered I.

"You are stupider. Case in point: the last time you were here you weren't tiptoeing about for no reason like a stupider person."

"But I have a reason. I'm on my way to rescue the little pigs."

"And is that the only reason you've come back?"

"Now you mention it, no it isn't. I've come for you."

"I see. So now you've added *thief* to your list of issues. Tut, tut, tut."

"How *dare* you tut me thrice! Little Red said I can have you."

"Why would she?" said the mirror.

"As a thank-you, for saving her from the Big Bad Wolf. What have you to say to that?"

"That your meddling has placed the three little pigs in grave danger."

"Precisely. And it's my intention to rescue them. Why did you *think* I was tiptoeing towards the kitchen?"

"I imagined that one so plump must tiptoe towards a lot of kitchens."

The mirror's observation was one I could not argue with. So instead I nodded and said, "I'm going to save the three little pigs now."

"Then you'd better get a move on, the Big Bad Wolf is due back any minute."

I stood straight and spoke up. "You mean to tell me the wolf isn't even here?"

"That's right. He's gone to market to get herbs and stuffing."

"You might have told me that earlier. There's obviously no time to lose, then." I grabbed the mirror and ran to the kitchen with it under my arm. I removed the apples from their piggy mouths, and all three said how they'd much prefer being rescued to being digested. They said they simply couldn't understand it, that according to *the book* they were supposed to be safe inside their house of brick. I told them that I *might* have had something to do with their story being changed. And from under my arm, the mirror piped up and said, "That's what's known as an understatement." It also said that they should take a long hard look at me, and when they asked the mirror why they should do so, the mirror said so that they could avoid me in future. As the three little pigs scampered into the woods, the mirror said that I was by far the most repulsive creature ever to be reflected in its glass. "Where are you taking me?" it added peevishly.

I'm going to take you somewhere where your opinion of me might actually be useful."

"And where might that be?"

"My stepmother's palace."

The Found Diary of Orange Orange

The very next morning, I set out on foot with the mirror under my arm. It was wrapped in a black cloth and, covered thus, the mirrors of the land have much in common with parrots in covered cages: they too stop chattering and remain silent when hidden. I had not gone far when I came upon a little girl in a blue dress. She was sitting in the shade of a tree and eating from a bowl with a wooden spoon. I went straight over to her and said, "That smells nice. What is it?"

"Curds and whey," said she, licking her spoon.

"What does it taste like?"

The little girl scooped up another mouthful of curds and whey and began to eat it. "It tastes… cheesy," said she, thoughtfully.

"I like cheese. What's your name?"

"Little Miss Muffet. And you are?"

"Snow White."

"The fairest in the land?" she murmured between swallows.

I shook my head, put down the mirror, and folded my arms. "As tasty as that dish doubtless is, it's obviously done nothing for your eyesight. I suggest you add carrot to it in the future."

She wrinkled up her nose and said, "Add carrots to *cheese*?"

"Yes."

"And make what, exactly?"

"I'm rather partial to cake myself."

"Make *cheese* cake?" said she, wincing. "Sounds horrible. What have you got there?" she asked, pointing to the mirror wrapped in a cloth under my arm.

"It's a mirror. Not just any mirror, but the only mirror in the land that doesn't think me the fairest of them all."

"I expect you're off to smash it, then."

"Goodness gracious me, no. I'm going to give it to my evil stepmother as a present."

Little Miss Muffet nodded, then lowered her voice and said, "I've heard about you, you know, Snow."

"About me? What have you heard?"

Little Miss Muffet looked left and right, checking that we were alone. "Well," said she, "I have heard through the grapevine that you've been... how can I put this? Rather meddlesome."

"I cannot deny it. But I have only tried to do right by others," said I, proudly.

Little Miss Muffet dropped her voice to a whisper. "That's

not all I've heard about you through the grapevine."

"It isn't?"

"No. According to the grapevine, you've made enemies of the Big Bad Wolf *and* Rumpelstiltskin."

I nodded. "But you know what they say: you can't make an omelette without breaking some eggs."

"I believe they do say that, yes. Aren't you worried about being alone? Out here in the woods, I mean."

"Well, I wasn't…" I felt a shiver run down my spine, then heard it land with a crunch upon the dry leaves and scurry off into the undergrowth.

"Perhaps you should consider a disguise," said Little Miss Muffet helpfully.

"I think perhaps you're right," said I. "Any ideas?"

She put down her bowl and pointed at her face with both of her forefingers.

"You're offering me your *face*?" said I.

"You must have noticed it."

"Noticed it? I've spent the last few minutes talking to it."

"Not my face. My tan."

"Oh. Yes. Have you never thought of spending more time in the shade? Only, sunshine can be horrid to the skin."

"It's fake."

71

"The sun's fake?"

"My tan's fake."

"Really? How's that possible?"

Little Miss Muffet reached into her pocket and pulled out a small tube. "Thanks to the powerful magic inside here."

"Whatever is it?"

"It's called fake tan, and it comes from a land called *Essex*."

"Essex? I don't believe I've heard of it."

"They absolutely swear by it there," she said, handing it up to me.

I looked closely at the tube, and read the warning printed on its side: *For medium to dark skin only.*

Little Miss Muffet observed the expression on my face. "What's the matter?" she asked.

"I think you'll find the clue to the matter is in my name. I'm so pale that I can be seen from space most nights."

She nodded as though she'd read my first diary. "All the better to disguise yourself with, then," she pointed out.

"I suppose drastic times call for drastic measures," said I, unscrewing the lid. "How should I apply it?"

"Liberally," said she.

"Liberally?" said I.

"Use the whole tube."

"If you think it best." With the contents of the tube relocated to my face, I pulled the cover from the mirror with a flourish, and picked it up. "Oh, my," said I, gazing at my reflection. I turned my head this way and that, and that way and this, but it mattered not how I turned my head; the result was the same: I was orange. So orange, in fact, that I looked nothing like my former self – a point reinforced by the mirror, which enquired, "Who are you? And what have you done with Snow White?"

I was about to explain that it was I, when Little Miss Muffet cleared her throat as though it contained an obstruction of considerable size. I looked down at her to see if she needed me to perform the Heimlich manoeuvre. If you've never heard of the Heimlich manoeuvre, it involves grabbing a person from behind and squeezing them until their blockage pops out. But far from needing this manoeuvre, her eyes were narrowed and she looked rather confident. She pressed a finger to her lips, and either she had something in her eye or she was winking and trying to tell me something.

"Oh!" said I, as the penny dropped. *She thinks it a good idea to keep my true identity a secret from the mirror. I've made so many enemies of late that I quite agree.*

"Answer my question. Who are you and what have you done with Snow White?" asked the mirror again.

"Isn't it obvious who I am?" said I, playing for time. "If not Snow White, then I can only be…" I looked at my reflection and hoped for some inspiration. Only one word came to mind, so I thought it best to say it twice. "…Orange Orange."

"Orange Orange? I've never heard of you," said the mirror.

"She's a new character," said Little Miss Muffet helpfully.

"Where *exactly* did you come from?" the mirror asked me suspiciously.

"From inside here," said I, holding up the emptied tube of fake tan.

"And where's Snow White?"

"She's inside the tube," said Little Miss Muffet. "Orange Orange is Snow White's cousin, and…"

"And?" pressed the mirror.

"And they're on an exchange programme," said Little Miss Muffet.

"Really?" said the mirror.

"Yes, spending time inside this tube has been at the top of Snow White's bucket list for years," said I.

"I always did think her peculiar. What is she doing in there?" asked the mirror.

"Very little, I should imagine," said I. I put down the mirror and covered it again, thereby rendering it deaf and silent. "Thank you for being such a help, Little Miss Muffet."

"That's quite alright."

"Is there anything I might do for you in return?"

"Actually, now you ask… I'm rather worried."

"You *are*?"

"You sound surprised, Snow. I mean, Orange."

"If I sound surprised it's only because, in all my wanderings, I don't think I've ever come across a more confident character. What is it? Whatever is the matter?"

"Well, the thing is, I've been sitting here and eating curds and whey for a long time…"

"How long, exactly?"

"For as long as I can remember."

"Oh. And?"

"And I have a horrible feeling something's going to happen. Something horrid."

"Like what?"

Little Miss Muffet shrugged, and her gaze fell to *the book* in my pocket. "I know it's against the rules to enquire about how one's own story ends, but…"

I looked left and right to check that nobody was around, then pulled *the book* from my pocket. "Rules schmules. It's not as though I haven't done this before," said I, flicking through its pages until I found Little Miss Muffet's nursery rhyme.

"That's what I'd heard. I wouldn't have dreamt of asking you otherwise," said she, hugging her knees to her chest.

"Here it is," said I, and I started to read her nursery rhyme to myself. It only had one verse, and while I read it she waited patiently. I closed the book and put it back in my pocket. "What... ah, what's the worst thing you can imagine?" I asked.

Little Miss Muffet shuddered so hard that she rustled the

leaves of the tree against which she was sitting. Her eyes opened wide and she said, "Please. *Please.* Tell me it's not a spider."

"Alright. It's not a spider," said I, looking up into the tree and trying to spot the spider that planned to come and sit down beside her. Little Miss Muffet gulped. "It *is* a spider, isn't it?"

Was a spider, thought I, reaching up for the closest branch and pulling myself up.

Two branches higher up, I came face to face with the spider in question. It stretched four of its eight legs and said, "Get out of my tree. You're in my way."

"What are you going to do?" I asked.

"Climb down and sit beside her. What else?"

"You can't."

"Why not?"

"Because you'll frighten her."

"So you *can* read. I'm surprised."

"How rude."

"Who are you? And what are you doing on this branch?"

"Don't you recognise me? I'm none other than Sn-ot… Orange Orange."

"Snot Orange Orange? What a ridiculous name. It suits you."

"It's *just* Orange Orange."

From below, Little Miss Muffet called up, "What's going on? Who are you talking to?"

"No one," replied I, chirpily.

"*No* one?" said she, suspiciously.

"Just to myself."

"Do you climb up trees and talk to yourself often?"

"Yes."

"But why?"

"On account of my many issues."

"Oh, right. I've heard about your issues."

"Have you? From who?"

"The grapevine."

"And what else did the grapevine say about me?"

"That you're insecure, meddlesome, inconsolable, awkward, and not particularly hopeful about living happily ever after with Prince Charming."

"The grapevine is awfully well informed," said I.

"Well, it *is* the grapevine."

The spider stretched its other four legs and said, "I'm sorry to interrupt your little tête-a-tête, but you need to go away so I can climb down and get on with my job."

"If you ask me, you have a horrid job."

"Nobody asked you."

"I think you should find another job."

The spider sighed. "I have thought about it. After all, it's not as though the prospects for promotion are good in this line of work. All I do is drop down and sit beside her." The spider checked the ends of two of its legs, as though it had fingernails and wanted to check them for dirt, then continued, "It's not like she's even going to hang around for a chat."

"That's because Little Miss Muffet is *petrified* of spiders."

"And how does she think that makes me feel?"

"I don't suppose she'll be thinking much about your feelings, not while she's running away and screaming."

"Rub it in, why don't you? The last girl I had a crush on ran in front of a herd of charging elephants. I was only chasing her because I wanted to tell her how beautiful she was."

"I'm very sorry to hear that."

"You should be. It wasn't exactly the crush I had in mind."

"Are you *sure* you're not talking to a spider up there?" asked Little Miss Muffet.

"Quite sure. I'll be down presently," said I, turning my attention back to the spider. "Look," I told it, "I'm on my way to visit the queen."

"No you're not. You're sitting in my tree."

"I will be presently. How about this? I'll hide you under that

78

blanket down there."

"What's under it?"

"A gift for the queen. A mirror. When we arrive at the palace, I'll set you free. It's a big palace and you'll find lots of job opportunities there."

The spider shook its head.

"Do you have a better idea?"

"Maybe… just maybe."

"Maybe what? Spit it out, spider."

"If truth be told," said it, bouncing a little on its web, "I've been sitting above Little Miss Muffet in this tree for as long as I can remember, and…"

"And?"

"I've grown rather fond of her."

I shook my head. "I'm very sorry, but if you want me to arrange a date for you with Little Miss Muffet, I think it quite out of the question."

"Why?"

"I should have thought it obvious."

"Not to me."

"I'm no expert in dating, trust me, but even I can see it's not possible to date someone while they're running away and screaming."

"Maybe if you introduced me, she wouldn't run away."

"Introduce you?"

"Yes. As a long-lost relative."

"A long-lost relative with eight legs who just *happened* to be up in this tree?"

"Stranger things have happened."

"True. But not a whole lot stranger, if I'm honest."

I have to admit, I had my doubts at first. But once I'd explained to Little Miss Muffet that the spider was an eight-legged uncle of mine, and that he'd keep his distance for as long as she wanted, she agreed to meet him. I said my goodbyes to both and, once a good distance away, I turned to see that all was well. And indeed it was. The spider must have told Little Miss Muffet a very funny joke, for she was laughing so much she had to wipe the tears from her eyes. I got the impression that the spider could be quite the little charmer. And so it was that I continued my journey to my evil stepmother's palace disguised as Orange Orange, the mirror tucked firmly under my arm.

A little later that day…

As I said in my previous diary, my evil stepmother's palace is very large and her butler very small – about the same height as a miniature poodle. I knocked on the door for what felt like an age before he finally opened it. "Yes?" said he, gazing up at me like I was a complete stranger.

"I have come with a gift for the queen," said I, and indicated the covered mirror with a pointed finger.

"Is her Royal Highness expecting you?"

"Not as such, but she's going to love her present," said I, attempting to brush past him. In this he expertly thwarted my every attempt, and pretty soon it began to feel as though we were out on a date, dancing. I stopped trying and, after he'd complimented me on my ballroom skills, he said, "Wait here while I go and see if the queen's available. Whom shall I say is calling?"

"Orange Orange."

"Orange Orange? I've read *the book* many times, and I've never heard of you."

"I've never come across you in *the book* either. But that's hardly the point."

"What is the point, Miss?"

"Beats me. Look, I'm Snow White's cousin."

"Snow *White's* cousin?"

81

"That's right. We're on an exchange programme."

At the very mention of Snow White, the butler grimaced and shuddered. "You'd better come in then," said he, stepping aside.

The butler lead me through the palace and out the other side to an apple orchard in the garden. It was there I came upon my stepmother picking apples and placing them in a basket. The butler cleared his throat to get her attention and said, "You have a visitor, Your Highness... may I present Orange Orange."

My stepmother turned and beheld me. For a moment, I imagined she could see through my orange deception, but then she almost smiled and said, "Have we met?"

I curtseyed and said, "No, Your Highness."

"You look familiar."

"I am Snow White's cousin."

"I've never knew she had a cousin."

"I'm a new character."

"I see. And what have you got there?"

"It's a gift for you."

"For me? You shouldn't have," said she, extending a hand. I removed the cover from the mirror and handed it to her. The mirror, that is. Not the cover. The cover I handed to the butler (well, I say handed, but it covered him completely). As she held it up and looked into it, I said, "Its opinions are the most up-to-date in all the land, Your Majesty."

"The most up-to-date in all the land, you say?"

"I do say. Maybe you have a question you'd like to ask it?"

My stepmother tossed her head so that her pretty black curls fell about her face. "Mirror, mirror, soon to be on my wall, who is the fairest of them all?"

"You are," replied the mirror.

"*Me*? But what about Snow White?"

To this, the mirror produced a strangulated mew, like it was about to projectile-vomit all over the orchard. Then, through gasps, it said, "What about Snow White?"

"Is *she* not considered the fairest in the land?"

"By *whom,* Your Majesty? The no-eyed, no-brained toad that sells curds and whey at the enchanted pond?"

I must admit that on this point, I found myself nodding in agreement with the mirror.

My stepmother looked at me and said, "Where is she? Where is Snow White?" Her eyes narrowed. "Has she left the land?"

"No. How could she? It's not possible to leave it."

"She's lying. They're on an exchange programme," said the mirror helpfully.

"So where *is* Snow White?"

"She's inside the empty tube that Orange Orange has hidden inside her pocket, Your Highness."

"Give it to me," said she, snapping her fingers at me.

"Give what to you, Your Highness?"

"You know very well. The tube! The tube in your pocket."

"What? *This* tube?" said I, taking it from my pocket and handing it to her.

My stepmother snatched it from my grasp and held it before the mirror. "Snow White is inside of *here*? Are you sure?"

"Orange Orange told me so herself," said the mirror. My stepmother examined the empty tube of fake tan closely. "The land inside it must be very *small*. Smaller even than Lilliput. What's she doing in there?"

"Very little, I should imagine," said the mirror, repeating what I'd told it in the woods.

"What are you going to do?" said I, clasping my cheeks in mock horror.

My evil stepmother chose to answer my question with actions rather than words. She dropped the tube upon the ground, and giggled as she stamped it into oblivion.

Tuesday

This morning, when I sat before my mirror and asked it, "Mirror, mirror on the wall, who is the fairest of them all?" and it replied "Not you, that's for sure," it felt as though a great weight had been lifted from my shoulders – so much so that I felt able to shrug properly for the first time in ages. "Something wrong with your shoulders?" asked my mirror.

"Why do you ask?" said I.

"They appear to be trying to swallow your head. Maybe they're confusing it with an actual orange. Easily done, I suppose."

"I suppose," said I, standing up.

I was determined that nothing would ruin my good spirits. Emboldened thus, I went out onto the porch, handed each dwarf his pick-axe and lunch box, and waved them off to work. Earlier during breakfast, they'd looked terribly downcast, and had spoken hardly a word to Snow White's cousin and replacement, Orange Orange. Not Particularly Hopeful said he'd *never* been particularly hopeful about Snow White outwitting her stepmother forever. Meddlesome raised a glass of milk by way of a toast, and said he was bursting with pride for Snow. "Some might call it meddling," said he, "but she only ever tried to help others." Awkward blew his nose into his hanky, and then rubbed snot into his eyes as he wiped away his tears. Blinking thus, he stumbled over a footstool and landed in a heap, sobbing. Insecure had been almost as inconsolable as Inconsolable, who had curled up into a wet little ball of misery. But, for the time being at least, I was resolved to follow Little Miss Muffet's advice and tell no one of my orange deception – except for the little lamb who skips past my cottage every morning. For the little lamb is famous throughout the land for keeping secrets.

Outside on the porch, I looked to my right and fully expected to see the little fellow hop, skip and jump out of the forest. Not a peep. "How strange," said I to myself, "I have never known the little lamb to be late. He's just not written that way. Always on the move and quite unable to slow down." There was much that I wanted to tell the clever little fellow: for instance, how I'd used my disguise to outwit my evil stepmother, and how she believed me crushed underfoot in her apple orchard. And how, now that she no longer needed apples to poison me, her orchard was being replaced by a croquet lawn. I was keen to tell the little lamb that news of my demise had been spread by the grapevine throughout the land (for once it seemed that the grapevine had got its facts wrong). *Maybe the grapevine isn't so reliable after all?* I thought. I was desperate to tell the little lamb that my Prince Charming wasn't so charming after all. About how easily he'd fallen for Cinderella's fluttering eyelids, and how he'd read my diary and thought me peculiar. It was then that I heard a rustling in the undergrowth, and hoped to see the little lamb pop out of it. But alas, it wasn't the little lamb, but Barry the boar. So downcast was Barry that he didn't even notice me.

"Whatever is the matter?" said I.

At the sound of my voice, Barry practically jumped out of his skin. "*Snow*?" said he, expectantly. But when he beheld my orangeness, his snout fell into the dirt.

"Barry? What's the matter?"

"For one happy moment, I thought you were Snow White.

But how could you be?"

"But I–" I bit my lip.

"Poor, *poor* Snow. Her evil stepmother finally got the better of her."

"But I–" I bit both my lips.

Barry gazed up at me. "You must be Orange Orange. I heard about you through the grapevine. Although the grapevine never mentioned that your mouth tries to swallow itself whenever you speak."

I unfurled my lips. "I had no idea you cared so much for Snow White, Barry."

"Being a new character, I don't suppose you know much about anything. Not even where I'm going."

"Where are you going?"

"To Snow's funeral."

"Her funeral?"

"That's right. They're burying the tube she was in when... well, when she had her *accident*..."

"You must be the only person who's going. Thank you, Barry."

Barry shook his head. "Shows how much you know. Why are you thanking me, anyway?"

"Snow *was* my cousin. And I'm going with you," said I, climbing onto Barry's back.

In a clearing, not far from the enchanted lake, we came upon a gathering of people. Just about everyone I'd ever met was there. Even the dwarves had taken the morning off work, and the dwarves *never* took time off. Little Red stood beside them looking downcast under her bonnet, and next to her stood Cinderella with my Prince Charming. They held hands as though they were on a date. Cinders was crying, and every time my prince leaned in close to offer a comforting word, she fluttered her eyelids and splashed him with her tears. Thelma Mavis Doodlebug was there with her baby, its poop-filled nappy made from the Panocci dress that Cinders had swapped with her. You may remember that the dress had belonged to one of Cinderella's sisters, and how Cinders had borrowed it to meet my Prince Charming. She hadn't been able to return it, and that explained why her sisters had turned up wearing her guts for garters.

Even though she knew about my Orange deception, Little Miss Muffet had come along with her new best friend the spider. The trees were filled with the songbirds who helped me with my chores every morning, and although such a thing should not be possible, their chirping sounded miserable. Hansel was there with Gretel, and poor Gretel's eyes were puffy from crying. Of all people, the Big Bad Wolf was there, and he alone was smiling. As far as I could tell, the only people who weren't there were Rumpelstiltskin and the little lamb who hops past by my cottage. Rumpelstiltskin made sense, but what had become of the little lamb?

They had all gathered around a hole in the ground (well, I say a hole, but it was more of a scraping just large enough for a squashed tube of fake tan). Out of the woods came a skunk harnessed to a tiny carriage, and upon the carriage, wearing a top hat and holding the reins, was my evil stepmother's butler. Walking behind, towering above the carriage, was none other than my evil stepmother. She was dressed in black with a black veil, sobbing and clutching a hanky to her veiled nose. I looked at the gathering, and hoped to see scorn and disbelief upon their faces. But Cinderella alone amongst them had the look of someone who wanted to bop a fake mourner on her nose. The butler climbed down off the tiny carriage, and placed the squashed tube (and I have never seen anything flatter) upon the backs of four baby mice. They were the pallbearers and they bore the pall (or in this case the flattened tube) about half a foot to its final resting place. They dropped it in, spun about, and used their back paws to kick dirt all over it. My evil stepmother, apparently overcome with grief, collapsed to her knees and placed an apple upon the little mound of dirt. I realised my hands had balled into fists, and the sight of that apple, doubtless the first from her orchard that hadn't been poisoned, was too much to bear!

I stepped forward, picked it up, and was about to bite into it when my stepmother wrestled me to the ground. "Don't eat it, Orange!" said she. "It is the last apple from my orchard and it is poisoned!" A sigh rose from the crowd as she helped me to my feet.

"*Poisoned?*" said I, making my point like a lawyer in court room. "But why ever are the apples in your orchard poisoned?"

"To kill slugs and termites," said she, checking her black nail polish for imaginary blemishes. "Why else?"

I placed my hands on my hips. "To poison slugs, was it?"

"Yes, that's right. And termites."

"So you haven't been trying to poison *Snow White* with

apple-based dishes for years?"

"How could you say such a thing?" She pressed her hanky to her veiled face and blew her nose (into her veil). As she sobbed, she mumbled something about how Snow had always been her favourite stepdaughter.

"Snow was your only stepdaughter," I pointed out.

"And so beautiful!" sobbed my stepmother.

I had a hunch and, stepping up on tiptoes, I pulled her veil from her face to reveal a smile that not only covered it but overflowed from its edges. "Something amuses you?" said I.

Her smile vanished so fast that it practically pulled her face inside out. "Beauty can be such a curse," said she, pulling out a compact and gazing into it. "Compact, compact in my hand, who is the fairest in the land?"

"You are," said the compact. She snapped it closed.

"Happy now?" said I.

She turned her gaze upon me. "Count your blessings," said she.

"My blessings?"

"Yes. That you resemble a mutated orange."

Later that day…

Later that day, I returned to my cottage only to find a note stuck to the door with a dagger. It read: *I have the little lamb that hops, skips and jumps past your cottage every morning.*

"And!?" said I.

And, the note went on, *unless you bring me Thelma Mavis Doodlebug's first-born child, I'm going to make a hotpot for my supper. I presume you get my meaning?"*

"I do!"

Good, said the note. It was signed *Rumpelstiltskin.*

I tore it from the door. "But why have you chosen me to bring the baby?"

PS, said the note. *Because as Snow White's closest relative, you're answerable for her crimes."*

"What crimes?"

Her meddling!

"What a conundrum!" exclaimed I. If you're wondering what a conundrum is, it's like a problem with knobs on. I reasoned that I could hardly let that horrid little imp make a hotpot out of the little lamb, no matter how tasty. And neither could I take him Thelma Mavis Doodlebug's baby. I sat down on the porch and placed my head in my palms. *If only the little lamb were here, he'd know what to do,* thought I.

It was then that a little hedgehog walked from the undergrowth and said, "You know what *They* say, don't you?"

"Yes, that you can't make an omelette without breaking some eggs. But how is that useful in this situation?"

"It isn't," said the little hedgehog, scratching its ear.

"Then why bring it up?"

"Because that's not the only thing They say."

"It isn't? What else do They say?"

"Lots of things. In fact, there's nothing They don't know."

"You mean, They might have the answer to my conundrum?"

"Of course They will."

I stood up. "Any idea where I might find They? I mean, Them?"

"Not exactly. All I know about They is that They live in the Forest of All Knowledge."

"And is it far?"

"Not as the crow flies, no."

"What about as the Orange rolls?"

"The Orange would do well to hitch a ride on the crow."

I gazed up at the sky and placed a hand over my eyes to shield them from the sun. "I haven't seen the crow in ages."

"Maybe so, but he's easy to summon. All you need to do is trot up and down on the spot, flap your arms so that your elbows knock against your sides, and squawk like a two-headed chicken."

"And why will that summon the crow?"

"Beats me. It's a conundrum. If you find Them you can ask Them."

"I will. And thank you, little hedgehog," said I, trotting up and down on the spot, flapping my arms and squawking like a two-headed chicken.

"Only too pleased to help," said he, continuing on his journey.

I was engaged in summoning the crow thus, when I heard Barry the boar 'whistling.' Barry trotted from the undergrowth, and when he saw me, he stopped *dead* in his tracks and said, "Have you ever considered therapy, Orange?"

Already a little out of breath, I said, "You are mistaken, Barry, for I am not bonkers."

"Having issues is nothing to be ashamed of. They obviously run in the family."

"Whatever do you mean?" said I, trotting and flapping on the spot for all I was worth.

"That your cousin Snow had her fair share of issues, too."

I added a nod to my trot and flap. "You're not wrong there, Barry. But you really are mistaken, for I am engaged in summoning the crow."

"That's not how you summon the crow," said Barry.

"I think you'll find that it is…"

"I think you'll find that's how you summon the men in white coats."

I was about to argue the point when two men in white coats emerged from the forest, one holding a syringe and the other a straitjacket. "Somebody summon us?" said the one with the syringe.

"No. It's a false alarm," said Barry. "She's trying to summon the crow."

"Oh," said the man with the straitjacket. "You must have met the little hedgehog."

I stopped nodding, trotting and flapping and stood quite still. "He was here just a minute ago," said I, craning my neck in the direction he'd gone.

"That little hedgehog is quite the practical joker," said the man with the straitjacket.

"Was he also lying about They?" I asked.

"What about They?" said Barry.

"The little hedgehog said that They live in the Forest of All Knowledge. And that They have the answers to any conundrum."

"If you have a conundrum, you'd better jump on, Orange, and I'll take you to see Them."

The Forest of All Knowledge was full of whispering trees,

and no matter how hard I tried to listen, it was impossible to hear what they were saying. We came upon They fishing in a little brook. As it turned out, They was a groundhog called Frank.

Frank cast his fishing line and said, "I knew you were coming. There's actually not a lot I don't know about anything."

I climbed off Barry and said, "Where are the others?"

"There are no others. I am They," said Frank, twirling his whiskers.

"What? *All* of them?"

"Every single one."

"But you *can't* be They," said I.

"And why not?"

"I should have thought that obvious. *They* is plural. It means *more* than one."

"Think about it," said Frank. "If I called myself I, then people would sound like English gentlemen every time they quoted me. For example, *I say, you can't make an omelette without breaking some eggs.* Or, *I say, good things come to those who wait.* Or, *I say, you should never count your chickens before they're hatched.* Need I go on?"

I sat down on a tree trunk beside Frank and scratched my head. "I do see your point."

"Good. I presume you haven't just come to point out that I'm singular?"

"Indeed, I have not. Something terrible has happened, and it has given me a conundrum. I was hoping you might be able to solve it." I explained to Frank how Rumpelstiltskin had kidnapped the little lamb, and how he was going to turn him into a hotpot unless I brought him Thelma's baby. Once I'd explained all, Frank said, "You know what They say, don't you?"

"What do you say?"

"That you can lead a horse to water but you can't make it drink."

"Is that useful?"

"Not particularly. But luckily for you, I'm only just getting warmed up."

"Pleased to hear it."

"You've met the little hedgehog, also known as Mr Wind-Up?"

"Indeed I have. He wound me up so much that he had me summon the men in white coats. It's a good thing Barry was there, or they would have locked me away somewhere horrid. What of the little hedgehog?"

"He's the answer to your conundrum," said Frank thoughtfully.

"I hope you're going to explain *how*."

"Alright. You're going to give the little hedgehog to Rumpelstiltskin."

"Why? Does Rumpel want him?"

"Of course not. That's why you must tell Rumpelstiltskin that the little hedgehog is Thelma's baby."

I sighed and shook my head. "He looks *nothing* like her baby. For starters, he's a lot more prickly."

"That's because he's a little hedgehog."

"Good to see you're coming round to my way of thinking."

"That's why you must ask Cinderella's fairy godmother for help."

I sat down on the ground, crossed my legs, and rested my heavy head in my palms. "I came here today thinking you were going to help *unravel* the confusion, but you seem intent only on adding more knots."

"I need you to bear with me, Orange."

"I'll try. But only if you jump to the part of your plan that's in some way helpful."

And that's precisely what Frank did when he said, "Cinderella's fairy godmother can cast a spell upon the little hedgehog, and make it the spitting image of Thelma's baby – at least until the clock strikes twelve. But that should give you plenty of time to exchange him for the little lamb."

"Oh! I see. And when the clock strikes twelve, I suppose the little hedgehog is going to turn into a pumpkin," said I, making what I considered to be quite a funny joke.

Apparently *They* have no sense of humour, for They (or to use Their correct name, Frank) shook his head and said, "No. When the clock strikes twelve, the little hedgehog will turn back into a little hedgehog."

"But why would the little hedgehog agree?"

"Because he'll grasp any opportunity to wind up Rumpelstiltskin. He isn't known as Mr Wind-Up for nothing. What's the matter?"

I considered my words very carefully and said, "The thing is, Frank…"

"There's a thing?"

"Indeed there is."

"Well, if there's a thing, you'd better tell me what it is."

"The thing is this: my cousin Snow *might* have upset Cinderella's fairy godmother. And, in a land such as this, a person's deeds are inherited by their closest relative. And that would be me."

"And what *might* your cousin Snow have done to upset her?"

"You obviously haven't spoken to the grapevine recently."

Frank shook his head. "Not since I heard through him that you should take everything They say with a pinch of salt. So? What has your cousin done?"

"She arranged for Cinderella to go on a date with *her* Prince Charming – Snow's Prince Charming, that is. And they really hit it off."

"And?"

"And that means that the whole thing with her turning a pumpkin into a carriage must be off now. I believe it was to be her fairy godmother's big moment."

Frank began to reel his fishing line in. "Don't worry," said he. "Before I fell out with the grapevine, I heard through him that Cinderella's fairy godmother is not one to hold a grudge."

"Oh, that's marvellous news!" said I, standing up. "However can I thank you, Frank?"

"Think nothing of it, for you know what They say."

"What do you say?"

"That kindness brings its own rewards."

"Can't say I've seen much evidence of that," murmured I, as I climbed back onto Barry's back.

Later that day …

I knew I had no time to lose, for if Rumpelstiltskin intended to turn the little lamb into a hotpot for his supper, he would start his cooking preparations early. I hightailed it over to Cinderella fairy godmother's place (or, more accurately, Barry hightailed it while I clung to his tusks for dear life). We came upon the fairy godmother sweeping her front porch. I say sweeping, but, in truth, her broom was doing all the work while she waved her wand about as though conducting an orchestra. Barry was panting when I climbed off him and said, "Thank goodness you're here, for I need your help!"

Cinderella's fairy godmother, who, from now on, I shall refer to as CFG as a labour-saving measure, rested her ample hands on her ample hips and said, "Do you now?"

"Yes, I do."

Rather than enquire what had vexed me so, she simply said, "Follow me, young lady." CFG moved her ample self off her porch, and headed around the back of her house and into her back yard. Once there, we came upon something large covered in a sheet. She removed the sheet to reveal the biggest pumpkin you've never seen.

"My, what a large pumpkin," said I. "It's easily as big as a..." I closed my mouth.

"You were saying?" said she, folding her arms and tapping her wand against her chin.

"It's easily as big as… well, as…"

"A carriage?"

I nodded.

"Do you have any idea how long it took me to grow this pumpkin?"

"A while, I suppose."

"For*ever*. And now, thanks to your meddling cousin introducing Cinderella to the *wrong* Prince Charming, I've absolutely no use for it." CFG frowned and, if truth be told, fairy godmothers are particularly difficult to make frown. And making one as grumpy as this was unheard of.

I cleared my throat and said, "If Snow were here, I imagine she would say how sorry she is for introducing Cinders to her Prince Charming. She might also say, were she here, that she only had Cinderella's best interests at heart."

"*Would* she now."

"Yes, she would. And that she acted out of good intentions."

"Well, you know what *They* say about good intentions, don't you?"

I shook my head. "I just saw Frank, and he didn't mention anything about that."

"Well, I'll mention it for him. They say that the road to hell is paved with good intentions."

"But whatever does that mean?"

"That meddling doesn't always turn out for the best. Which reminds me, why have you come to see me?"

"I need your help."

"That much I had gathered. This would be your opportunity to elaborate."

"Elaborate?"

"Tell me what has you so agitated, young lady."

"It's Rumpelstiltskin…"

"What about him?"

"He's kidnapped the little lamb that hops, skips and jumps past my cottage. And unless I take him the baby that Thelma Mavis Doodlebug promised him, he's going to turn the little lamb into a hotpot for his supper."

"Oh."

"I know."

"And what might I do about that?"

"*They* said you might turn the little hedgehog into a duplicate of Thelma's baby. And that I might exchange him for the little lamb."

"Is that what Frank said?"

"It is."

"I suppose They know best." CFG waved her magic wand and the little hedgehog appeared at her feet. "Fairy godmother," said it, doffing a top hat. "What can I do you for?" CFG pointed her wand at me, and the little hedgehog turned to face me.

"You look surprised to see me," said I.

"I am."

"And why is that?"

"I thought you'd be spending quality time with the men in white coats."

"Quality time? I think not. Thankfully, Barry explained to them that *you* were responsible for my on-the-spot trotting, arm-flapping and squawking like a two-headed chicken."

"Ah, well. Glad you see the funny side."

"Do I *look* like I see the funny side?"

The little hedgehog shrugged, placed his top hat back upon his head, and looking back and forth between CFG and myself, asked again what he could do us for.

"Rumpelstiltskin has the little lamb that hops, skips and jumps past Orange's cottage," said CFG.

"So?" said the little hedgehog.

"So this," said I. "He's planning on turning him into a hotpot."

The little hedgehog's reaction could be considered insensitive, for it leapt into the air, clicked its heels and said, "I *love* hotpot. *Please* tell me Rumpel has invited us all for supper?"

"No. He has not," said I, making fists and planting them firmly on my hips.

"What then?" asked the little hedgehog.

CFG extended her magic wand towards me and said, "Need you ask?"

The little hedgehog shook his head. "Meddling runs in the family, does it, Orange?"

"I prefer to call it having good intentions."

The little hedgehog scratched itself. "The road to hell is paved with good intentions," said he.

"I have been made aware of that possibility, yes."

"Then I suggest you let Rumpel enjoy his hotpot."

"I'll do nothing of the sort. You're going to help me save the little lamb *and* Thelma's baby."

"And why would I do that? What's in it for me?"

"An opportunity for the wind-up of the century," said CFG, waving her wand and turning the little hedgehog into a duplicate of Thelma's baby.

Not only was the little hedgehog the spitting image of Thelma's baby, but he was nestled in a lovely pram. Upon his little head was a bonnet, and in his mouth a dummy, which he spat out. "Ga! Ga!" he said, urgently.

"What's that?" I asked.

"GA! GA!"

"Saying the same thing, only in capitals, leaves me none the wiser, little man-hog."

"GA! GA! GA!"

"Similarly, neither does saying it thrice." I looked at CGF, who said that she *supposed* he'd need a larger vocabulary if he was to wind up Rumpelstiltskin. With that she waved her wand and "GA! GA!" became a string of words that have no place in a young woman's diary. So I have found no place for them.

Once the little hedgehog had calmed down, he asked for his dummy back. Not something I'd expected. I picked it up and handed it to him, one eyebrow raised. "It's comforting," said he, snatching it away. CFG pointed out that the time for supper was fast approaching and, with that, she waved her magic wand and transported the little man-hog and myself to Rumpel's tower.

As described in my previous diary, Rumpel's tower is tall and thin, and has vines growing all over it. At its top is a single room with a single window, out of which wafted the aroma of cooking. I gazed up at the window, and was relieved to see the little lamb appear… then disappear… then appear… then disappear… "Thank goodness we're not too late," said I.

The little man-hog removed the dummy from its mouth and said, "More's the pity. I'm famished." I snatched away his dummy and, before he had time to elaborate, I shoved it back into his mouth.

The tower contained a great many steps – one hundred and eighty-six, to be precise. All of these I had to navigate backwards while pulling the pram. Once at the top, I knocked upon the door. The door had a great many locks, and while Rumpel turned a great many keys, I pulled the little man-hog from the pram and cradled it to my breast. I removed the dummy from its mouth and it said, "Like I told you downstairs, I'm hungry."

"Don't push it," said I. The door opened to reveal the horrid little imp and, beyond him, the little lamb jumping about at the window. I barely recognised the little lamb, for all his lovely wool had been plucked out. "How *dare* you pluck the little lamb that hops, skips and jumps past my cottage!"

"I do dare. Did you expected me to cook a woolly hotpot?" I gazed down at Rumpel, who was wearing a Panocci apron with the letter P all over it. He rose up on tiptoes and peered closely at the 'baby' in my arms. "You did it... you have brought what was promised me... what is rightfully mine. Now hand it over," said he, extending his grubby little hands.

"Don't do it, Orange!" cried the little lamb.

"But I must, otherwise he's going to turn you into a hotpot."

"A common fate for little lambs such as I," said the little lamb, philosophically.

"But you deserve better, my little friend."

"*Friend?*" bounced the little lamb. "But we've only just met. We haven't even been formally introduced." I folded my arms and looked down at Rumpel, who said, "Well, *excuse me* if not in the habit of introducing visitors to my dinner."

"He's not your dinner," said I, handing the little man-hog down to him.

"You can't!" bounced the little lamb. "Snow would never

approve!"

"It's done," said Rumpel. He held the little man-hog aloft, danced about his lome and added, "It would be a terrible shame to let all my herbs and stuffing go to waste!"

"We'd best be going," said I to the little lamb. The little lamb barely bounced past me, and refused to say even a single word as we descended the tower's many steps. Once we reached the bottom, I caught him mid-bounce and, holding him stationary with arms outstretched, I whispered, "Fear not! For I have not given Rumpel Thelma's baby!"

At first, the little lamb, who was not accustomed to being stationary while airborne, opened his eyes wide and looked towards the ground. He swallowed hard and said, "But I saw you."

"You only think you did. What I actually gave him was the little hedgehog, also known as Mr Wind-Up."

"How's that possible?" asked the little lamb, eyeing the ground.

"Thanks in no small part to Cinders's fairy godmother. Need I say more?" Had the little lamb features, I imagined he would have arranged them into a smile.

The next morning…

The next morning, I awoke with the feeling that all was well in the land. Yes, I was deluded, but They say ignorance is bliss. And having met Frank, I felt inclined to agree with him. However, my blissful ignorance was not to last long, for the grapevine slithered through my bedroom window and said, "I've come to do a background check."

"On whom?"

"On you, Orange Orange." In case you haven't heard much through the grapevine recently, he sounded much like a policeman conducting an interview with a criminal.

I sat up in bed, yawned and said, "A background check? On I? Whatever for?"

The grapevine sprouted a tentacle, and it hovered close to my face.

"Take a picture, why don't you?" said I to it.

"I like to get my facts straight before I spread them about."

"*And?*" said I as the tentacle touched the tip of my nose, making me go boss-eyed.

"And I've never heard of you, Orange Orange."

"That's because I'm a new character."

"That's what I heard."

"Through your*self*," said I, stifling a chuckle.

"No. And therein lies the problem."

"So who did you hear it through?"

"Little Miss Muffet."

"Lovely girl. Crazy for curds and whey."

"Quite so. She keeps the no-eyed, no-brained toad who sells curds and whey at the enchanted pond in business."

"Does she now."

"Yes. And if anybody asks, you can tell them you heard it through me."

"Alright. Look, if Little Miss Muffet says I'm a new character, then her word ought to be enough."

"Her word might have been enough, once upon a time, but..."

"But what?"

"She's been acting strangely lately."

"How so?"

"For starters, she hasn't been spending all her days eating curds and whey."

"A lifestyle improvement, if you ask me."

"That isn't all. She's also spending more and more time away from her tree, and has become quite inseparable from the spider that was *supposed* to drop down and sit beside her."

"They're friends now. What's wrong with that?"

"Spiders aren't supposed to have friends."

"Oh, that's grim, even by the standard of the land." I pushed the tentacle away. "I hope you're satisfied that I am who I say I am. I have chores to attend to now."

"I suppose I'll have to be for the time being. But I'll be keeping an eye on you, Orange. Something about you smells fishy."

I stifled a burp. "That would be the clams I had for supper. Oh! While you're here, I don't suppose you have any news of the woodcutter?"

"Woodcutter?"

"Yes, the one who was supposed to kill Snow but decided to let her go."

"What's it to you?"

"I wanted to explain one or two things to him on Snow's behalf."

"Regarding the woodcutter, the news is not good," said the grapevine.

"Is the poor fellow alright?"

The tentacle that had hitherto been trying to peer up my left nostril pulled back and shook itself. "He's very worried about his son, Edward."

"Has something happened to Edward?"

"As a punishment for not killing Snow White, the queen has taken Edward to be her slave, and is quite determined to

110

work the poor boy to death."

"Is that in *the book*?"

"Of course not, but all sorts of strange changes have been taking place throughout the land of late. Due in no small way to that meddling cousin of yours."

I felt in some small way responsible for poor Edward's fate. After all, it had been entirely my fault. If only I'd accepted my own fate, been philosophical about it, and allowed the woodcutter to kill me, then his son Edward would have been spared his terrible fate. My conscience was eased a little when I remembered that letting me go had been written in *the book*. So whoever wrote *the book* ought to shoulder at least *some* of the blame.

During breakfast with the dwarves, I discussed my plan to rescue Edward. Not Particularly Hopeful said I should stop my meddling ways, for no good would ever come of them. At which Inconsolable burst into tears and pointed out that it had been Snow who had meddled so, not her cousin Orange. At which point, Meddlesome banged his fist upon the table and told Not Particularly Hopeful that *plenty* of good had come of Snow's meddling ways. Insecure said that it didn't matter either way, because I'd make a mess of whatever I decided to do. Awkward remained perfectly composed and perfectly still, surprising everyone present. After Not Particularly Hopeful had checked Awkward for a pulse, and had been surprised to find he still had one, I left. My destination? The front porch, where I whistled for Barry.

"Where can I take you, Orange?" said he.

"Snow's stepmother's palace."

111

"You sure that's such a good idea?"

"I have no choice, Barry. For it is there that I will find Edward."

"Edward?"

"The woodcutter's son. Thanks to Snow *and* the writer of *the book* for allowing his father to release her, poor Edward has been enslaved by the queen. And she is quite determined to work the poor boy to death."

"So what are you going to do?"

"I'm going to save him."

Barry produced a little squeal that sounded very much like a stifled sob.

"Whatever is the matter?" I asked.

"It's just you remind me of your cousin, Snow." Barry 'whistled,' kicked up some dirt with his hind legs, and we set off for my stepmother's palace.

After the debacle at the funeral, I felt certain I would not be welcome, so I told Barry to drop me off at the end of the drive and made my way on foot towards the palace through its beautiful grounds. I came upon a gardener, hard at work digging a hole. The man was toiling dreadfully, and I had no wish to startle him. I crept up and from behind a bush I whispered, "Would you, perchance, be the woodcutter's son, Edward?"

The gardener, who looked nothing like the woodcutter due to his bald head and pug-like face, wiped the sweat from his brow and said, "I thought I'd uprooted all the talking hedges." He climbed out of the hole and rubbed a crick in his neck. "It's a good thing you spoke to me and not the queen. She'd have had what's left of me for garters," said he, poised to drive his shovel into the bush's roots.

"Don't!" exclaimed I.

"Why not?"

"For you are mistaken. I am not a whispering bush."

"I know, you're a talking hedge. It's all the same to me."

"I am neither hedge nor bush," said I, poking my head above the hedge/bush. At the sight of me, the gardener stumbled back and fell in his hole, disappearing from sight. From the hole there came a low groan, like the sound of a gardener in pain. This was reassuring, as it seemed to me entirely appropriate. I tiptoed out from behind the hedge/bush and peered down at him. "I imagine you mistook me for an orange troll. Take heart, for it bodes well for your eyesight."

The gardener shook his shiny, pug-like head. "I thought you a mutant orange, something hideous that escaped from the orchard."

"That makes sense also. Need a hand?" I crouched down and extended mine into his hole.

"No, thank you," said he.

"So?" I pressed.

"So what?"

"Are you Edward, the woodcutter's son?"

At the mention of Edward's name, the gardener shuddered. "I'm not him. And every day I thank my lucky stars that I'm not."

"So Edward hasn't been having the best of times, then?"

"You think I was toiling hard?"

I nodded heartily.

"This enormous hole? Nothing. A mere trifle when compared to what the queen makes Edward do every day."

"Bad, then?"

"I'll say. She won't be satisfied until she's worked him to death."

I cast my gaze about the beautiful gardens. "Then I must find him as soon as possible."

"What good will that do?"

"I'm going to rescue him. Where is he?"

The gardener pulled a pocket watch from his waistcoat and observed its hands. "Twelve o'clock," said he. "He'll be starting his afternoon session on the electricity wheel."

"The electricity wheel?"

"Biggest wheel you've never seen. Provides electricity for the whole palace. Before Edward arrived, it was turned by eight oxen."

I jumped up. "Where is it? You must point me in the general direction of the wheel! For I fear there may be no time to lose."

"It's that way," said the gardener, pointing.

Like his eyesight, the gardener's sense of direction was first-rate, and it was not long before I came upon the enormous wheel. It lay flat, close to the ground, and was easily the circumference of a house. I made my way around it and came upon a bare-chested young man, drenched in sweat and grasping a wooded handle. "Excuse me?" said I. "Are you Edward, the woodcutter's son?"

The young man paused mid-toil, and gazed at me over his bare shoulder. His hair was of the brightest gold, his eyes of the deepest blue, and his dimpled jaw of the squarest kind. What's more, his cheekbones were high and chiselled as though from marble, and... and... and that's when I passed out. From hunger, you understand. When I came round, I beheld the face as just described looming over me. "Do not attempt to speak, for you have suffered a nasty fall. You must drink some water," said he, pulling a canteen from his belt. He placed it to my lips and smiled. I must have been absolutely *famished,* for I passed out again. He splashed water on my face, and when my eyelids fluttered open he said, "Who are you? And what has brought you here?"

I cast my gaze over his sinewy torso, doubtless made so by all the toil he'd been forced to endure thanks to my wilful selfishness, and all I could think to do was apologise. "I am truly, *truly…*"

"Truly who?"

I shook my head and murmured, "Orange."

"Truly Orange. Your name is an apt one, but you shouldn't

be here. Don't you know that no one is permitted to speak with me?"

I was about to explain the confusion over my name, but he smiled again and I passed out again. When I came round for the second time, he asked if I had an underlying medical condition. I shook my head and requested that he not smile. "At least, not until I've had something to eat," said I, sitting up.

"It was from hunger that you fainted, then?"

"What else?"

"A problem easily rectified with my sandwich," said he, opening his lunch box and taking out the smallest sandwich I had never seen.

I beheld it and wondered if a single slice of bread, with nothing on it, could reasonably be described as a sandwich. "Is that *all* you have to sustain you?" said I.

"It is. But I will gladly give it to you, for it's clear that your need is greater."

I gazed at the enormous wheel that he had to turn, and then at the tiny 'sandwich' that must sustain him. "*You* must eat it."

"I have no need of it, for I was permitted a similar meal only last week," said he.

"Last week? What has a woodcutter's son to do to get a break in this land?" I looked away from his face in case he should smile, and then decided to take Prince Charming's advice and get a grip for once in my life. So, and despite my famishment, I stood, brushed myself down and asked him

116

politely again if he would refrain from smiling.

"But why?"

"Apparently it makes me *very* hungry when you do."

"My smile makes you hungry, Truly?"

I thanked my lucky stars that I was orange, for it prevented me going red.

"You have turned the colour of sunset," said he, covering his mouth to hide his smile. "Despite my ridiculous hue, you're coming with me," said I.

"I cannot. I have been enslaved by the queen and cannot leave here."

"Haven't you heard?"

Edward shook his head. "The grapevine has not passed through here in sometime."

"I see. Well, I've been making some small changes to stories, and–"

"You? I heard it was Snow White that has done so."

"Yes," said I, brushing myself down needlessly and purposefully and looking away from the object of my desire. Did I just say *desire*? I meant famishment. "I'm Snow's cousin, and I share her determination to make changes where changes are required."

"Required by who?"

"By anyone who can't seem to get a break in this land."

"With the exception of the queen, that could be just about anyone."

"Tell me about it. Which is why my cousin Snow and I have had our work cut out for us."

"And you imagine that I require your assistance?"

I looked at his forehead, it being the least hunger-inducing thing about him, and murmured softly, "I do."

"You do?"

"I *do* think you need my assistance. And that is why you are coming with me, away from this dreadful place."

"Truly, is that your heart's desire?"

"It is."

"Then we'd best get going, for I am due a flogging any minute."

We had not gone far when came upon a pretty spot where Edward suggested we had lunch. "Lunch?" said I.

"You said yourself how famished you are. And I still have my sandwich," said he, producing his lunch box and removing the lid.

I gazed down at our intended meal and said, "Are you sure that's a sandwich? Only, does not a sandwich require *two* slices of bread, and something between them?"

Edward looked at his sandwich and sighed. "Truly, it requires a little imagination to make it a sandwich."

I sighed too and stumbled slightly. Edward reached out a hand and steadied me. We sat upon the ground, surrounded by bluebells, and Edward divided the sandwich that required a little imagination to make it so in two. I say in two, but he gave me the lion's share, and the piece he kept for himself could hardly be described as a piece. It was a morsel. As I nibbled upon my larger morsel, I felt his gaze upon me. "Why do you watch me so?" said I. "Am I not hideous to gaze upon? I wouldn't for all the land want to put you off your sandwich."

Edward shook his head. "That is not possible."

"You are too kind. For I resemble a mutated orange at the best of times," said I, getting the obvious comparison out of the way.

"I believe it important to see beyond colour…"

"Beyond?"

"Yes. To the person within."

"To… to… to… the person within? *Please*. You must refrain from doing so in my case. I fear the person you see will be a terrible disappointment."

Edward raised an eyebrow and shook his head.

"For starters," said I, "the person within is chronically meddlesome."

"If that is so, it is only to right the wrongs of this land." He gazed upon his morsel and added, "Mmm, it is delicious. And so filling."

"Imagination?" said I.

"Truly."

"Yes?"

"Truly it requires imagination to make it so."

"I see. We should be going. The queen will soon discover you're missing," said I, standing up.

"Where will we go? For I fear there is nowhere in the land that the queen will not find me. It would therefore serve you better if I returned to my wheel. I would not for all the land wish to get you into trouble."

"Nonsense. We will make haste and find somewhere to hide you."

"Truly, is that your heart's desire?"

I replied by nodding and making off with haste.

It may or may not have come to your attention that, since meeting Edward, I have been more hungry than usual. And that the closer Edward was to my person, the more faint (from famishment) I felt. For this reason, as we made our way through the forest, I remained several paces in front. Striding purposely, every so often I would hear Edward call, "Truly, is hiding me your heart's desire?" In response, I would nod, and the back of my head would convey that it was. This went on for some hours, and I lost count of the number of times the question was posed. Then he asked another question entirely. "Truly, is that a house I see yonder?" I stopped walking and, as I looked through the many trees, Edward caught me up and stood beside me.

"Look," said he, pointing.

"Yes. I see it," said I, standing on tiptoes. Edward looked up and gauged the position of the sun, and also the position of the second moon (for there are two in this land). "Given our position relative to the sun and second moon, that house can only be the property of three people."

"Really? How ever do you know?"

"Before I was enslaved for the crimes of my father, I had made *the book* my life's study. I see you are surprised." I was about to explain that I was not in the least bit surprised, when he raised a palm and said, "I am just the son of a poor woodcutter. I have not the education of a Prince Charming. But I was fortunate to grow up in a shed that was close to where the little lamb hops, skips and jumps on his daily travels."

"You know the little lamb?" said I.

"I do. And he was kind enough to spare me a few minutes each day, to teach me how to read." Edward shook his head. "It was not easy."

"Learning to read?" said I.

"Learning to read whilst hopping, skipping and jumping about the yard. But I persevered. And so did my joints," said he, rubbing the small of his back.

As I watched him, I heard myself murmur, "Prince Charmings aren't so clever. Did you know they can only count to eight?"

"I had no idea."

"It's true."

"Of course," said he, rubbing the other side of his back. "It explains why they only ever cut figures of eight out of the air." Edward forgot his promise and smiled at me. Not long after, I came round and Edward apologised for doing so. He said he must try harder not to smile, at least until my acute hunger had been satisfied. "Truly, do you like porridge?" he asked.

"Yes. The dwarves say it's particularly nourishing."

"Quite so. As do the bears."

"The bears?"

"Yes. The three bears who live in that house yonder."

Some minutes later …

Some minutes later, we approached the house. It was a large brown house with a white front door, and large windows with white window frames. As I peered in through the window, Edward turned and rested his back against the side of the house. "Don't tell me," said he. "You see a table, and upon the table are three bowls."

"Yes."

"The bowls are different sizes: one is small, the second medium-sized, and the third large."

"Yes! Clearly, you have studied hard."

"As I said, I have made *the book* my life's passion. The bowls belong to the three bears. And now we must be going for she might arrive at any moment, and she should not for all the world discover us here."

"Who?" said I.

"Goldilocks."

"*Goldilocks?* Now you come to mention her, I believe I've heard of her." I shuddered. "What's wrong?" asked Edward.

"I just wondered what horrid fate *the book* has in store for her. I expect she's destined to fill those bowls many times over."

"Fear not, Truly, for the three bears are a kindly family. Goldilocks will be safe here. Now we really must be going."

"Safe here? Are you sure?"

"Quite sure."

"Safe sounds a very unusual fate for this land. But that being the case, I have an idea." I looked at Edward's golden hair. "Your name might have been Goldilocks," murmured I.

"It might. Although, I would have taken issue with my parents if it were."

"Be that as it may–" Edward held up a palm and silenced me.

"But don't you wish to hear my plan?" said I.

"It has already grown from an idea into a plan?"

"It has."

"Then you are correct. I do not wish to hear it."

"Not even if telling you my plan is my heart's desire?"

"Truly, you drive a hard bargain. If it's your heart's desire, then you must tell me."

"The three bears have not yet met Goldilocks?" said I, casting my gaze about for her arrival.

"They have not."

"So it seems to me that this is the perfect place for you to hide. At least until the queen grows tired of searching for you."

"I need not point out that this is not my story."

"It's true. You needn't. But you have studied her story, so

why not pretend to be her?" Edward cast his gaze down upon himself. He shook his head and said, "While it may be true that the colour of my hair may resemble hers, its length and style are wholly different. And as for the rest of me? I need hardly point out the obvious."

"But if the bears are yet to meet her, what does it matter?"

Edward looked at me and I could tell he was doing his best not to smile. "Truly, is it your heart's desire that I remain here with the bears?"

"Where you'll be safe from the evil queen. Yes."

"Then I shall do as you wish."

We entered the house and Edward sat before the smallest of the three bowls of porridge. He indicated the larger bowl with his eyes and said I should satisfy my hunger at once. Once all three bowls had been emptied, I followed Edward upstairs, where he lay first upon the smallest bed, then the medium-sized bed, and then the largest bed where I tucked him in. "Promise me you will remain here until it's safe to leave, *Goldilocks*," said I.

"Truly, is it–" I silenced him with a finger pressed to my lips.

On my way home, I kept my eyes peeled for Goldilocks, and made a point of trying to keep my mind *off* Edward. It was not easy, and even though I'd had a hearty bowl of porridge, whenever I pictured his smile in my mind's eye, I grew faint (with hunger). I therefore reasoned that my mind's eye was a distraction from my actual eyes, and my eyes needed to be alert if they were to spot Goldilocks. So, firmly but politely, I had a word with my mind's eye and asked it, "Would you kindly stop conjuring images of a smiling Edward?" My request must have worked because, out of the corner of my actual eyes, I beheld a flash of gold moving at pace. I turned and called, "Goldilocks?" A young woman with golden hair slowed to a stop and looked at me. I waved and beckoned her over and, having considered her options, she shrugged and made her way towards me.

"I must be close. Am I close?" said she, expectantly.

"Close to what?" asked I.

"To the house where I will find porridge?"

"You like porridge?"

"Of *course*. I'm also rather partial to a bed. For I find that forty winks are just the thing after a hearty bowl of porridge."

"Are porridge and beds your favourite things?"

"In the whole world."

"I see."

She drew a deep breath and looked about anxiously. "I don't think you do. For I must find porridge and then go to bed as soon as possible."

"You sound very serious, Goldilocks."

She nodded. "How do you know my name?"

"I'm a student."

"Of *the book*?"

"Is there any other?"

Her eyes grew wide, and she pleaded, "Then you *must* know where I will find my porridge and a bed? Please say they are close by."

"Indeed they are. I have just come from both."

"You *have?*"

"Yes. And I have a confession to make. I have eaten your porridge."

"You've done *what*? But why?"

"My options were scant, for I have passed out at least three times today from hunger."

"Who are you? And what in the name of oats is wrong with you?"

"My name is Orange Orange and, of late, my appetite has been humongous."

"That may be so. But do you even belong in my story?"

"As a rule? No."

She clapped her hands to her cheeks. "So my story's been changed? And Orange Orange has eaten all my porridge? Have you also slept in my bed?"

"No. But another has. His name is Edward, and he's in grave danger. So, if you don't mind, he'll be hiding in your story and pretending to be you. At least for a short while."

"But I do mind! For without porridge and a place to sleep, I shall go bonkers."

"Fear not, Goldilocks, for I shall take you home with me," said I, stepping in the direction of home.

"Why? Do you have porridge?"

"Oh, yes. All the porridge you can eat," said I over my shoulder.

"And a bed?"

"I'll make one up in the spare room as soon as we get back."

"And what about three bears?"

"No bears. But there are five dwarves."

"Are they kindly dwarves?" she called out.

"Yes. Very kindly." So it was that Goldilocks caught me up, and we locked arms and set off for home.

The next morning…

The next morning, I awoke to find Edward in my mind's eye, smiling. A little later, Not Particularly Hopeful shook me awake and said he'd never known me to sleep so late. "I'd convinced myself you must be poorly, or worse still, gone to a better place," said he.

"I'm neither ill nor have I gone to a better place. I'm just sorry for having neglected you all," said I, stretching. "I will get up and make breakfast."

Not Particularly Hopeful patted his stomach. "There's no need."

"You've had breakfast?"

"That's right. Best porridge a dwarf ever tasted."

"You must have met Goldilocks, then," said I, looking around him through my open bedroom door.

"You won't see her," said Not Particularly Hopeful. "She emerged from the spare room first thing this morning, saw the five of us sitting at the table holding our spoons, and…"

"Were introductions made?" I enquired.

"No. There was no one to make them."

"So what did she do?"

"She went to our supply oats and set about making several gallons of porridge. She sat with us and spooned down about a gallon herself, and then went straight back to bed."

"And she uttered not a word?"

"Not a word."

After the dwarves left for work, I told the songbirds to sing quietly as I did the housework. "Goldilocks needs her rest between porridge binges. It's the way she was written," said I, dusting. "And on no account are you to sing anything evenly *remotely* romantic. Love songs have a way of making me faint from hunger lately. And for some inexplicable reason, they return Edward to my mind's eye. And I need not remind you of the consequences should he smile." I laughed philosophically. "I have not been feeling myself lately." To which one of my songbirds tweeted that a walk in the fresh air would do me the world of good.

Later on, I stepped out onto the porch and looked to my right. The little lamb popped over his usual fence, and then skipped and bounced up to me. "I still haven't thanked you properly for saving me from Rumpelstiltskin, Orange," said he.

"Think nothing of it. Oh, what a lovely day! The weather is so very clement, don't you think so?" said I, appreciating its clemency. The little lamb bounced up to me and observed me at close quarters. "As I said to the grapevine yesterday, why don't you take a picture? It will last longer."

"Your cousin Snow would have expected me to help you."

"Help me? But why ever should I need help on a fine morning such as this? The finest of mornings!" I knelt and picked a bluebell from the ground. "*Help me*? I can't think what you mean," said I, holding it to my nose and breathing in its sweet scent.

"The grapevine tells me you have not been feeling yourself lately," said the little lamb.

"I suppose there has been the odd occasion when I have felt faint from hunger."

"It's not from hunger, Orange," said the little lamb, as though my diagnosis were ridiculous. I laughed in a good-natured way and said, "*Obviously* it's from hunger. What else could make a girl so light-headed?"

"Love," said the little lamb.

"*Love?*" said I, taking a step back.

"Love," repeated the little lamb.

"*Love*," said I, taking another step back and gripping the door frame for support.

"You're in love, Orange. With the woodcutter's boy, Edward."

"I most certainly am n–!" The sound of Edward's name brought an image of Edward's face to my mind's eye, and he smiled…

Some minutes later, I regained consciousness to discover that in his eagerness to wake me, the little lamb had been licking my face between bounces. As he descended to lick it once again, I rolled over and he licked up a mouthful of dust from the front porch. He bounced thrice, spat thrice, and said, "Do you believe it now? You're madly in love with the woodcutter's son."

I sat bolt upright and spluttered, "But,,, but,,, but,,, but…"

"Why else would you be talking about his butt?"

"I most certainly am not talking about *that*," said I, standing up.

"The sooner you accept that you're in love with Edward the better," said the little lamb as he hopped away.

"I thought you wanted to help me!" I called out.

"I did."

"How is this helping me?"

"It's the truth."

In response, I stamped my foot. It was in this mood that I began my walk. "Love Edward? Stuff and nonsense. I don't *do* love. Never have done love. Never will do love. Far too many issues for *love*. The notion alone is just too preposterous. One need only spend *two minutes* with my dwarves to know that!" I had not gone far when I spied two men in the distance. They were fighting over a single object and, sitting on a log and painting her toe-nails, was a girl whose face was obscured by her long blonde hair. As I drew nearer, I saw that *two* Prince Charmings were engaged in a tug of war over one slipper.

"Hello, Orange!" Cinders called from her log.

"Oh, it's you. What's going on?" I asked.

Cinders grabbed her ankle, raised her toes to her lips, and blew on the polish. "I'm making my foot as pretty as possible for the winning Charming to slip the slipper onto," said she between blows. I observed the Charmings who, for all intents and purposes, could have been identical twins. Cinders added, "My Prince Charming arrived early, just like yours did."

"Which one is which?"

"Beats me."

"Are we to be deluged by early Charmings?" said I.

Cinders admired her pretty foot and said, "Apparently, when news reached my own Charming that I'd fallen for another, my own Charming couldn't get here quickly enough."

I folded my arms and watched as one Charming tugged the slipper to his chest, and then the other did the same, and while they tugged they said things like, "The slipper *and* the girl are mine!"

"Were yours! But now they belong to me!"

"We'll see about that!"

"Indeed we shall!"

I looked at Cinders and said, "How long have they been tugging over you?"
"For what feels like an age," said she, sighing.

"Why don't you just pick one?"

"How to choose?"

"They're identical. So what difference would it make?"

Someone sitting on the branch of the tree above us cleared their throat and said, "Your cousin Snow has promised Cinderella's Charming to me. So I suggest you pick *Snow's* Charming, Cinderella." I looked up and beheld Little Red.

"Is that true?" Cinders asked me.

"My cousin may have made such an arrangement, yes."

"May schmay," said Little Red, climbing down and standing beside Cinders.

"I don't believe we've been formally introduced," said Cinders. Both looked to me for the introduction.

"Cinders, Little Red. Little Red, Cinders," said I. They shook hands and said the pleasure was all theirs. The formalities out of the way, I stuck two fingers in my mouth and whistled to get the attention of the Charmings. They paused mid-tug and held firmly to the slipper. "You must have noticed?" said I to them.

"Noticed?" repeated the Charmings in unison.

"That some changes have been made to the land of late."

The Charmings growled at each other under their breaths and said, "We've noticed."

"Chief amongst these changes is that the ladies of the land are now able to *choose* the Charming of their heart's desire."

The Charmings both looked gravely concerned and, when I asked what had perturbed them so, they said in unison, "For the love of all that's perfect, *please* don't choose either of us, Orange."

Little Red chuckled. "Haven't you heard?" said she. "The grapevine has spoken of little else of late. Orange Orange has found her one true love." I looked at Little Red, and my expression must have been grave, for she quickly averted her gaze.

Cinders slipped her shoe back on and said, "I'm so happy for you! Unlike your cousin Snow, you have found your heart's desire."

I felt suddenly confused and spluttered, "But... but... but... but... and *but* with just one 't'." I glanced at the Charmings, who scattered like startled rabbits and flew into a nearby bush. "Don't pick either of us! Please! For we would not have our children resemble satsumas for all the world!"

"I have no intention of picking either of you," murmured I.

Cinderella stood up and moved to my side. "Little Red and I will choose our Charmings when we're good and ready," said told the Charmings. "In the meantime, we must take a walk with our friend Orange. For there are some things that girls must discuss in private."

"What *things*?" said I.

"Matters of the heart," said Little Red pointedly. With that the girls interlocked my arms with their own, and marched me away.

Once beyond the earshot of either Charming, Cinders said, "Do you know, your cousin Snow was exactly like you when it came to matters of the heart."

"I'm sure I don't know what you mean," said I, glancing down at Cinders's arm, which held my own.

Little Red nodded. "I only met her a couple of times, but I got the impression she was *very* insecure."

"How perceptive you are!" said Cinders. "Snow never could get to grips with her fairest-in-the-land status."

"It must have been quite the burden for one with so many issues," said Little Red.

I straightened my back and said, "So we both have our fair share of issues. If you have a point to make, then please make it."

"The point is this," said Cinders, tenderly squeezing my shoulder. "Feeling insecure about your appearance and being unable to love yourself must run in your family."

"Rub it in, why don't you?" said I.

A well-intentioned Little Red did just that when she pointed out, "Neither you nor Snow think yourselves worthy of another's love."

"The *point*, please?" said I, straightening my back to the point where a backwards cartwheel was a distinct possibility.

Cinders and Little Red glanced at one another and Cinders said, "The point is going to come as somewhat of a shock, Orange."

Little Red grasped my shoulder and, having supported me thus, she said, "We have heard through a most reliable source…"

"The grapevine, no less," said Cinders.

"Yes, the grapevine," continued Little Red, "who assures us

that he's spoken to the young man in question…"

"Edward," said Cinders helpfully.

"Yes, Edward, so his facts have come straight from the horse's mouth…"

"What *facts*?" said I.

"That Edward is in love with you too," said Little Red.

"…He can't possibly be," said I quietly, "for I resemble a mutated orange. And if he did, it would mean…"

"That he has fallen for the person within," said Cinders, placing her hand upon my heart.

I glanced down at her hand. "And he still thinks me worthy of… of…"

"His love, yes," said Little Red.

Tears overflowed from my eyes and rolled down my cheeks as I babbled, "The poor boy is clearly bonkers, but… no matter, for we will get him the *very* best help, but on no account is anyone to call the men in white coats."

"Hush, now," said Cinders. "Edward is perfectly sane. He's just the poor son of a woodcutter."

"Poor and perfect," murmured I.

The Return of Snow

I write this at midnight on the following day, and nothing has changed. And believe me it's not an easy thing to say, and more difficult still to write, but… I am in love with Edward. We had a date at the enchanted lake this afternoon. Cinders had arranged it, and she hid inside the hollowed-out tree, whispering words of encouragement through its peephole.

The fact is that before *you-know-what* happened to me, life seemed so much simpler. I did the housework each day, and then set off to help some poor character in need. Some might call it meddling (and many do), but this land is a cruel and terrifying place, and so many of its inhabitants need a happier ending. But since meeting Edward, I have been distracted. I blame my mind's eye, for it has been loath to let me think about much else. It is as though an enchantment has been placed upon me – an enchantment that I love *and* hate. Is it any wonder a person can't think straight when they fall in love?

This morning when I sat before my dressing table's mirror, I was no longer Orange Orange; I was Snow White again. My mirror welcomed me back (I presumed from the dead) as though I'd returned from the living room. It wasted no time in telling me that I was the fairest in the land. I didn't believe it, of course, but with my date with Edward only a few hours away, hearing it was a comfort of sorts.

My mirror might have taken my return in its stride, but the same could not be said of the dwarves. I decided it would be best to break the news to them quickly, like ripping off a plaster. Thus resolved, I drew a deep breath, flung open my bedroom door and shouted, "I'm back!" The dwarves, who had been waiting patiently at the kitchen table for their breakfast, spoons in hands, threw their spoons away and leapt for cover as though their spoons had become hand grenades. Goldilocks, who you may remember had come to stay with us, glanced up from the oats she was turning into porridge, observed my change in person, shrugged, and then returned to the serious business of porridge production.

Once I'd apologised to the dwarves for my Orange deception, and explained why it had been necessary, they gave me a hug and then returned to the table for breakfast. Insecure was quick to point out, "Once your evil stepmother discovers you're back, you're still going to be in terrible danger, Snow."

Not Particularly Hopeful drew a deep breath, as though a very large penny had just dropped. He began shaking his head and waggling his finger at me. "You've fallen in love with the woodcutter's son!"

Insecure smiled nervously. "No, she hasn't. It was Orange Orange who fell in love with the woodcutter's son."

"But Snow *is* Orange Orange!" pointed out Not Particularly Hopeful, not particularly helpfully.

Insecure looked at me like I'd betrayed him, and I could see the cogs turning behind his widening eyes. "You must be crazy," he murmured. "For while the woodcutter's son may be poor, according to the grapevine he's also perfect!"

"And?" I stammered.

"And?" said Insecure, turning as white as a sheet. "Don't you think that one so perfect deserves someone considerably less peculiar!?"

"Yes, of course I do, but…"

"But what?" said Insecure and Not Particularly Hopeful in unison.

I knew I had to think fast, otherwise they would ruin everything. And if everything was to be ruined, I would rather ruin it myself. The seed of an idea came to me. I grew it hastily and replied, "But I was Orange Orange when I fell in love with Edward."

"And?" said Insecure.

"And when I was Orange Orange, I wasn't feeling at all myself…"

"*And*?" pressed Insecure.

"And don't you see? It was *more* than just an orange disguise. Much more. The enchantment was so powerful that it turned me *into* Orange Orange. And it was she who fell in love with Edward. But, I'm Snow White again now, as you can see, so when I meet Edward today, I'm going to tell him there's been a terrible mistake."

"Would you like us to come with you?" asked Insecure.

"No! I mean, that won't be necessary. You've been taking far too much time off work because of me as it is. What with attending my funeral." As I smoothed out my apron, a general calmness fell over all. Which meant that Insecure and Not Particularly Hopeful must have believed me at least a little. Meddlesome, however, was in a dreadful mood. I knew why: I'd not had meddling on my mind. In fact, when it came to meddling, and without pointing any fingers, Cinders and Little Red had been the ones meddling in *my* affairs.

A little later, when the dwarves set off for work, I watched them until they were out of sight. I heard someone scream, and turned to see Cinders crumple to the ground, unconscious. Having just arrived at the cottage, she'd expected to see Orange Orange, not Snow White back from the dead. I hurried over and turned her onto her back. "Cinders? Cinders!?"

Cinder's eyes fluttered open. "*Snow*," said she softly. "You're alive?"

"Yes, it's me," said I, helping Cinders into a sitting position and sitting cross-legged beside her. She gazed at me askance, and slowly her senses returned. I placed a hand on her shoulder and squeezed gently. "It was I all along. I used powerful magic called fake tan, and with it I turned myself into Orange Orange."

"Fake tan?" she repeated, uncomprehendingly.

"Yes. They swear by it in a place called Essex."

"But why ever would they?"

I shrugged. "They must aspire to be orange there."

"But why? Orange is not the least bit an attractive colour for a person to be."

"That's why it was the perfect magic for me. I was no longer the fairest in the land, and my stepmother had no need of poisoning me."

"You could have told me, Snow. I'm your best friend."

"Little Miss Muffet thought it a good idea to keep my true identity a secret from all."

"Did she now? I can't say I'm surprised. That one's been acting very strangely of late. Hardly ever is she by her tree and eating her curds and whey. Now she spends all her days with the spider who was supposed to sit down beside her. Did you know that the no-eyed, no-brained toad that sells curds and whey has gone out of business?"

"Oh dear! No, I didn't. And it's all my fault for giving Little Miss Muffet a life beyond curds and whey."

Cinders brushed a stray hair from my face and said, "You do know what They say, don't you? That you can't make an omelette without breaking some eggs. It's so good to have you back, Snow!" *Technically speaking,* I thought, *I haven't been anywhere.* I opened my mouth to make that very point, but closed it again when Cinders lowered her voice and confided, "Truth be told, I wasn't particularly keen on Orange Orange. Oh, my!" She clasped her cheeks in surprise. "OH, MY!" she repeated, only louder and in capitals. "So it is *you* who has fallen in love with Edward!"

"Hush, keep your voice down," said I, glancing over my shoulder in the direction the dwarves had gone. "For Insecure and Not Particularly Hopeful must not find out for all the world."

"Snow in love? Oh, this is *big*. Perhaps you're destined to live happily ever after, after all!"

I shook my head. "Edward is sure to tire of me, particularly when he discovers that I've turned from Truly Orange into truly peculiar."

"Whatever is the matter, Snow? You've turned the colour of an icicle."

"Which reminds me, Edward is expecting to meet Truly Orange today, so he will also think me a liar."

"Word on the grapevine is that Edward is poor and perfect. And perfect people are colour-blind."

"You don't think he has a thing for orange girls, then?"

Cinders shook her head. "That would make him as peculiar as you are."

Later that day…

Later that day, Cinders accompanied me to the enchanted lake for my date. I didn't make it easy for her, and kept coming up with excuses for turning back. The closer we got to the enchanted lake, the more I wanted to take flight and the tighter her grip on my arm became. And when the willow tree, within whose tumbling branches my date with Edward was to take place, came into view, poor Cinders had literally to drag me towards it.

Under its canopy, Cinders had laid out a magnificent spread: strawberries with cream, cream buns, cream cheese, cheese cakes, cheese toasties and many more cheese-based dishes besides. "What's with all the cheese?" said I.

"I know how much you love it. And you will recall how the no-eyed, no-brained toad had gone out of business?"

"Yes, of course. It was all my fault."

"Well, the toad had all this cheese to sell, and…"

"Say no more. What a lovely gesture," said I, squeezing Cinders's hand.

Cinders opened the secret door in the tree. "He was so *desperate* that he sold me all his cheese for an absolute bargain!" said she, stepping inside and closing the door.

"Oh, I see," said I.

Cinders waggled a finger through the little peephole. "Sit," she said sternly. I glanced behind to see the dog she must be talking to. "Sit!" said she again. "Edward is due at any moment."

The notion of seeing Edward at any moment turned my legs to jelly, and I didn't so much sit as collapse into a heap. "I really don't need this," groaned I from within my heap.

"For goodness's sake!" said Cinders. "Rearrange yourself out of that heap. Didn't you hear what I said? Edward could arrive at any moment." The reminder didn't help, but I managed to emerge from my heap somehow. "Do you hear that?" said Cinders.

"Hear what?" said I, my heart skipping a beat and my breath leaving me.

"Footsteps!" whispered Cinders.

I stuck my fingers in my ears until I saw Cinders's thumb emerge from the peephole and point downward, then withdrew them. "*Yes*," whispered I. "Dry leaves are being trodden underfoot…"

"Under Edward's foot," said Cinders, "and here he comes!"

A hand pushed aside the willow's hanging branches, and I beheld Edward wearing a strapless red dress and stockings. I had hoped Edward would not smile when he saw me, and those of you who read my last diary will know how his smile had a tendency to make me faint from famishment. On this point, I was relieved, for it was clear from his expression that there was very little chance of him smiling. I supposed it was his disappointment at finding me no longer orange, but pale enough to be visible from space most nights. But then he glanced down at his dress and shook his head as though he would have preferred one with straps. He looked at me, did a

145

double-take, and said, "Truly, there is no cause for alarm. But it could be that you need a blood transfusion."

I shook my head and confessed. "I am supposed to look like someone in need of a blood transfusion. You see, my name isn't Truly Orange, it's Snow White."

"The fairest in the land," murmured Edward.

"Well, yes, and *obviously* no. I have deceived you, Edward. And having deceived you, I would understand if you wanted nothing whatsoever to do with me…"

I was silenced mid-babble by Edward's raised palm. "Your colour, or lack of it, is unimportant, as I am colour-blind."

"Metaphorically speaking?"

"Quite so," said he. "Although the same could not be said for the eyesight of the three bears, whose own story mentions not a word of their acute myopia."

"I see."

"Like the three bears, I do not think that you do. They were expecting Goldilocks to be a girl, and would accept nothing I told them to the contrary."

"Oh. So you aren't wearing a strapless dress and stockings by choice, then?"

"Is that a serious question, my love?"

"Deadly. For I know for a fact that the Big Bad Wolf likes to dress in women's clothes."

"Perhaps you are mistaken, for the reputation of the Big Bad

Wolf is fearsome to say the least."

"Maybe so, but it's not as though anyone *forced* him to put on a nightdress and bonnet. He might just as easily have stood beside the door and devoured Little Red the moment she walked through it. I'm babbling, aren't I?"

Edward nodded. "And so fast that I barely caught a word of it." I opened my mouth, but closed it again when Edward added, "However, from the word or two I did catch, it seems that the Big Bad Wolf has more issues than your average wolf."

"Precisely so. And to think I wanted to go on a date with someone who wears a dress!" said I, glancing at Edward's.

"I am pleased to hear it isn't a preference, for I don't believe I can keep up this pretence for very much longer."

"It's a very nice dress," I pointed out.

Edward sighed. "Just one of the many that Mummy Bear has made for me... or rather, made for *Goldilocks*." Edward pulled at the side of the dress as though in discomfort.

"What is it?" asked I.

"Mummy Bear is so short-sighted that she mistook my muscular chest for something else... and *insists* on my wearing a training bra whenever I go out."

"I see," said I, endeavouring not to smile.

"I do not think that you do, for if you did you would know that for anyone to go through humiliation on a scale such as this on behalf of another could only mean that that person thought the world of that other person."

When I regained consciousness, I began to mutter, "But you cannot think the world of me, *must* not think it, for if you do it can only mean you are bonkers." I sat up and gazed beyond the branches of the weeping willow tree for the men in white coats who must surely be coming for him. "The men in white coats came for me once, but *that* was a misunderstanding," said I.

Edward brushed a stray hair from my cheek and said, "What has happened to make one so fair and so charitable so insecure?"

"I suppose I must have been written this way."

"Then I for one would like a word with the Author."

"Really? And if you met him what would you say to him?"

"I would give him a piece of my mind."

"Have him rewrite me, you mean?"

"Rewrite you? Never. Sooo," said Edward, sighing.

"Buttons on your training bra?" said I, feeling awkward and making a terrible joke.

"What was that?" asked Edward.

"Nothing. Just a terrible joke about embellishing your training bra with buttons."

"It already has buttons, believe me." Edward almost smiled, but stopped himself in time. "This cannot be easy for you," said he.

I nodded wholeheartedly. "The truth is that making jokes

under such stressful circumstances is extraordinarily difficult."

"Then maybe it's for the best if you do not try."

"So you don't think I'm the least bit funny, then? You will soon learn that not being the least bit funny is perhaps the most attractive thing about me." Edward's gaze seemed to take in every feature of my face, then settled on my lips. I rubbed at them vigorously. "Is there's something unsightly stuck to my mouth? Yesterday's porridge, perhaps? I'm such a messy eater. Compared to me, Insecure says that Awkward has excellent table manners. You may raise an eyebrow, but Awkward regularly stabs himself in the eye with his fork, and…" Edward leaned towards me, his lips parting close to mine. "I've had an idea," said he. I watched him, quite unable to move or speak. I blinked in a way that suggested he continue explaining his idea. "Perhaps," said he, "in a land such as this, where frogs can be turned into princes, and princesses can be woken from a hundred years of sleep with a single kiss…" He stopped talking and his gaze once again found my lips. I blinked, blinked again, and then sighed. "Well," he went on, "perhaps a kiss can magic away all your insecurities about living happily ever after." Edward leaned in closer, and I could feel his sweet breath upon my lips, and… *that's* when someone outside the tree yelled: "Edward, son of the woodcutter! Come out! You're under arrest by order of the Queen!"

A fraught moment later…

A fraught moment later, Edward was on his feet and I lay sprawled on my back. In my haste to join him, I had tripped over not just one but both of my size nines.

"You'd better stay there," said he, backing away.

"No! I'm coming with you. They are my stepmother's guards, so maybe I can help!" said I, clinging to his dress and pulling myself to my feet.

Edward backed away from me. "No," he said firmly. "It's much too dangerous. When the Queen discovers you're still alive, she'll start trying to poison you again. You know as well as I that she's written that way."

From beyond the tree's tumbling branches came the cry of the same guardsman. "This is your last chance! Come out with your hands raised above your head!"

"I will go and see the Queen!" said I. "I'll promise her *anything* if she'll let you go."

"Please. Do nothing foolish on my behalf…" said Edward, disappearing through the hanging branches.

He was greeted on the other side by laughter. I heard the door to the willow tree open behind me, and felt Cinders's hand upon my shoulder. "What has an insecure and not particularly hopeful girl to do to get a break in this land?" said she.

"You are not wrong."

"So what are you going to do?"

"Go straight to my stepmother and ask her to release Edward."

"You heard him. It's much too dangerous."

"That woman is going to find out I'm back sooner or later. She has so many spies that I suspect it will be sooner." I stuck my fingers in my mouth and whistled.

"Barry?" said Cinders.

"Yes. There is no time to delay."

Barry came trotting under the tree's canopy as though he'd been waiting to do so. Barry is faultless that way. When he clapped eyes upon me, he turned pale – not pale enough to be visible from space most nights, perhaps, but believe me when I tell you I have never seen a paler boar. "Is that really *you, Snow?*" said he, his piggy eyes welling up.

"Yes."

"But *how?* And where is Orange Orange?"

"Orange Orange was me all the time. Little Miss Muffet gave me powerful magic that transformed me into her. I am very sorry for having deceived you, Barry, but I believed myself in great danger."

"From your stepmother?"

"Yes. And I'd like you to take me to see her now."

Barry looked at Cinders, who shrugged her beautiful shoulders. "She means to help Edward, the woodcutter's son.

And you know what Snow's like when she's minded to help someone in peril."

Barry nodded enthusiastically. "You'd better jump on. You wouldn't be Snow otherwise." I did just that, and Barry glanced at me over his shoulder. "It's good to have you back! I don't care what anyone says, this land needs you."

"Like a hole in the head, I should imagine. But thank you, Barry."

Forty-seven anxious minutes later…

Forty-seven anxious minutes later, I climbed off a hot and panting Barry. "You sure you want to do this, Snow?"

"I must. Edward needs me."

"Alright, but I'm not going anywhere. I know swine are not permitted inside royal palaces unless roasted and served on a bed of rice, but if I hear you whistle, I'll batter down that door and find you."

"Thank you, Barry."

I knocked upon the door. My stepmother's butler opened it. You will remember how he is vertically challenged – so much so that he barely reaches my knobbly knees. Speaking of which, he must have recognised them right away, for he stumbled backwards, beheld my pale face, clasped his own and cried, "It can't be you!"

"I think you will find that it is me."

"But if you're alive this is dreadful news! The very worst news imaginable!"

"You're pleased to see me, I can tell."

"The Queen's been in such good spirits since she crushed you underfoot. Shoo!" said he, shooing me with his little hands. "Go! Just go. And if you know what's good for you, you'll go as far away as possible."

"While I appreciate your advice, it isn't about me…" I

153

attempted to brush past him and, like the last time I visited, he thwarted my every attempt, and pretty soon it felt like we were out on *another* date, dancing. The idea of being on a *second* date was even more irksome than when it felt as though we were on our first date. I'm ashamed to admit that, when he did one of his impressive twirls, I stuck my foot in the small of his back and shoved him for all I was worth. I must be worth quite a lot when it comes to shoving vertically challenged butlers, for he shot away so fast on the polished floor that, when he finally made contact with something (it sounded like a cabinet filled with china cups, but who knew?) I could no longer see him. "Whoops," said I, brushing myself down.

As mentioned in my previous diaries, my stepmother's palace is very large. I might easily have got lost, if not for a loud party taking place in one of its many ballrooms. I followed the sound of merriment and eventually came upon two guards standing outside a set of gigantic doors. The guards were very tall, and held staffs that were taller still. The one on the right peered down at me. The fellow couldn't have been much of a scholar, for he didn't even recognise me. "By what name should I announce you, madam?" he asked.

"Snow White."

I had clearly underestimated his scholarly ways, for he opened the doors, banged his staff thrice upon the ground, and announced my arrival thus: "Snow White, the fairest in the land!"

Well, it would be no exaggeration to say that you could have heard a pin drop. And once the guest who had dropped a pin muttered an apology, the guests began to part and my stepmother emerged from among them like a spider from its lair. She fixed her evil gaze upon me and the colour drained from her face. "Orange Orange? Is this some kind of joke? Did you imagine this a Halloween party?"

I held my head high and shook it.

"Then have you recently been submerged in a vat of flour?" said she, looking past me into the hall as though expecting to see the vat of flour from which I had emerged.

I stood up as straight as possible and said, "No, I didn't. The truth is… I *am* Snow White."

"But I…" My stepmother glanced behind her and cast her gaze over her open-mouthed guests.

"You what? *Killed* me?"

"Don't be absurd. I was about to say I… I went to your funeral."

"It was not really my funeral. You buried an empty tube of fake tan." My stepmother smiled, and so false was her smile that it looked to have been painted on her face by an artist who could paint only glares. "Oh, it matters not! Thank goodness you're alive!" said she, summoning a servant with a crooked finger. When the servant was beside her, she leant in close and whispered, "Have the croquet lawn dug up immediately."

"Dug up, Your Majesty?"

"Yes, immediately. And then re-plant my apple orchard." Her servant bowed and left to carry out her orders.

"Sounds awfully urgent," said I.

"What does?" she asked.

"Your need for apples."

"What splendid hearing you have. You know what They say, don't you?"

"No. What does Frank say?"

"That an apple a day keeps the doctor away. They have never said that about a round of croquet," said she, getting a round of applause for Frank's insight. "Your father is going to be so relieved when he hears you're back. Where have you been?"

"Nowhere. I was disguised... as Orange Orange."

A dreadful penny must have dropped then, for she began laughing and pointing at me like I was the most ridiculous thing ever to disgrace her palace. Then she remembered her charm offensive and said sweetly, "So it is you, then."

"Yes. I believe we have already established that it is I."

"*You* and not Orange Orange have fallen in love with the woodcutter's son!" This she could not help but find funny, and her laughter must have been infectious for it quickly spread amongst her guests.

I stood as straight as possible under the circumstances and said, "I suppose I am quite fond of him, yes. Which brings me to the reason for my visit: I want you to let Edward go. For unless being poor and perfect is a crime, which I do not believe it is, then he has done nothing wrong and must be freed."

"Freed, you say?"

"I do say. And preferably into my custody. And right away."

"But my dear, Edward must be punished for the crimes of his father."

"And what crime did Edward's father commit?"

"The woodcutter was supposed to…"

"Yes?"

My stepmother glanced behind her at her assembled guests, all of whom were hanging on her every word.

"He was *supposed* to do what?" I pressed.

"It matters not what he was *supposed* to do, for his son has committed a serious crime in his own right now. And he must therefore remain in my dungeon until his trial."

"*Crime?* The crime of being poor and perfect?"

"No. If that were the case, I'd be half guilty of the same crime."

"Then what has he done?"

"He has impersonated another character – a very serious crime, and punishable by death."

"But that was all my idea!"

"Then maybe you'll be less meddlesome in future."

"How did you find out?"

"My soldiers knocked at your cottage this morning, and discovered that Goldilocks was living there. So they put two and two together, and then paid the three bears a visit. You are aware that Edward delights in wearing stockings and a training bra?"

"He does *not* delight in it. He only agreed to it because it was a part of..."

My stepmother leaned forwards on her throne. "Of what? Of his terrible deception?"

I removed my foot from my mouth and reattached it to the end of my leg. "I want to see him," said I.

"And so you shall. At his trial – a trial at which I am to be his only judge. A word of step-motherly advice: do not to get your hopes up. I have already found him guilty."

"And is that your final word on the matter?"

"It is."

I felt tears come to my eyes and, before I grew inconsolable, I turned and walked slowly from the ballroom.

I walked back through the palace with hands clasped behind my back and head bowed low. I soon came upon a green vase lying on its side in the middle of the corridor. The vase had on a pair of patent leather shoes, and it was talking to itself in muffled tones. This struck me as odd. I picked it up and put it back on its feet, whereupon it darted away and smashed against the wall. Out popped the butler like a booby prize. I say a booby prize, for any prize that bellows a string of words unrepeatable in a young woman's diary before it shoves you out the front door could only be described as booby.

The following morning…

I would like to say that I awoke the following morning with renewed hope in my heart that all would soon be well, but I didn't manage even a wink of sleep. This was due in no small part to my mind's eye, which *insisted* on showing me poor Edward in his dungeon every three seconds. I had never seen his cell (and neither had my mind's eye, come to that) but that did not prevent it conjuring the most horrid things. And as my mind's eye was quick to point out, Edward would never have been chained by his ankles to the ceiling over a pit of snapping alligators, if not for my meddling.

At breakfast the dwarves were all relieved not to have porridge again. "I'm glad Goldilocks has gone to live with the three bears," said Inconsolable.

"A real space-cadet. I fear for her," added Not Particularly Hopeful.

"You are wrong to fear for her," said I. "For Goldilocks is one of the few characters in this land who was always going to live happily ever after."

"It's alright for some," said Insecure.

Not Particularly Hopeful almost smiled. "It's just as well you're not Orange Orange anymore," he said.

"And why is that?" I asked.

"I should have thought that was obvious. Orange Orange fell in love, and nothing good ever came from falling in love."

"That's right," added Insecure. "You need look no further than Edward the woodcutter's boy to see that."

"Poor Edward!" cried Inconsolable, apparently on my behalf. "With all the trouble he's in, you're so lucky you're not Orange Orange anymore." He blew his nose and then looked at me with tears in his big green eyes. "Poor Snow," said he. "She looks miserable enough as it is."

"Why *do* you look so miserable?" enquired Awkward. Insecure and Not Particularly Hopeful leaned forwards and looked at me, while Awkward leaned too far back on the bench and fell off onto the floor.

"Poor Awkward!" said I, standing up and rushing to his aid.

"Well?" pressed Insecure.

"Well what?" said I, helping Awkward to his feet.

"Why the long face?" asked Insecure.

"That is surely a question for *the book*'s illustrator," said I firmly.

"Your face is actually more round than it is long, Snow," said Not Particularly Hopeful.

"I wish you would make up your minds," said I. "My face is either too long or too round, but I don't really see how it can be *both*. Although, come to think of it…"

"Where are you going?" asked Inconsolable, welling up.

"I'm taking my long round face out for a walk," said I, heading for the door.

160

Inconsolable burst into tears. "But you haven't finished your breakfast!"

"She hasn't *started* her breakfast," pointed out Meddlesome. And then, true to his meddlesome nature he added, "In my experience, a lack of appetite can indicate that a person is in love."

"Not this time, it doesn't," said I, crossing my fingers and walking out the door.

I strode purposely through the woods. I didn't know where I was going but I knew wherever it was I needed to find answers there. *If only I knew the questions*, thought I. *Edward's fate is sealed? He's to be found guilty of impersonating Goldilocks – put to death for a crime that I practically* forced *him to commit.* I kicked a pebble and, as it sailed away, I thought, *Who says Edward's fate is sealed and can't be changed? Surely They must know better than Who?* It was then that I decided I must hear it from the horse's mouth. By that I didn't mean the horse's mouth in the west wood, but Frank the groundhog, known to all the universe as They.

I came upon Frank reclining in a hammock reading. "Hello Frank," said I, "what are you reading?"

"A very rare and old copy of *the book*," said he, licking a paw and turning the page.

"You don't seem the least bit surprised to see me returned from the dead," I said, standing at the end of his hammock.

"I'm not. And you know what They say, don't you?"

"No. What do you say, Frank?"

161

"That the early bird catches the worm."

"I must be the worm," nodded I. "I certainly resemble a worm first thing in the morning."

Frank rolled his eyes. "You are the bird, Snow."

"So who is the worm?"

"The worm is the useful information you seek."

"You know why I've come to see you, then? You have good news about Edward? That his fate is not sealed?"

"How can Edward's fate be sealed when we have an expert in the art of meddling in our midst?"

"And who might that expert meddler be?"

"Do you really need to ask?"

"It is *I*?"

"It is."

"So there is hope for Edward, then!"

"Yes. But at the same time you know what They say."

"No. What do you say?"

"That you should never count your chickens before they've hatched."

"I have chickens!"

"Just one chicken."

I held out my hands and turned them palms up in anticipation of my chicken.

"Your chicken is the Eighth Fairy," said he.

"The *who* fairy?"

"No, the Eighth Fairy. Have you heard of her?"

I shook my head. "Who is she, and how can she help Edward?"

"You've heard of Princess Aurora?"

"No."

"Many know her by her other name, Sleeping Beauty."

"I believe I have heard of *her*, yes."

"Sleeping Beauty is to be pricked by a cursed spinning wheel."

"Ouch," said I.

"It gets worse."

"It usually does in this land."

"The spinning wheel's curse will place her into a coma from which she can only be awakened by a kiss from her Prince Charming."

I scratched my head. "If you replace the spinning wheel with an apple, her story sounds very similar to my own. Are you *certain* you're not confusing her with me? For the deluded – and there are a great many in the land – think that I am a great beauty, and if my stepmother gets her way, then I'm to become a beauty of the sleeping variety."

Frank shook his head.

"So you mean there's a *genuine* beauty who is to sleep for a great many years?"

"There's another one, yes," said Frank.

"And does she have an evil stepmother who hates her?"

"No."

"Then who hates her enough to curse the spinning wheel?"

"The Eighth Fairy."

"The same Eighth Fairy who can help change Edward's fate?"
"That's right."

"But if she's as mean as you say, then why would she?"

"She won't, but she knows of a place where it can easily be done. And she will lead you there if you follow her."

"Follow her where?"

"To it."

"*It?*"

"Yes, to *it*." I placed my hands on my hips and fixed Frank with my most determined stare, and it must have done the trick, for he added, "*It,* the Author's Cabin it: the place where *the book* was written. It is where you'll find *the book's*

164

original manuscript."

"Really?"

"Yes. And that's where you'll also find the Author's pencil and eraser. With them you can rub out Edward's current fate and replace it with one more to your liking."

"That's sounds *so* much to my liking! Not to mention right up my alley!"

Frank twirled his whiskers. "It has your name written all over it, Snow."

"And so too will *the book* if I get my hands on it."

It was Frank's turn to fix me with his most no-nonsense stare.

"Just my little joke," said I. "Of course I won't write my name all over it."

"If you do you'll write your name into every story in the land."

"I would never impose myself on the land in such a way. This land deserves better."

"Only rub out and alter the paragraph that relates to Edward's fate. Have I made myself clear?"

"As the finest crystal. So where might I find the Eighth Fairy?"

"She resides in the land that lies to the east, beyond the mountains."

"I wasn't aware there was a land to the east and beyond the

mountains."

"Well, there is one. Why the long round face?"

"Because if that's true, I could have kept my promise to the woodcutter and left this land. So all this really *is* my fault."

"And now you must leave this land to put things right."

"Put things right…" murmured I. "Has the Eighth Fairy cursed the spinning wheel yet?"

"Oh, yes. She cursed it sixteen years ago when Princess Aurora was just a baby."

I felt a chill run down my spine. "So Princess Aurora has already been pricked by the cursed wheel?"

"Not yet. Her father the king found out about the curse and ordered that all the spinning wheels in his land be destroyed. If they don't spin they can't prick her." I opened my mouth in readiness to ask the obvious question, but closed it again when Frank held up a paw. "But *one* spinning wheel is still in use," said he.

"One?" said I. "And where is it located?"

"In the palace where Princess Aurora lives."

"But why? Could there *be* a worse place?"

Frank shrugged. "It's the way her story was written."

"I see. Who is this cruel Author? Might I find him at his cabin? I'd like a word with him."

"The Author left his cabin as soon as *the book* was finished.

And nobody has seen him since."

"Too ashamed to ever show his face, I should imagine."

"Perhaps."

"So how does Princess Aurora come upon the spinning wheel?"

"First thing tomorrow morning, she's going to feel restless and explore the palace."

"Tomorrow morning!" I stuck two fingers in my mouth and whistled for Barry. "Then I should not delay for all the world."

"If you want my advice, it would be best if you didn't meddle with Princess Aurora's story."

"When her story is so much like my own?" I glanced about and could see no sign of Barry. I whistled again, and sure enough he emerged from the undergrowth.

"We must make haste to the land beyond the mountains, Barry."

"Who said there's a land beyond the mountains?"

"No. *They* said there is. Tell him, Frank."

"No doubt about it," said Frank.

"Well, I never," said Barry. "If that's what They say, then it must be true."

"If we've quite established that it's there, could we please make haste?"

Barry shook his head. "You know I'd help out if I could. But I'm not equipped to make that journey."

"Equipped?"

"With wings to fly over the mountains."

"Then how am I to get there?" said I, looking back and forth between Frank and Barry.

They came up with the solution: "You'll need to summon The Crow."

Barry nodded. "Frank's talking about The Crow as in as *the crow flies.*"

I jumped and flapped my arms, then remembered that that was how you summoned the men in white coats. I stopped and peered about nervously for them. Frank snatched a hair from his cheek and flicked it over his left shoulder. "Is that how you summon The Crow?" asked I.

Barry snorted. "If that's how They do it, then that's how it must be done." And lo and behold, The Crow appeared. It was considerably larger than your average crow – and it needed to be, what with all the weight I imagined I'd put on recently.

A good many fields and a mountain range later…

A good many fields and a mountain range later, The Crow landed in a forest clearing. I thanked it for getting me there in double-quick time and, in response, it squawked how the pleasure had been all mine – at least, I assumed that was what it said – then it flapped its great wings and took flight.

There was a well-trodden path that wended its way through the forest and, taking into account the way The Crow had brought me, I continued in that direction. I had not gone far when I came upon a little house. Outside of the house an old lady swept her porch while her dog danced a jig. "Hello!" she called.

"Hello!" replied I.

"I'm Old Mother Hubbard. And who might you be?"

"Snow White. My, what a talented dog you have! It's dancing a very impressive jig."

"It's the star of our nursery rhyme," said Old Mother Hubbard, rolling her eyes.

"That's nice."

"Not for me. All I do is run errands for it." Old Mother Hubbard looked at her dog and sighed. "I went to the barbers to buy him a wig, and when I came back he was dancing this jig."

It was then that I noticed her black dog had a mop of blonde hair. The old woman put down her broom and began to walk away. "Where are you going?" I asked.

169

"To fulfil the next verse, where else?"

"Which is?"

"*She went to the cobblers to buy him some shoes, and when she got back he was reading the news.*"

"Might I trouble you for some information before you go?"

"The dog troubles me all the time, so you might as well. I'm used to being troubled."

"I'm sorry to hear that. If you answer my question, perhaps I might do something for you in return."

"What might you do for me?"

"Oh, I don't know. Maybe change your nursery rhyme?"

Old Mother Hubbard rubbed at a crick in her bent back. "I don't think such a thing is possible."

"I am certain that it is possible. I have had to make *teensy weensy* changes to stories before, and what's more, the place I must eventually find will make it easier than ever to change your rhyme."

"Where must you eventually find?"

"The Author's Cabin."

"I hope you're not going to ask me for directions to the Author's Cabin. No one knows where that is."

I shook my head. "They say there is one person who does know, which is why I must find the Princess Aurora – aka the Sleeping Beauty – for she is acquainted with this person.

So my question to you is, do you know where she lives?"

"The Princess Aurora?"

"Yes."

"Her Royal Highness lives in the Grand Palace, of course."

"And is it far?"

"Not as The Crow flies."

"The Crow dropped me off a few minutes ago, and seemed in a great hurry to return to my own land."

"It's lucky for you I know a shortcut, then," said Old Mother Hubbard, walking back towards her house.

"Where are you going?" I asked. "I need to reach the Princess Aurora without delay, for she is in grave danger of being pricked."

"I'll be back in a mo. Just going to fetch a pencil and pad."

"Whatever for?"

"So I can rewrite my poem on the way, just in case you should find the Author's Cabin."

Sometime later

I waved goodbye to Old Mother Hubbard and put the new
poem she'd written in my pocket. The path that led up to the
Grand Palace was steep and winding, and when eventually I
saw it, it stole my breath away. It was magnificent, and much
grander than any in my own land. Its turrets were so high that
they pierced the pink clouds floating over it. These same
clouds were reflected in the water of its moat. A drawbridge
began to lower and many men on horses rode out, paying me
little attention as I crossed it – one of the benefits of being
plain.

In the courtyard there were a great many doors leading into
the palace. Some were grand, and I suspected that were I to
knock upon one, a butler would refuse to let me pass. And I
had to pass, so before long it would doubtless have felt as
though we were out on a date, dancing. I therefore chose the
smallest and shabbiest door I could find. Inside was a
corridor lined with pegs, and he peg at the far end held a
maid's costume. As I approached it, a portly woman
appeared as if from nowhere and handed it to me. "You're
late!" she said.

"Late? Oh, no! Has the Princess Aurora been pricked? Has
she fallen into a coma?" The woman did not answer my
question, opting instead to ask one of her own: "Are you
quite normal?"

I shrugged. "Well, I'm obviously not *normal*, but I find that
I'm able to function on a rudimentary level. Why do you
ask?"

"Not only are you talking absolute *gibberish,* but you're dreadfully pale."

I nodded. "I'm visible from space most nights. So, Princess Aurora hasn't been pricked by a spinning wheel, then?"

"Of *course* she hasn't. The king banned them all."

It was clear that as well as being rude, this woman was considerably less well informed than I. "I won't be needing this costume," said I, handing it back to her. "And now, if you could just point me in the direction of Princess Aurora, I'll be on my way." I don't know if you've ever been boxed about the ears by a portly woman who is less well informed than you are, but I would not recommend it. It makes your lobes smart. "Get off me!" cried I, for that seemed the appropriate thing to cry under the circumstances. I crouched down, scrambled under her legs, and sprinted for all I was worth.

When I eventually slowed to a trot, I caught sight of my reflection and wondered why I was running like a pony. I stopped doing so and stood before a mirror. It was tall and grand, and I thought that boded well for my location in the Palace. I sensed that the mirror was about to speak, and stopped it with a raised palm. "Before you prove that you need your eyes tested, could you please just tell me where I might find Princess Aurora?"

The mirror yawned.

"Am I keeping you up?" I asked it.

"Now you come to mention it, yes."

"Hard work being a reflective surface, is it?"

"Of late. I blame the location."

I looked left and right down the ornate hallway. "What has the location to do with it?"

"It's the ideal place to stop for a chinwag. And whenever people stop and wag their chins, they keep me awake."

"I don't see why this should be such an ideal location."

"Really? Did you not just choose it to stop and wag your own chin?"

I could not deny it. "If you'd just tell me where I might find Princess Aurora, I'll be on my way."

"You're in luck. She wandered by here not five minutes ago."

"*Please* tell me that she didn't look the least bit restless."

"Now you come to mention it, I've never seen her look so restless. In fact, I've never seen her before. She's supposed to remain in her rooms."

"Then she must be about to come upon it!"

"Come upon what?"

"A room where an old lady is making clothes with a spinning wheel!"

"Relax. There is no such room. The king banned the use of spinning wheels sixteen years ago when the Princess was born. The Eighth Fairy placed a curse on her, you know."

"I had heard about the curse, yes."

"That Eighth Fairy is bad news. Wagging chins inform me that it all started when she went away to assist The Author at his cabin. She had been gone for such a long time that the king forgot to invite her to the Princess's christening. The Eighth Fairy was so angry that she placed a curse on the poor little Princess. That curse is the reason she's been confined to her rooms for sixteen years. It's the fear of her coming into contact with a spinning wheel, you know."

The mirror's reminder of that which I already knew was timely. "You must tell me which way she went!"

"That way," said the mirror.

"Past that grandfather clock?"

"No. The *other* that way."

"Past the cabinet filled with china cups?"

"If there's a third option in this corridor, I'd like to hear about it."

Several anxious minutes later…

Several anxious minutes later, I heard voices coming from behind a door that was slightly ajar. "Are you *sure* you want to touch my spinning wheel?" asked an old woman.

"Oh, yes please!" replied a younger woman.

"But why?" asked the older woman.

"It's just something I've always wanted to do," replied the younger woman.

"Be my guest, then…"

I burst into the room and saw Princess Aurora reaching for the spinning wheel. "Step away from that wheel!" I cried.

The Princess looked at me with the dulled eyes of someone who, having been confined to her rooms for sixteen years for fear of being pricked by a spinning wheel, reaches for the first one she sees having left it. "But why shouldn't I touch it?" she asked, looking down her beautiful nose at me.

"Two reasons," said I, endeavouring to look down my fat nose and still see her.

"And they would be?"

"Well, firstly it's a wheel."

"And the second reason?"

"It's *spinning.*"

"So?"

"So the curse so!"

"Oh, that," said she, glancing down at her beautifully manicured nails. "Surely touching it *once* couldn't hurt."

I took hold of her hand and pulled her from the room into the corridor. She protested loudly but stumbled after me nonetheless.

I went back into the room, closing and locking the door. I picked up the spinning wheel and hurled it through an open window. It splashed into the moat, where it bobbed about on the surface. "Oh, now you've really gone and done it," said the old woman. "The Eighth Fairy is going to be furious."

"Maybe so," said I, sucking on my pricked finger, "but you know what They say: you can't make an omelette without breaking some eggs."

"*You* just volunteered to be the eggs," said she, pointing a gnarled finger at me.

"And not the first time," said I.

"You must be Snow White."

"I cannot deny it." We heard another splash, and when I poked my head out of the window, I saw Princess Aurora swimming towards the spinning wheel. "You have got to be kidding!"

"Has she jumped into the moat after it?" asked the old woman.

"Yes!"

The old woman nodded sagely. "She's been told so many times and by so many people to avoid spinning wheels that she's grown up to find them irresistible…" I've no idea what the old woman said next, for the very next instant I leapt from the window. Down I fell, my nose pinched between thumb and forefinger in anticipation of the smelly green water that fast approached it.

Several moments and a splash later...

Several moments and a splash later, we must have made quite a sight: two fairytale characters who were never even supposed to meet, let alone end up splashing about and screaming together in a smelly green moat. The reason for our screaming (and to a lesser extent our splashing about) was this: neither of us could swim. Apparently, we hadn't been written that way, so it came as a relief when we realised the moat was only four feet deep and we could stand up. Aurora made a splashing lunge for the spinning wheel, and I made a lunge for Aurora. Despite my efforts, the princess landed flat upon the wheel. Fortunately for her, the wheel was no longer a spinning wheel but a bobbing wheel. I folded my arms and asked the Princess what she was bobbing and sobbing about.

"How am I to become the Sleeping Beauty now?"

"That wheel was *cursed*. Wouldn't you rather be a waking beauty than a sleeping one?"

Princess Aurora stood up. "Like you, you mean?"

I shook my head. "All that bobbing and sobbing must have affected your vision. But all things considered, you're a very fortunate person."

"Yes, you are!" said an angry voice.

I looked up and beheld a young woman with short dark hair. She was wearing a pink dress and holding a purple wand. "The Eighth Fairy, I presume?" said I.

"Snow *White*, I presume?" said she. We placed our hands on

our hips, a body language that said we'd presumed correctly. "Well, this is a first," said she. "Not only are you in the wrong story, but also the wrong land!"

"I will travel anywhere to prevent an injustice." The Eighth Fairy pointed her wand at me and went red in the face. "You can't frighten me with a silly wand," said I, preparing to duck.

She lowered her wand. "There is somewhere I have to be, so I'll decide what to do with you later. Unlike you and your *meddling*, some of us have useful work to do." With that she turned and stomped off.

I moved swiftly to the edge of the moat and tried to climb out. The edge was steep and muddy, and no sooner had I hurled myself upon it than I had slid back down into the water. I turned to Princess Aurora. "Would you mind giving me a hand?"

"Not at all," said she, wading over to me. "Where are you going?"

"After the Eighth Fairy," said I, craning my neck and watching her stomp into an immense forest.

The Princess cupped her hands, and a glance from her pretty green eyes told me it was quite alright to place a foot in them. As I climbed out, she said, "She's headed into the forest of a million and one trees."

"A million and *one?* Sounds awfully precise."

"It's the *one* that counts the most."

"And why is that?"

"It leads to the Author's Cabin. And you must not for all the world even behold it."

"And why not?"

"Because it's forbidden. Don't you know Anything?"

I shook my head. "I've never had the pleasure of meeting him, but if there's one thing I do know, it's that *nothing* should prevent us from changing things for the better." I reached down and pulled her from the moat.

"You must be very brave," said she.

"Brave? No. Just meddlesome."

As I walked away, she called out, "Thank you! All things considered, I think being a waking beauty might be better after all."

I nodded. "You know what They say."

"No. What do They say?"

"That no one has ever had a fabulous time in a coma."

"Is that what They say?"

"I expect it is what Frank would say if he were here, yes."

"And what of my Prince Charming? He's expecting to come upon me in a coma."

"If he loves you he'll understand."

"And if he doesn't?"

"Then you hold out for a Charming who does."

"Alright! I will."

About an hour and some ten thousand trees later…

About an hour and some ten thousand trees later, I observed the Eighth Fairy stomp up to a cluster of five trees. As I watched her, it occurred to me that perhaps she wasn't in a bad mood after all. "Maybe she just has a ridiculous walk," murmured I. I crouched behind a tree and watched the Eighth Fairy cast her gaze about to check that she hadn't been followed. She must have considered the possibility a slim one, for she quickly stomped through the centre-most of the five trees and vanished.

I stood before the tree – which, to all intents and purposes, resembled a normal tree – and reached out to touch it. I was not surprised when my hand vanished inside, and relieved when the rest of me followed it…

I emerged into a pretty little garden with a picket fence. At one end of the garden was a white house, and at the other end a log cabin. The Eighth Fairy stomped up the steps towards the white house, opened the door with a key on a chain, and went inside. I breathed a sigh of relief and turned towards the log cabin. "That must be the Author's Cabin," said I, walking towards it. The door to the Author's Cabin had a round brass knob, which to my delight turned. The door opened…

Inside was a study with a desk, and upon the desk was a single book. Closer inspection revealed it to be a manuscript held together by a brass clip on its left-hand side. On the front was written, "*The Manuscript of The Book*, sole property of *The Author*." By the manuscript's side was a pencil with an eraser tip. The notion of holding *the book* alone was enough to give me goose bumps. After all, this was where the world of fairy tales had been created. Over time, and through word of mouth, its stories had been told in many lands, including your own. I opened the manuscript and flicked through its many pages until I came upon one where the names Happy, Grumpy, Sleepy, Bashful, Sneezy, Dopey and Doc had been written in the margin. They had been crossed out, and on the actual page were the names of my dwarves.

I remembered why I was there. "I must save Edward," said I. I was about to turn the page and find the part where the Queen was to find Edward guilty, when I paused and looked over my shoulder to make sure I was alone. I was. Steeling myself, I picked up the pencil and changed Insecure's name to Secure, then erased the *Not* in Not Particularly Hopeful's name. Even as I looked upon their new names, Secure and Particularly Hopeful, I felt different: as though I might as well feel secure and hopeful as feeling any differently was counter-productive. I added brackets above the changed names and in the brackets I wrote: "*and feeling secure and particularly hopeful should also apply to anyone who reads these words, for they are an important part of this story too.*" "It's a good thing I didn't change Meddlesome's name," said I, smiling and turning the page. *And it's a very good thing I came*, I thought, as I read how the Queen was to find Edward guilty and sentence him to death by a thousand wolf bites. *Talk about overkill.* I erased all of that and replaced it with: '*and it came as a complete surprise to everyone in the land when the Queen found Edward innocent. And what's more, all the mirrors in the land were gifted with improved vision and as a result could see that they'd made an error: Snow White was not the fairest in the land at all, the Queen was, and from that day on they told her so.*' "I'm hopeful that will do the trick," murmured I.

184

I flicked through *the book* and made one or two more changes. Sometime later, I yawned and stretched and said, "Meddlesome will be very pleased."

When I left the cabin, I came upon the Eighth Fairy using her wand to water flowers in the garden. When she saw me, she looked very confused. I had read in The Book how, when I left the cabin, she would discover me and, in true fairytale style, would transform me into a rat as punishment for following her. And not just any rat: the rat *I* was to become was the fairest rat in the land. The poor rat was to live with four mice, and their names would reflect its – that's to say *my* – personality. The names of the mice were to be Flea-Ridden, Festering, Claustrophobic and Agoraphobic. Which basically meant that I would spend my days in a festering, flea-ridden panic whether I stayed in or went out. I had erased all that, choosing new words and actions for the Eighth Fairy. I therefore had an excellent idea of what she was going to say and do when she saw me. "Oh, it's you!" said she, as though surprised to see a long-lost friend.

"Yes, it is I."

"Have you just visited the Author's Cabin?"

"I have."

"Hope you found it to be clean and tidy?"

I nodded.

"Did you make any changes to *the book* while you were there?"

"Yes. And I have tried my best to do right by others."

"And having done right by others, I expect you're keen to get back to your own land to see how it's all panned out?"

"That's right. So, if you wouldn't mind waving that wand of yours and doing the honours…"

A moment later…

A moment later, I was back in my own land, and the first two people I came upon were Little Miss Muffet and the spider. They were in the midst of a passionate embrace, the spider's arms wrapped around her and their lips pressed tightly together. I imagine you must be grimacing, but there really is no need. Thanks to a *small* alteration on my part, the spider was no longer a spider but a handsome prince. And Little Miss Muffet's prince was no one-dimensional Charming either: he was a person of great imagination and wit. Indeed, he had the personality of the spider. When they saw me, they broke their embrace and before he had a chance to ask I said, "Yes, it was I who turned you into a handsome prince."

The prince bowed low. "However can I thank you?" he said.

"You can thank me by always remaining true to Little Miss Muffet."

"Consider it done," said he who had no name, and then asked if I might give him one.

Without a moment's hesitation, I replied, "Prince True of Hearts."

"Thank you!" said Little Miss Muffet, hugging her Prince True of Hearts.

"You have turned my worst fear into my true love!" said she, releasing her prince and opening her book of fairytale poems. She read aloud the amendments I had made to her poem (for they were in every copy of *the book* now): "*Little Miss*

Muffet sat on her tuffet eating her curds and whey, along came a spider who was turned into a handsome prince and they lived happily ever after."

"I'm sorry it doesn't rhyme, but I was pressed for time," said I, rhyming after I needed.

"Who needs a rhyme when you can live happily ever after with your one true love?"

"That was my thinking," said I. "While you have *the book* to hand, would you mind looking up Old Mother Hubbard's poem? I pasted a new one she'd written over the top of the Author's, but had no time to read it."

Little Miss Muffet flicked though *the book*. "Here it is," said she, scanning the poem.

"Well?" said I.

"It seems Old Mother Hubbard has a maid who waits on her hand and foot... yes, her maid brings her presents in every verse."

"And what of her dog?"

"Dog? There's no mention of a dog." I felt a little guilty for allowing Old Mother Hubbard to erase the dog from existence, but fortunately Little Miss Muffet was on hand with the most famous of They's quotes: "You can't make an omelette without breaking some eggs."

As I went on my way, I thought about that and decided that, despite the dog's erasure from existence, I was rather chuffed with the way my omelette was turning out.

188

The next character I came across was the no-eyed, no-brained toad. You may recall how he used to sell curds and whey down by the enchanted pond? And how, since Little Miss Muffet no longer spent her waking hours eating curds and whey, he had gone out of business. Having no eyes and no brain had proven an obstacle to starting a new career, but thanks to my alterations that was no longer the case. The no-eyed, no-brained toad now had 20/20 vision and an IQ of 240, which meant he had perfect eyesight and the biggest brain in the land. This went some way to explaining why he was hurriedly writing equations while simultaneously examining the surface of both moons without the aid of a telescope. I thought it best not to disturb the perfect-eyed, big-brained toad and continued on my way.

I hadn't gone far when I heard the most beautiful whistling I had ever heard. Barry the Boar came trotting from the undergrowth with his lips pursed. "My, what a fine whistle you have, Barry!"

"Thank you, Snow. No idea how it happened. One minute I was blowing raspberries, and the next…" Barry pursed his piggy lips and whistled the most enchanting melody. He stopped and said, "There's something different about you too, Snow."

"There is?"

"Yes. You look… happier."

"I cannot deny that I am feeling particularly hopeful."

"No one deserves to feel particularly hopeful more than you," said he. Then he pursed his lips and whistled on his way to work.

I little further on, I met the dwarves on *their* way to work. Meddlesome hurried over and shook my hand. He sounded awestruck as he said, "We heard through the grapevine that you found *the book*, and did some rewrites!"

Awkward, who was not far behind him, tripped over his own feet and stumbled to the ground. "Couldn't you have changed *my* name too?" he lamented, glancing over his shoulder at Secure and Particularly Hopeful.

"I didn't see the need," said I. "You are so very endearing the way you are, and everybody loves you."

Particularly Hopeful and Secure took hold of an arm each and lifted Awkward back onto his feet. "And you will always be well liked," said Particularly Hopeful.

Secure reached out and squeezed my shoulder. He smiled and said, "And the same goes for you, Snow."

"Thank you. And you no longer have any objections to my falling in love with Edward?"

Secure and Particularly Hopeful glanced at one another and shook their heads. "Why should we object?" said they.

I waved goodbye to the dwarves and set off along the path that led home, and had not gone far when I came upon the little lamb. My rewrites doubtless had something to do with the fact that he was no longer hopping about like a crazy thing with fleas. The little lamb was reclining in a hammock and enjoying the shade of a sunny day with a glass of milk. "Hello, Snow," said he, sipping from his glass.

"Hello, little friend," said I.

"I can tell by your smile that you've noticed there's something different about me."

"I have noticed."

"And do I have you to thank for my being able to relax and enjoy the moment?"

"I may have made a *small* amendment to *the book* concerning you, yes."

"I cannot thank you enough. This feels like what life ought to be about. Not rushing about and never sparing a moment to appreciate anything. Thank you."

"It was my pleasure."

"Where are you off to?"

"To find Edward."

The little lamb nodded. "The Queen pardoned him."

"I thought she might."

The little lamb smiled knowingly. "He's a lovely young man. I've known him since he was a boy."

"So he told me. You taught him how to read."

"Yes. And here he comes now."

"He does…?" said I, turning as Edward stepped from the woods into the clearing. He smiled as he walked towards me, but his smile no longer made me faint from famishment. Now it just made me smile too – which I considered not only a vast but also a workable improvement.

"Hello, Snow," said he.

"Hello, Edward," said I.

"Little lamb," said Edward.

"Edward," said the little lamb. "It seems we both owe a debt of gratitude to Snow and her meddling ways."

"Agreed," said Edward. "And what a sight for sore eyes you are," he told me, which I believe to be a compliment. He approached me, took hold of my hands, raised them to his lips, and kissed them. I felt a little famished and wobbled slightly, but managed to stay on my feet. He raised a perfect eyebrow. "I wondered," said he, pausing to ponder his wonder.

"You wondered?" enquired I.

"Yes. If you might spare me a few minutes of your time and walk with me."

I had no timepiece, but had I one, I would not have had any great need of it at that moment. "Yes," I replied. Edward offered me his arm and I took it – that's to say I held onto it as we walked.

"I bumped into your dwarves earlier," said he.

"You did?"

"Yes. And I couldn't help but notice that a great change had come over two of their number."

"And which two might that be?" said I, as though I had not even the first clue.

"Let me explain," said he. "You can imagine my surprise when Not Particularly Hopeful patted my back and said he was *particularly hopeful* about our future together."

"Yours and his?"

"Mine and yours."

"I see. I can only but wonder at your confusion."

"And that wasn't all."

"It wasn't?"

"No. Secure shook my hand – very firmly, I might add – and told me that you were up to the task of living happily ever after."

"With my dwarves?" said I.

Edward shook his head. "With me."

I drew a deep breath and smiled. Edward stopped walking and turned to face me. He studied my face and looked deeply into my eyes. "It's true, then? You do feel ready to live happily ever after?"

"Yes, I believe I do."

"Tell me," said he. "How did this miraculous change occur? And why are you smiling?"

"I am smiling because I discovered how to change those things within myself that stop me being happy and, having discovered how to change them, I ..." I stopped talking because Edward had moved his head closer to mine, and wherever his head went his lips tended to go also. "Are you going to kiss me?" I asked.

"Truly, is that your heart's desire?" I could not answer, but something about my expression must have answered for me, for the next moment our lips touched. It would be inappropriate to go into too much detail about our first kiss. But when I tell you what They say about it, I think you'll understand: that no kiss before or after was ever as gentle or as passionate.

After our kiss, Edward walked me home. He was about to kiss me goodbye when Awkward stumbled out of the front door and landed in a heap. As we helped Awkward to his feet, he apologised for being so clumsy. Edward would hear nothing of it. "To be flawed is to be human, and beyond those flaws that would keep us apart, I would not change any of Snow's for anything in the land."

"Is that true?" said I.

Edward brushed a stray hair from my eyes. "You would not be the person I love without them."

That night when I went to bed, I thought about how fortunate I'd been to find and change *the book*, and also about all the friends who have accompanied me on this journey. It occurred to me that there might be one or two changes you'd make if you could find your own book. Well, you know what They say: that everyone has a book inside them. Frank assures me that people have misinterpreted what he said, and that he didn't mean that anyone can write one great novel. He said that's ridiculous. What he *actually* meant was that everyone has a book inside their imagination. And once conjured, changes can be made to those things that stand between them and their happiness. Frank has assured me that those things are almost always in the mind, and that anything in the mind *can* be changed. Best wishes. And goodnight to all. Snow.

The end

Thank you for reading! Snow is set to return in May 2017 in a new adventure: Snow & Alice in Wonderland. When, at her wedding to Edward, Snow is about to say her vows, Edward vanishes only to be replaced by a young woman called Alice who enquires, "Did you see which way the white rabbit went?" So begins an extraordinary adventure as Snow and Alice must work together to reach wonderland, rescue Edward and find the only rabbit who can lead Alice back to the real world.

In March 2017, The Lost Diary of Snow White Trilogy will be available as an audio book, with acting talent Hannah Cooper-Dean bringing all these weird and wonderful characters to life.

I Am Pan:

The Fabled Journal of Peter Pan

by Boyd Brent

I Am Pan

One day, someone from the real world called J.M. Barrie is going to write my life story. Tiger Lily is certain of it. She said she saw him in a dream, hunched over a desk and scribbling things about me. "He isn't even going to hear about you first-hand from someone who *actually* knows you, Peter. But *fourteenth*-hand from someone who's heard about you in the vaguest of terms."

"How vague, exactly?" I asked her.

Tiger Lily peered at my ears. "Pointy-ears vague. Is that vague enough for you?"

I scratched at my ear, which is perfectly round. "I see," I said. "And?"

"And how accurate can his book be?"

I placed my fisted hands on my hips. "Well, let him write it! And knock himself out if he wishes." And by that I did not mean he should punch himself in his own head until he loses consciousness; I meant let him do his worst and write whatever he likes.

Tiger Lily sat down on a rock and sighed. "But you're a real hero, Peter. You owe it to the world outside the Neverland to tell them the *truth*."

I drew my sword and lunged at an imaginary pirate. "What would you have me do?"

"Find this J.M. Barrie."

"Why?"

"How else are you to challenge him to a duel for making up stories about you?"

I froze mid-lunge and narrowed my eyes at her. "Is J.M. Barrie a *pirate*?"

"No, Peter. He's an author."

I slid my sword back into my belt. "I can't go around challenging authors to duels."

"Why ever not?"

"It doesn't sound very heroic."

Tiger Lily adjusted her Indian headdress. "Oh, I know! Why don't you keep a journal? That way you can tell your tales of derring-do the way they actually occurred." If you have my journal in your possession, I must have liked her suggestion.

Journal entry no. 1

I flew beyond the Neverland today, to a place in the real world called London – a great city where grown-ups rush about like headless chickens trying to earn a crust. And by *crust* I don't mean pies without filling. It is money they seek, to pay things called *bills*, and to buy things to impress others – those who live next door, mostly. It's not all dreadful in the real world, though, because children live there. I watch them at play, and marvel at how they use their imaginations to escape it. I try my best not to think about how they're morphing into grown-ups. It makes me break out in a cold sweat whenever I do. You may think that I too must grow up one day. Think again! I promised myself long ago that I would never allow myself to morph into a man who chases a crust by day, and allows his imagination to wither by night.

I have a secret to tell. Come closer now, and I will whisper it: there is one family in particular I like to watch. They are called the Darlings – a family of two grown-ups and three children. The children are called Wendy, John and Michael. They live in a grand red-brick house on a street lined with tall oak trees. I was attracted to their bedroom window by the glow of their night lights. Did I mention that I can fly? I can, and without the aid of wings or a motor. If not for this ability, I would never be able to leave the Neverland, which is located amongst the stars. We have no space programme here – at least none that I am aware of, although, I would put nothing past James Hook in his quest to plunder worlds beyond our own. But more of Hook later.

When I first looked through the window into the bedroom of the Darling children, I beheld a room with lime-green walls and lush red carpet. I saw three beds, each with its own night light. In the middle of the room was a doll's house big enough for a child to shelter in. I visited their window regularly, and realised their parents were creatures of habit. After their father kissed them goodnight, their mother would read them stories until they fell asleep. I always arrived in time to watch their mother read to them. Tiger Lily said that makes me a Peeping Peter, but Tinker Bell told her that there is no such thing as a Peeping Peter. "Peter is a Peeping *Tom,*" she said. Tiger Lily placed an arrow in her bow, took aim at her, and told her to admit she was wrong. Tinker Bell waved her wand and said she would not. I thought it best to change the subject before they came to spells and arrows. "I sometimes wonder," I said, "what it would be like to have someone kiss you goodnight every night, like those Darling children have." My question seemed to cheer Tink and Tiger Lily. They cast aside their weapons and said I should choose one or other of them to conduct an experiment. "What kind of an experiment?" I asked suspiciously.

"A goodnight kiss experiment," they replied. I said I would need time to think about that, and flew quickly away.

Once again, I have interrupted my own train of thought. And so back to the Darling house…

Yesterday, after their mother had finished reading to them, she opened their bedroom window. I hovered below it, pressed my body against the brickwork, and waited until the coast was clear. Once I was certain that they were asleep, I flew in through the window and landed on the carpet in my bare feet. The carpet was as lush as a bed of dandelions in spring, and so I spent some time pinching it with my toes. As I picked the fluff from between my toes, I hovered from bed to bed and took a closer look at the children. When I told Tink what I'd done, she clasped her cheeks in horror, and told me I was worse than a Peeping Tom now. "In the real world they call what you did *breaking and entering*. And they lock people up who do it!"

"Calm yourself, fairy! They wouldn't lock me up. I didn't break anything."

"It doesn't matter. You entered and that's just as bad," said Tink.

"Of course I did. How else was I to get a closer look at the children?"

Tink sighed. "If you *should* end up in court before a judge, accused of breaking and entering, it might be best if you didn't make that your defence."

"We have no courts in the Neverland, Tink."

"Lucky for you. What's so interesting about this *Darling* family, anyhow?" she asked.

"They make me wonder…"

"About what?"

"Do you think I ever had parents that kissed me goodnight?"

"Don't you remember?"

I shook my head. Tink sat beside me and placed a hand on my shoulder. "Are you sad, Peter?" she asked. "Only I don't think I could stand it if you were."

I stood up, placed my fisted hands on my hips, and turned to face her. "You imagine that great heroes have time for sadness?"

"Your modesty knows no beginnings, Peter," she said.

"You imagine you will win me over with flattery?"

"You think that *flattery*?"

"Hush now and let me explain: I have decided to make some friends in the real world."

"Friends with who?"

"The Darlings, who else?"

"What are they like?"

"Who could say? Wendy, Michael and John were all sleeping soundly."

Tink sprouted her silver wings and fluttered up into the air. I looked up at her. "How do you know their names?" she asked.

"They are carved into the wooden headrests of their beds."

"Are they horribly spoilt, then?"

"Maybe so. But I shan't know until I meet them."

Tiger Lily had been hiding on the branch of a tree above, and now she made herself known. "Isn't it forbidden even to *talk* to anyone in the real world?"

"Forbidden? By who?" I said, drawing my sword.

"Hook, I believe," said Tiger Lily, placing an arrow in her bow and casting her gaze about for pirates.

I laughed. "Since when did we take orders from James Hook?"

"Since never!" said Tiger Lily, letting an arrow fly into the night.

"Both of you listen," I said. "Hook only makes such rules because he cannot reach the real world himself."

At that moment, the sun's first rays peeked over the mountains to the east, and the first cock began to crow. "It's time to find them, Peter," said Tink.

Journal entry no. 2

I left Tink and Tiger Lily, and flew to the Lost and Found Lagoon to find the Lost Boys. They rely on me to find them every morning, and only then can their day begin. Finding them is not so difficult, as they've taken to losing themselves in the same place every night. I flew down and landed on the usual rock, folded my arms, and cleared my throat. "I hereby declare the Lost Boys to be found."

"What time do you call *this*?" asked Nibs, looking up at me.

"I thought the right time. Did the first cock not just crow?"

Tootles got up and stretched. "No, it didn't. The first cock has probably forgotten it crowed. What have you got to say to that?" he asked.

"That I must have got lost in my imagination, and time passes so quickly there. Although, cocks aren't best known for their excellent memories," I said.

"Peter's not wrong," said Slightly. "I talked at length to a cock once, and it had precisely nothing to say for itself. I got the impression it couldn't remember a single thing, not even when I asked it what it did in the two seconds before I arrived."

Nibs shook his head. "What did you expect from a cock? All they remember is how to walk, peck and crow."

"I'm starved," said Nibs, reaching for his fishing rod.

At the edge of the lagoon Slightly, Nibs and Tootles cast their fishing lines. You may be wondering about the other Lost Boys. If so, then wonder no more. There are only three, but that's not to say we're not on the look-out for new Lost Boys – although finding new Lost Boys is as hard as finding a cat in a dog pound. I flew up onto the precipice above them, and shielded my eyes from the sunlight that glinted off the water.

"It's still there?" asked Nibs.

"Yes," I said.

Nibs cast his line. "What's it doing?"

"It's floating. What else would a pirate ship be doing in a harbour?"

"And just to confirm: it's not floating in our direction?" said Slightly.

"Relax. Its sails are down. And so too is its anchor."

"So why were you late this morning, Peter?" asked Tootles.

"I visited the real world last night."

"Again?" said Nibs.

"That's right, and it's a long way away."

"The further the better, if you ask me," said Tootles.

I crouched down and picked at some moss on the rock. "It isn't all bad in the real world," I said.

"It must be nearly all bad if it's full of grown-ups," said Nibs.

"It's true: the grown-ups have allowed their imaginations to wither." At this terrible truth the Lost Boys shuddered.

Slightly skimmed a stone across the water in the direction of the pirate ship. "Even pirates haven't allowed that to happen."

"Why *do* you keep going back there, Peter?" asked Tootles.

"To see the children, of course."

Tootles pulled at his braces, which grow tighter by the day. "But why?" he asked.

"Because they are turning into grown-ups, and I fear for their imaginations."

"Not a lot you can do for the imaginations of children in the real world," said Nibs.

"Maybe I can't help them *all,* but…"

"But what, Peter?" asked Tootles.

"But the *Darlings,*" I murmured.

The Lost Boys looked one to the other and sniggered. Between sniggers, Slightly said, "While it may be that the children of the real world are *darlings*, perhaps you shouldn't refer to them as such."

"No," chuckled Tootles, "not unless you want to grow pigtails."

I stamped my foot. "Silence! Do you imagine that I, Peter Pan, am going soft?"

"No. Of course not," said Nibs, shoving the other two.

"*Darling* is the name of a family. Two parents called Mr and Mrs Darling, and three children called Wendy Darling, John Darling, and Michael Darling."

"That's an awful lot of *darlings*," said Tootles, and all three fell about laughing.

I stood up straight and filled my chest with air. "Grow up!" I said.

My ill-thought-out instruction brought looks of horror to their faces. Nibs, who had turned slightly redder in the face than the others, said, "Did you just tell us to *grow up*?" He grabbed his heart as though to prevent it from bursting.

"Too cruel," said a horrified Slightly.

"Take it back, Peter! Or it might come true!" cried all three.

I reached up and grabbed three imaginary backs from the air. I took a fourth for good measure, then apologised for the worst instruction any young person can give another. Nibs worked at calming his breathing. "You're spending *much* too much time in the real world, Peter."

"It can't be helped. The Darlings need my help."

"To do what?"

"To prevent the loss of their imaginations."

"Does that mean you're going back to see them again?"

"Oh, yes. Tonight."

Journal entry no. 3

That night when I arrived at the Darlings's house, I was pleased to find the window open again. I shot high over the house and looked across the rooftops to the clock tower called Big Ben. It was midnight, and I felt certain they would be sleeping by now.

I flew through the open window and landed on the carpet. I turned and looked back out of the window at the full moon. And because I know *how* to look, I watched the moon-fairies that fly across it on the hour. This particular hour meant there should have been twelve, but I counted thirteen, and made a mental note to stop and shake a finger at them on my way home. Barely had I made this note, when I felt a tap upon my shoulder. I turned quickly, and looked into the face of the youngest of the Darling children, Michael. Michael has a shock of blond hair, and high and rounded cheekbones like those of a cherub. "I was hoping you'd come back," he said, rubbing his eyes.

"You *were*? But why?"

"So you can teach me," he whispered.

I motioned to the window behind me. "Teach you how to count the fairies that float across the moon every hour?"

Michael glanced up at the moon, furrowed his brow and shook his head. "No," he whispered. "I hoped you'd teach me how to fly."

"Fly? You mean so you can soar with the birds?"

"Yes! Would you?"

"I suppose I might."

"It would serve John right if you did."

"Why him?" I said, glancing at John in his bed.

"Because he doesn't believe that children *can* fly."

"Does he not?"

Michael frowned and glanced at his sleeping brother. "He laughed at me when I told him we'd been visited by a flying boy."

"So, you were only pretending to slumber when last I visited?"

Michael nodded.

I ruffled his hair. "You pretend well!"

"I practise every Christmas eve. Are you a pixie? Only when I told Wendy about you, she said you must be one."

"Oh? And what gave her that idea?" I said, glancing at her sleeping form.

"I told her how you wear clothes that are made from green leaves and moss." Michael stepped closer to me, and examined the moss that is stitched over my heart.

I made a hook with my hand, and it threw a shadow up on the wall. Michael glanced at this shadow and drew a deep breath.

I leaned closer to him and whispered, "The moss hides the tears that Captain Hook made when he slashed at me."

"Hook sounds like a rogue!" gasped Michael, then slapped a palm to his mouth.

I glanced at the beds. "It's alright. I don't believe you've woken them."

Michael lowered his voice again. "If not a pixie, then what are you?"

"Not what, but who." I bowed low and stood up straight. "I am Peter Pan, and I am at your service."

"Does that mean you have to teach me to fly? It would really serve John right if you did."

"For what?"

"For what he said about you."

"What did he say?"

Michael scratched his head. "That you're a *figment* of a child's over-active imagination."

"And what is a figment?"

Michael shrugged. "A *fig* that's *meant* to do something silly, perhaps?" Then he peered above my head all the way up to

211

the ceiling.

I followed his gaze. "What is it you seek?"

"The strings… the ones that John says are always attached to children who *appear* to fly."

"Don't you believe?"

"Yes, of course. But now at least I can tell John that I had a good look… and couldn't see any."

I ruffled his hair again, and then floated up until my head almost touched the ceiling. "See? No strings," I whispered down at him.

"Michael? Who are you talking to?" said the voice of a sleepy girl.

"No one," whispered Michael. "Go back to sleep, Wendy."

I flew into the corner of the room where the light from the moon was weakest, and the shadows most pronounced. I watched Wendy sit up in bed and rub her eyes. "Have you been dreaming about pixies again?" she asked.

"I most certainly have not."

"Then go back to bed and stop talking to yourself. You know what John says about people who talk to themselves… that they'll go mad unless they stop it right away."

I tutted from the shadows. "And what does *John* know?" I whispered.

Wendy scrambled up onto her knees as though someone had pinched her. "Who… who said that?"

I floated down and landed on the carpet, bowed low, and then straightened up and assumed my most heroic pose. "I said it. Peter Pan."

Wendy's pretty mouth opened wide – so wide, in fact, that I put my fingers in my ears to block her coming scream.

"It's alright!" Michael whispered, preventing her. "This is Peter. And he's going to teach me to fly. Show her, Peter. Show Wendy how you can fly!"

I rose up and did several laps of the room like a fish darting around its bowl. I landed at the foot of her bed, and was surprised to see that far from closing, her mouth had opened wider still. She realised I was staring at the gaping hole in her face, and snapped it shut. I leaned forwards and whispered, "Answer me this: are you, perchance, any relation of the crocodiles?"

"A relation of the *whats*?" she replied loudly. Michael and I glanced at John, who shuffled a little under his blanket but did not wake.

I leaned closer still to Wendy and asked her again, "Are you a relation of the crocodiles? Only he snaps his mouth closed *just* as you do."

Wendy's mouth fell open again, and Michael shook her by her shoulders until it closed. "Peter's going to teach me to fly, and if you ask him nicely, maybe he'll teach you too."

Wendy looked at me, but her eyes failed to focus. "To answer your question," she murmured, "I don't believe that I am a relation of the crocodiles."

"It was a compliment," I said, "for the crocodile is a force for good in the Neverland. It hates pirates, you see. And it hates no pirate more than it hates James Hook. And if not for the ticking of the clock that the crocodile swallowed, it would have crept up on the captain and eaten the rest of him long ago. Do you follow?" The expressions on both their faces led me to believe they had difficulty following even the simplest things. "Well, then," I continued. "You'll just have to come to the Neverland and see for yourselves."

Wendy climbed off her bed and stood before me. I raised myself up on tiptoes and made myself slightly taller. She observed my face, then took a step back and studied my clothes.

"Don't call him a pixie. I don't think he likes it," said Michael.

"I didn't think he was a pixie," she said, looking closely at my ears. "How *old* are you?" she whispered.

I shrugged the shrug of the unfathomable. "None could say for sure, and some say I am as old as time itself."

Wendy's brow furrowed and she scratched her head. "But you're just a boy. No more than fourteen. My age."

I straightened my back and raised my chin. "Then I must have been fourteen when I decided *not* to grow any older."

"I'm afraid that deciding such things isn't possible," said Wendy.

"Neither is flying without wings, but you just saw Peter doing it," Michael pointed out.

"True," she said, stepping towards me and poking my chest.

"Stop that, Wendy! It's rude to poke people," whispered Michael.

"I have to check…" she poked.

"Check what?" asked Michael.

"That he's real…"

"Of *course* he is. What makes you think he isn't?"

"Only *everything* he says and *everything* he does."

"How would you like it if he poked at *your* chest?" I asked.

"I wouldn't. I'm a girl, so it would be inappropriate," she said, withdrawing her finger.

"Will you teach us both to fly before John wakes up?" asked Michael.

I shook my head and glanced at the window. "I must be getting back. It will soon be sun-up, and the cock's crow must be answered."

"Back where?" asked Wendy.

"The Neverland, and I must return without delay."

"What for?" asked Michael excitedly.

I drew my sword and spun about, expecting to see that a pirate had followed me somehow.

"What are you *doing*?" asked Wendy. "You'll have somebody's eye out with that thing."

I slid my sword back into my belt. "In the Neverland,

whenever anybody says *what for*, it means someone approaches who must be given what-for."

"Although that's great, it isn't what I meant," said Michael. "Why must you hurry back to the Neverland?"

"To find the Lost Boys."

Wendy smiled at me. "Do you always find them, Peter?"

I nodded. "Their day cannot start until I do." I floated up off the carpet. "I'll return soon enough. And that's when we'll see if it's still possible."

"See if what's still possible?" asked Michael.

"I know I can teach you to fly. You are young and your imagination has yet to permit boundaries." I looked at Wendy. "I believe there is still hope for you, too. As for your brother John, we shall just have to wait and see." I floated backwards towards the open window.

"And what should we tell John? About you, I mean?" asked Wendy.

"Tell him that if he doesn't believe children can fly, it may be too late for him to learn."

"That's not what I meant. What should we tell him about *you*?"

"Tell him everything!"

"But what if he doesn't believe us?" said Michael.

"Then tell him to prepare for my return, when he'll have little choice but to believe!"

Journal entry no. 4

The Neverland is the brightest star in the galaxy. Despite this truth, only those who remember how to *see* may look upon it. Adults leave the ability to *see* in childhood, and that's why they fail to see it, even through their most powerful telescopes. Just as well, for if they could see the Neverland they might build rocket ships one day and visit us. A disaster! They would change *everything*, and before long the Neverland would become The Land Where No One Ever Stops Worrying About Everything.

The Neverland's address is: The Neverland, Third (not the second!) Star on the Left, and then Straight On Till Morning. For those who still know how to look, it's the brightest star in the constellation of Asia Minor, the one that changes colour depending on the mood of its inhabitants. When white, the population of Neverland is mostly at rest. When flickering blue, it means that our spirits are high, and there is fun to be had in every quarter. But beware, reader, for when it flickers *scarlet* it means that murder and blood-lust are afoot. It was this scarlet flicker that greeted me upon my return from the Darlings. I flew through the outer atmosphere and made for the blue, kidney-shaped lagoon where Hook keeps his galleon. It is also where the Lost Boys are waiting to be found. On this particular morn, I spotted Tink sitting on a cloud, arms folded and with an expression like thunder. I landed beside her on the cloud and folded my arms.

"Why do you wear the face of someone who's been licking bat droppings off a rancid toad?" I asked.

Tink stood up. "Do you mind? And what time do you call this?"

"I do mind, for it can only be the time that I arrived back from the real world. Did my eyes deceive me, or was that a glow of scarlet I saw? Is trouble brewing?"

"Is trouble brewing, he asks. Tell me, *Peter*, where are you going now?" she said, tapping her foot impatiently upon the cloud.

"You *know* where I'm going. Is your question a trick one?"

"To find the Lost Boys?"

"Given the hour, where else?"

"Well, good luck with that!"

"What is wrong?"

"Hook has already found them!"

"But he can't have. Only I can find them. That is the earliest their day can begin."

"Their day has begun in earnest without you, and it's turning into their worst ever."

"What were they doing when Hook found them?"

"What else would the Lost Boys be doing just after the first

218

cock has crowed, Peter? They were waiting to be found!"

Let that be a lesson to all who read this: if you're waiting to be found, chances are you will be. So remain alert, in case the finder should be not friend but foe.

"What are you going to do, Peter?" asked Tink. "Hook is going to make them walk the plank. They're to be the crocodile's breakfast."

I hurried to the edge of the cloud, crouched down, and observed Hook's galleon far below. "What do you *think* I'm going to do? I'm going to save them."

"Any idea how?"

"Hush now, fairy, and let me think."

I will leave myself there to think for a moment, reader, and share with you some facts about Hook's galleon. It is called the *Jolly Roger*, and it provides sanctuary to the most bloodthirsty pirates ever to roam the high seas. The *Jolly Roger* has three masts, the centremost of which is tall enough to pierce the clouds. Upon this mast hangs a sail vast enough to cast a black shadow the length and breadth of a football pitch. As I looked down from the cloud, this sail flapped and billowed over the hundreds of pirates manning its decks. I flew down from the cloud and saw Tootles, Slightly and Nibs, huddled amid a pack of baying pirates. The boys were stripped to their waists, and their hands had been tied behind their backs. It made my blood boil, reader, to see the red marks upon their backs where the cat o' nine tails had lashed at them. I scanned the calm waters for any sign of the crocodile, and beheld the beast some way off, moving at speed towards the plank. Hook likes to keep the belly of the crocodile always full. It has been his way ever since I cut off

219

his hand and threw it into the crocodile's jaws. Since then the creature has craved the rest of him, which only goes to prove that there can be no accounting for a crocodile's taste. Now you understand why Hook provides the crocodile with a hearty breakfast every morning: it is the hope that it will leave him alone for the rest of the day.

Back to the events of earlier today…

One amongst the crew of ruffians spotted the crocodile's approach and called out, "Fetch the captain! The croc's here!"

I flew down, landed high up on the rigging, and shouted above the high winds, "And so too is Peter Pan!"

The Lost Boys looked up at me with tears in their eyes. As I smiled down at them, their eyes filled with watery hope. Drawing my sword, I floated down and landed upon the deck. Hook burst from his cabin with his first mate Smee. While Hook is tall and thin with a foul, bristling moustache, Smee is short and round with spectacles that are rounder still.

"Bad form, Pan!" growled Hook in a voice that sounded like approaching thunder.

I stamped a foot upon the deck. "And feeding helpless boys to crocodiles is *good form,* I suppose?"

"Helpless?" cried Hook. "Don't make me laugh! These three assassins have killed almost as many of my men as have volunteered to be the crocodile's breakfast."

"I see. So your men volunteer to be the croc's breakfast, do they?"

Hook nodded. "Of course. They're good men. Always keen to please their captain. Is that not so, men?" Hook's men made a low murmur that did not answer his question one way or another.

"See, Hook? You delude yourself. They are volunteered to be the crocodile's breakfast by you. And so great is their fear of you that they would sooner end up in its belly than cross you."

"As I said, they are good men." Hook looked suddenly mindful of something: the crocodile, and he listened for the ticking of the clock in its belly. We were all reminded of the creature, and listened but could hear no ticking. The silence of that rogue's galleon was broken by Hook himself. "Your day will come soon enough, *Pan*. In the meantime, stop interfering in business that is not your own. Fly away, little birdie, lest I clip your wings!" With that, he drew his cutlass.

I cut a figure of eight from the air. "Oh, I think this is my business, *Hook*."

"Don't be absurd. Since when was croc business any business of yours?"

"Since you decided to feed it not pirates, cereal or oats this morning, but my friends Nibs, Slightly and Tootles."

"I *found* them, Pan. And possession is nine-tenths of the law, which means they belong to me now. Is that not so, Smee?"

"That's right, Captain," said Smee, pulling his wide belt up over his hanging belly.

"And thanks to my generosity of spirit towards the crocodile," continued Hook, "the croc is to have something different for its breakfast."

"Think again!" I cried, "for the Lost Boys belong to no one."

"I'll decide what belongs to me and what does not aboard my own ship!" Hook stepped forwards and slashed at the shrinking space between us. I flew up onto the plank and observed the approach of the crocodile. Its size is equivalent to *two* lifeboats lashed together, and a bigger or more ferocious-looking beast you will never see. It was close enough now that all could hear its ticking. As I looked, the sound drained the colour from Hook's face. More than this, it had drained the strength from his legs, for he staggered sideways and grasped the hair of one of his men for support. Hook pulled the man's hair, and both their faces contorted in agony. "Be quick, men!" cried Hook, "and force those boys to walk the plank!"

"I won't let you do it!" I cried.

"Not a lot you can do about it, *Pan*," he said, as a hundred pirates spilled onto the deck like a tide that pushed the Lost Boys towards the plank.

Below, the crocodile gnashed its teeth and swished its tail, while above the mammoth sail billowed in the winds that now sensed our peril. Perhaps I should explain: the winds have always been a friend to us boys, and now they whistled an idea to me through a hole in the rigging. The whistle cried, "Cut down the main sail and use it to your advantage, Pan!"

I leapt and flew up with sword in hand and set about cutting out a great circle from the sail, one big enough to engulf the band of pirates that bundled the Lost Boys towards the plank. The severed circle of sail broke free, and the winds came at it from all angles and held it in place. I grasped hold of its edge, and flew down towards the mass of pirates with the sail clasped to my neck – the biggest cloak ever to be conjured in the imagination of any boy! Its shadow engulfed the pirates first, and their frightened faces looked up to see a great dark blanket descend upon them.

"Tink!" I called. "I will need your light!"

"And you shall have it, Peter!" Tink appeared not as girl with elfin face and wings, but as a tiny light that hovered close to my face. Hook looked on from a higher deck and shouted down to his men not to panic, but as soon as the sail fell and engulfed them in darkness, they began slashing at one another's shadows, believing them to be The Foes That Come In Sudden Darkness.

I scurried between their anxious feet and, led by Tink's light at the end of my nose, I made my way to the Lost Boys. "Hold still while I cut you free!" I said, slicing through the ropes that bound them with my dagger.

"I'm free, Peter!" shouted Nibs above the shrieks of pirates as they mistook friend for foe. Moments later, I had freed the Lost Boys.

"Nibs, you grab hold of my belt. Tootles, you grab Nib's belt, and Slightly, you take hold of Tootles. Are you all arranged?" I called behind me.

"Yes!"

"Yes!"

"Yes!"

"Go then, Tink! Lead us through the darkness and out of here!" Tink led us expertly through legs that swerved and stumbled, and soon enough we all four emerged into a sunlight that blinded us momentarily.

"This way," said Tink, tinkling for all she was worth. We followed the sound of her bell, climbed over the side of the ship, and fell into a lifeboat.

Shielding my eyes from the sun, I drew my sword and cut the ropes that lashed the boat to the side of the ship. It plunged down into the water with a splash. "To the oars before someone spots us!" I commanded. We each took up an oar, and made our getaway to the sound of Hook's bellows for calm, and the cries of pirates.

Journal entry no. 5

When we reached the shore, we hid the boat in some reeds and ran up a steep embankment. From our raised position, we looked out over the lagoon to where the pirates now sought what had moments before been the crocodile's intended breakfast. But to no avail, for its breakfast stood beside me, and all three courses looked the worse for wear.

"Well!" I said, slapping Slightly on his back. "A close shave was had by all, but all is well that ends well."

Nibs pointed to the *Jolly Roger*'s plank. "Not for all," he said. I knew his logic to be sound when I spied three pirates on their knees, hands clasped before them as they begged Hook not to make them walk it. "Do you imagine he'll show them mercy, Peter?" asked Tootles.

I shook my head. "Those men's names might just as well have been Toast, Orange Juice and Porridge. For a similar fate awaits all three now."

Tootles gulped. "It was almost our fate."

"It won't happen again, for I shall never be late finding you again."

"If we *had* ended up as breakfast for the crocodile, those

Darling children would have had a lot to answer for," said Nibs.

"Don't blame the Darlings; it was my fault. She awoke and I lost track of time."

"Who awoke?" asked Tootles.

"Wendy Darling," I said.

We heard the sound of Tink's bell and she appeared to us in human form, albeit with pointy ears, transparent wings and fairy frown. She folded her arms and said, "She woke, did she? And what did Wendy *darling* do when she found you in her room?"

Slightly patted me on the back. "She must have been impressed to find Peter in her room," he said.

"Impressed?" said Tink, looking me up and down.

"Yes," said Slightly. "After all, I doubt she wakes to find a genuine hero in her room very often."

"Or a peeping *Tom*," said Tink.

"I was not peeping," I pointed out.

"Really?" said Tink. "Then answer me this: were your eyes closed while you were there?"

"Of course not."

"Then shame on you for peeping!"

"Pan is no peeper!" I said.

"If you weren't peeping at Wendy *darling* then you must have been staring at her," said Tink, making her eyes bulge. The Lost Boys looked away from Tink who can look fearsome when she wants to.

"So what did Wendy Darling do when she saw you, Peter?" asked Tootles.

"Oh yes, Peter, what *did* Wendy *darling* do when she saw you?" said Tink, her green eyes as big and as round as saucers.

I sat upon the ground, placed my chin in my hands, and cast my mind back. "I can't remember everything, but... I'm sure she poked me."

Tink went bright red in her face. "She did *what?*"

"Poked me."

"Where?" said Tootles.

"In my chest."

"Once?" asked Tink.

I shook my head. "Truth be told, Wendy Darling poked me so many times I lost count."

"I hope you poked her back," said Nibs.

"No. She said it would be wrong to poke a girl in the chest."

"That's called double standards!" said Tink. "You know you can poke me anytime, don't you, Peter?" said Tink, smiling sweetly. The Lost Boys began to chuckle, but a glance from Tink silenced them.

"What did Wendy do after she'd finished poking you?" asked Nibs.

"Well, as I recall, her little brother Michael told her of my promise to teach him to fly. And he said that I might teach her to fly, too."

"And did she like the idea?" asked Slightly.

"I believe she did," I said.

"I *bet* she did," said Tink. "Well, I think if you do teach her to fly it would be perfectly mean of you."

"Silence, fairy! Teaching others to fly would be a noble act."

"Really? If that's so, then why haven't taught the Lost Boys to fly?"

"That's not fair," I protested. "You know I'm the only boy who's supposed to fly in the Neverland."

"And why is that?" asked Tink mischievously.

"You know as well as I that it is one of the unwritten rules of the land."

"But why?" asked Tink, a twinkle in her eye.

"Isn't it obvious? If everyone flies about the Neverland it would be transformed into an aviary for people."

"Peter has a point," said Slightly, gazing skyward.

Tink huffed. "The same could be said of teaching the children of the real world to fly. Yet you seem intent on teaching those little *darlings*."

"I have no choice. How else are they to come here?"
Tink fluttered her wings urgently and took to the air. "You can't actually be considering bringing children from the real world here?"

"Considering? No. Decided? Yes."

"You mustn't!" said Tink. "Not bringing children of the real world here is another unwritten rule of the land. And you can't cherry-pick which rules to obey and which to ignore."

"If it is an unwritten rule, then I think it a stupid one," I said.

"Why?" asked Tootles.

"Did we not all come from the real world once upon a time? And did we not leave it because it did not agree with us?"

"But you all found your ways here *naturally*," said Tink. "Which is nothing at all like bringing people here who have no *right* to be here."

I folded my arms. "It doesn't seem fair to keep the Neverland all to ourselves. Not all the time, Tink."

Tink threw her arms wide. "You know as well as I that the Neverland is filled with children. They come here to stay young forever, and to play in worlds created by *their* imaginations – just as this world has been created by yours, Peter. We've all seen their shadows or spotted their reflections in water."

"I hear their laughter sometimes," said Tootles.

I patted him on the back. "We all do."

A voice above us asked, "Why are there so many

Neverlands?" We looked up at Tiger Lily. She was sitting astride a branch, bow in hand.

Tink fluttered her wings and flew up to her. "Because not all children want to live in a Neverland filled with dangerous Indians and pirates, a monster croc, and a hero called Peter Pan. They choose to inhabit the Neverlands of their own imaginations."

"Do you think that children from these other Neverlands see us sometimes?" asked Tootles.

"I know they do," said Tink. I rose to my feet, walked to the edge of the precipice, and gazed out over the lagoon.

"What is it, Peter?" asked Nibs.

"I've felt as though something has been missing from our Neverland of late."

"Missing?" said Tink.

I turned to face them. "Yes, child visitors from the real world… but not for long," I said, flying up over their heads.

"But what good will it do us bringing them here?" said Tink.

"I think it will do *them* good. For when they are to return to the real world and grow up, they might always remember us, and maybe that will help to keep their imaginations alive."

Journal entry no. 6

That night when I returned to the Darlings's house, I thought I'd find them excited about learning to fly. I landed on the carpet in the middle of the room, placed my hands on my hips, and looked from one to the other. Far from pleased to see me, Wendy and Michael looked as miserable as pigs deprived of dirt. And worse still, their brother John sat on his bed clutching a cricket bat, an expression of grim intent on his face.

"It's alright, Peter," said Wendy. "John isn't going to hit you with his bat."

"I might," said John nervously.

"See! I told you Peter was real, John," said Michael, pointing at me.

John got up, and although a year younger than Wendy, he stood just as tall. He was a serious-looking boy with reddish hair that lay upon a large forehead. He raised his bat with shaky hands and asked impertinently, "Are you friend or foe?"

I was taken aback and so took a step back. "Tell me this," I asked, spreading my arms wide, "would a *foe* fly astronomical distances across space and time to teach the gift of flight?"

As I said, John's forehead is large, and I deduced that his brain must be large also. I reconsidered this when he said, "Liar! Flying astronomical distances across space and time isn't possible."

I cocked my head at him and observed him as though he may be broken. "Why would you say such things to someone who does so regularly?"

"For starters," he said, clutching his bat, "you can't fly through space because nobody can."

"And why not?"

"Because there's no oxygen in space, so you couldn't breathe," he said uncertainly, looking to his siblings for agreement.

"Oxygen?" I said.

"Air! Air to breathe!" John's exasperation at trying to comprehend these things seemed to drain him of the very oxygen he needed, and so he sat on his bed, gasping for more.

"I stand before you as proof that these things *are* possible. And that is surely good news," I pointed out helpfully.

John shook his head. "How can finding out that everything I ever read in my science books isn't true be a *good* thing?"

"It's exciting, surely!" said Wendy.

John began to thump the side of his head with a flat palm. "*Good?* If it's really true, it means I must rearrange everything."

"Oh, stop beating yourself up," Wendy suggested.

"Sterling advice, Wendy!" I said. "And count your lucky stars, because it could be so much worse."

"My poor troubled brother won't stop thumping his own head. How could it be worse?"

"Well, he might be thumping his head with his bat. I remember how one of Hook's crew beat himself up with a bat once…" I paused and saw that I had their attention; even John had paused his thumping to listen. "I think it best if I say no more about it. He hit his own head with his bat until he could hit it no more and, well, let's just say the resulting sight was not a pretty one."

"But why would he beat himself up with a *bat?*" asked John.

I shrugged. "Hook told him to do it."

"By why?" asked Wendy.

"As entertainment, why else?"

"Hook? Who's Hook?" asked John.

"The captain of the pirates," said Michael, pleased to know something his brother didn't for once.

"Wendy?" I said, narrowing my eyes. "Why have you and Michael grown so heavy of heart?"

Wendy went to the window and gazed up at the stars. "What does it matter to you?" she whispered.

I stood beside her. "It is important that you reverse your melancholy, and without delay."

"Why is it, Peter?"

"Isn't it obvious? Learning to fly with a heavy heart is like setting sail with your ship's anchor dropped, or trying to ride a sledge back up a snow-covered hill. You do still want to learn, don't you?"

Wendy gazed at me with watery eyes. Michael came and stood beside her. He took hold of her hand and I watched a tear roll down his cheek. "What has happened to make you all so miserable?" I asked.

"Are you sure you want to know, Peter?" said Wendy. "After all, you're so carefree... I'd hate to ruin that by making your heart heavy."

"I do not think that you can."

"It's Kenneth," said Michael, squeezing his sister's hand.

"Kenneth?" I asked, looking from one to the other.

"He's the boy who lives next door," said Wendy. "He's been unwell, and about a week ago, just after your last visit, he lost his fight and left us."

My hand went to the hilt of my sword. "Was it pirates? Did they follow me?"

"Oh, Peter. Don't you know there are no pirates here? Kenneth hadn't been well for some time."

Michael wiped a tear from his cheek. "He'd been staying at Great Ormond Street," he said.

"Great Ormond Street?" I asked.

"It's a hospital," said Wendy. "One where they look after poorly children. We were looking forward to visiting him, but on the morning of our visit, Mother told us we must prepare for the worst."

From behind us John said, "They said we'd get a chance to say goodbye. And we all promised Kenneth that we would. We took oaths. So you see, we've let him down."

"How old was Kenneth?" I asked.

"He was to be thirteen next month," said Wendy.

"And did he possess a good imagination? Be sure and speak with an honest heart," I said, pointing at Wendy's.

Wendy smiled. "Oh, yes. He had the best imagination! He used to play with his collection of toy knights for hours."

John became animated. "Do you remember how he would imagine he was a knight in Camelot, Wendy?" He put down his bat and slid open the drawer of his bedside table. "He gave me his favourite toy knight," he said sorrowfully, taking out the wooden figure of a knight no larger than his thumb.

"It's a fine knight," I said.

"Yes. Kenneth swapped it for one of my toy soldiers. We made a pledge, you see…"

"A pledge?"

"To look after each other's toy, and to swap them back only once Kenneth was well again. Only that's never going to happen now." John wiped the back of his hand over his eyes.

"And what's more," he continued, "the hospital has lost Kenneth's favourite possessions, *including* the soldier I swapped with him."

I stepped towards John and looked down at the wooden knight in his grasp. "Listen well, all of you," I said. "Kenneth's possessions were not lost. He has taken them with him … cock-a-doodle-doo!" I whispered.

"Peter!" said Wendy crossly. "How could you be so insensitive when our friend has died?"

My smile broadened. "Were you not listening? Your friend is not dead. He has gone to a better place."

"Yes, we know. To heaven," said Michael with a sigh.

"There is no need to be glum. I'd wager one of the Lost Boys that Kenneth is in Camelot right now, and that he has become the brave knight he always wanted to be."

"Are you saying he's in the Neverland?" asked Michael.

I nodded.

"If that's true, then might you see him there?" asked Michael.

"I might, but only as a fleeting shadow. Or I might hear his laughter."

"Kenneth laughed a lot," said Wendy.

"Then I expect it's only a matter of time before I do."

"And if we go with you to the Neverland, might we hear him laugh?" asked Michael.

"If you listen for it, I don't see why not."

"I don't believe you," said John sadly.

"But you *must* believe me."

John lay on his bed and faced the wall. "Why? What difference will it make?"

"Don't you want to fulfil your pledge to say goodbye?" I asked.

John looked at me over his shoulder. "Of course. Wendy and Michael never told me how cruel you are."

"Cruel? How can helping you fulfil such an important pledge be cruel?"

John sat up and glared at me. "But you can't! Kenneth is gone and we'll never see him again. Stop saying these things."

"But we might," said Michael eagerly, "if we go to the Neverland."

"There is no Neverland. Not really. Don't be such a gullible child!" said John.

"John," implored Wendy. "Keep your voice down, otherwise you'll wake Mother and Father."

"Maybe I should wake them. At least they'd put a stop to this."

"Would you like me to bring *proof* that the Neverland exists?" I asked.

"Good luck with that," said John quietly.

I took off and flew three times around the room at such speed that I appeared as a blur. As I flew I plucked Kenneth's knight from John's hand without him knowing. The blur became Pan by the window. "How about I go one better? And return with proof that Kenneth lives on in the Neverland!"

"You're insane!" said John, sitting up.

"Maybe so, yet prove it I shall! Otherwise your heavy hearts will keep you grounded in the real world forever." I flew from the window, soared above London, and crowed so loudly that inhabitants for miles around might hear me. Then I fixed my gaze on the star I knew to be home, and sped towards it with Kenneth's knight in my grasp.

Journal entry no. 7

I arrived back just before sun-up, swooped down into the forest, and shot up the side of the tallest tree in Neverland: Tink's tree. She lives in a fairy castle way up in its highest branches. Although no bigger than a box in which a girl might crouch, when Tink transforms into a speck of light she has three hundred rooms to choose from.

If she is woken suddenly from her slumber, Tink is transformed into her human-fairy form. At such times, her palace becomes a single room, only large enough for her to sit with head bowed and legs drawn to her chest. I had just woken her by tapping on her castle's roof, and so this is how I found her. "Oh, it's you, Peter," she said, a green eye filling a window in the attic. "You woke me from a delightful dream, so this had better be important."

"It's of the utmost importance," I said, holding the toy knight up to the window.

Her eye narrowed. "All I see is stupid little knight."

"Look again, for this is no ordinary knight."

Tink yawned. "If you must wake me long before the first cock has crowed, I'd appreciate your telling me why before it has a chance to."

"As you wish. This toy knight belongs to *Kenneth*," I said, as though confiding a secret.

"I've never heard of him."

"Maybe not, but I'll wager you've heard his laughter. I am told he laughs often and loud."

Tink's eye focused on the toy knight in my hand. "Are you saying it belongs to one of the nether children?"

"That is precisely what I'm saying, and it will therefore have his aura all over it."

"That's nice."

"Nice? Don't you see? This is the first time we've had something that belongs to one of the nether children. And we might use it to find a way to into his Neverland."

"Why? Is there something wrong with our own Neverland?"

I shook my head. "We must return this toy to Kenneth."

"Why must we?"

"Because *he* is its rightful owner."

"I see. So you want to do that which has *never* been done, just to return a silly toy? Is that all?"

"No, it isn't. We must swap this toy knight for a toy soldier that belongs to John."

"John?"

"John Darling."

Tink's eye narrowed. "Wendy *darling's* brother?"

"Exactly. His heart has grown heavy, but will be lightened when I find his soldier and return it to him. It will help to prove that his friend lives on in the Neverland."

Tink's eye closed.

"Tink! Wake up! This is the perfect opportunity for us to help all the Darlings shed the burden of their heavy hearts."

Tink's eye opened slowly. "Ah well, just so long as all the little *darlings* are happy. Now, if you don't mind, I'm going to catch up on my forty winks." Tink's eye vanished from the window and I heard a faint tinkling from within as she returned to her bedchamber.

I stood and banged on the castle's roof. "Oh no, you don't! You're to come out and help me. You should have seen the gloom that losing their friend has caused the poor Darlings."

Tink's castle began shuddering, and her voice came from within. "If you want to help the *poor darlings,* then nobody's stopping you!"

I sat cross-legged on a branch and placed my head in my palms. "Tink," I said, "of all the fairies I have met, I believe you to be the wisest."

"Go on," said Tink, her voice softer now.

"And because you're the wisest, I shall need your help in finding the solution to finding Kenneth's Neverland."

There was a flash of light and Tink appeared, straddling the top of her fairy castle. "Do you mean it? Am I wisest fairy you know?"

"How could you ever doubt it?"

"Anything else?" said Tink, fluttering her eyelids and creating fairy dust that made me sneeze.

"Else?" I said.

"Look at me…" said Tink, leaning back on her palms and extending her long neck. "Am I not a beautiful fairy?"

"The most beautiful."

"And do you think me more beautiful than Wendy Darling?"

"Do you really need you ask? How can a human compete with a fairy when the competition is beauty?"

"It is Tiger Lily's help you need," she confided with a smile

"Tiger Lily's? She is best known for her skills with bow and arrow, not wisdom."

"It's her grandfather, Chief Hiawatha, that you must speak with. His soul is the oldest and wisest in the Neverland. If anybody knows of a way to move between Neverlands, it will be him."

"I knew I must come and speak to you first, and that you wouldn't let me down. Thank you, Tink." Tink's face was lit by a smile. Emboldened by it, I added, "We must go and speak with Tiger Lily now."

"Now?" said Tink, her smile vanishing.

"Yes. Were you not listening? There is no time to lose."

"But Peter, you know as well as anyone how dangerous it is

to go to Indian Creek before sun-up. Have you forgotten the last time? They mistook you for a pirate and shot you with an arrow."

I rubbed at my backside. "How could I forget? I am reminded of our misadventure every time I sit on a damp log."

"So we wait for sun-up?

"No. There'll be no sneaking around this time. We'll fly straight to Tiger Lily's tee-pee."

"We?"

"Of course. This adventure is much too important not to have you by my side." Tink's smile returned in spades.

There are hundreds of teepees at Indian Creek. Tiger Lily is the Chief's granddaughter, and she is a princess, so her teepee forms part of the centremost ring. The trees on the approach to Indian Creek are always full of snipers on the lookout for pirates. We waited for a cloud to float across the front of both moons, and then swooped down in the darkness and landed outside Tiger Lily's teepee.

Once inside, we found Tiger Lily asleep beside her sister Dainty Rose Petal. Whenever Tiger Lily complains that her name doesn't make her sound like a true warrior, I remind her of her sister's name. I tiptoed up to Tiger Lily, lying asleep upon the ground, and did my best not to wake Dainty Rose Petal, but I should have remembered how Tiger Lily says her sister likes to sleep with one eye open. The next thing I knew, Dainty Rose Petal was upon me with an axe, intent on cleaving my head in two. In a flash, I drew my sword and steel clanked against steel. The sound woke Tiger

Lily, who cried, "Dainty Rose Petal! Stop it! Don't you recognise him? He's my friend, Peter!" Dainty Rose Petal snarled at me and backed away. Nibs says she's so aggressive because she feels she has to compensate for her name. Once, the Lost Boys and I drew straws to decide who would put that question to her. I made sure that I drew the short straw, as Dainty Rose Petal would have killed any of the others for asking it.

"Why are you here, Peter?" asked Tiger Lily.

"I have come seeking your help."

Tiger Lily blushed. "You have?"

Tink flew from my pocket and transformed into her human-fairy self. "It was my help he sought first," she said, her nose raised high. Her nose lowered quickly enough when she noticed Dainty Rose Petal glaring at her. "That one has anger management issues," said Tink, producing her wand.

"Never mind her. What is it you need my help with, Peter?"

"I need to ask your grandfather the Chief something, and it has to be before the sun rises. It is a matter of great urgency." I explained the need to find Kenneth and swap his knight for John's toy soldier, and how John's soldier must be returned to him. "In this way the Darlings will know their friend lives on. Their heavy hearts will be lifted and they can learn to fly."

"Those poor Darling children," said Tiger Lily. "Their hearts sound so heavy with sorrow. Don't you think so, Dainty Rose Petal?" Tiger Lily's sister hurled her axe into the wooden tent pole as though she knew better than anyone how to put the Darlings out of their misery.

Only Tink was amused by this. "You know," said Tink, "I think your sister is onto something. If I were her I would hurl the axe at Wendy *darling* first. There's no need to look at me like *that*, Peter. Sometimes you have to be cruel to be kind."

Tiger Lily shook her head and stood up. "I'll go and wake my grandfather now."

Several minutes later, Tiger Lily poked her head inside the teepee. "Chief Hiawatha will see you now," she said.

Chief Hiawatha's tent was spacious and round, and smelt of tobacco and herbs. The Chief sat at its middle, puffing on a pipe, and looking just as old and wise as you would expect an Indian chief to. Tiger Lily, Tink and I sat down, forming a circle with him.

"Tell me, how may I help you?" he said, puffing away. I placed Kenneth's toy knight between my thumb and forefinger, and held it up so that Chief Hiawatha could see it clearly. "It is a fine toy knight," he said.

"Indeed. It has come from the real world, and I seek its owner who now resides in the Neverland."

"Finding him should not prevent any difficulty for Peter Pan," asserted the Chief.

"Normally, I would agree. But the boy I seek is not in our Neverland; he is in another."

The Chief smiled and nodded sagely. "Are your reasons for travelling to another's Neverland noble?" he asked.

"Yes, for there are children in the real world whose heavy hearts I wish to lighten. I believe that I can achieve this by taking them proof that their friend has gone to a better place. I must therefore swap this knight for a soldier that their friend has taken with him."

"Your cause is indeed a noble one," puffed the Chief.

"They really are *such* little darlings," said Tink through clenched teeth.

"This fairy has anger management issues," observed the Chief.

"Forgive her. She is a work in progress," I said.

"Oh, that's rich," said Tink. "I'm as sweet as a sleeping babe on a summer's morn compared to Dainty Rose Petal."

"It's true," said Chief Hiawatha. "Dainty Rose Petal is a work in progress too."

"And not a lot of progress has been made," murmured Tink.

"Hush now, fairy, please! This is important. Let Chief Hiawatha speak." I looked at the Chief, whose eyes were now tightly closed. "Tiger Lily? Is he sleeping?" I asked.

Tiger Lily shook her head. "He's thinking."

"About the problem at hand?" I said hopefully.

Tiger Lily nodded, then crossed her fingers.

Some minutes later, and with his eyes still closed, Chief Hiawatha said, "I have been away consulting with the spirits of my forefathers."

"And are they well?" I asked politely.

"The spirits of my ancestors are in rude health. Thank you for asking."

I leaned closer to the Chief. "Think nothing of it. And?"

"And they tell me there is but one way to move between our own Neverland and the others at this time." The Chief opened his eyes and looked at me. "But the way is dangerous."

I puffed out my chest, but given the late hour, I resisted the urge to crow. "It's a good thing that *dangerous* ought to be my middle name, then," I said.

"If it were, then people would mistake you for a faulty cooking utensil," mumbled Tink. Although true, the Chief and I ignored her comment.

"My ancestors have informed me that you must find the clock with four faces."

"And where is this clock?"

"Peter Pan should not need to ask such a question," he replied.

I slapped my forehead. "Of course! Hook's cabin!" The peculiar truth is this, reader: Hook has stolen all the clocks in the Neverland so as not to be frightened unnecessarily by a ticking that does not come from the crocodile's stomach. In this way, he can go about his daily business of theft and murder without a care.

Tiger Lily shifted nervously where she sat. "If Hook has such a powerful clock, why hasn't he used it to plunder other Neverlands, Grandfather?" she asked.

Chief Hiawatha shrugged. "It can only be that he is uncertain of how to harness its power."

I felt my heart begin to race. "Then it must be removed from Hook's cabin without delay. And once we have it, how might *I* harness its power?"

"It must be conveyed to the highest point in the Neverland," said the Chief. "Once there, the toy that belongs to the boy you seek must be placed inside it. If the object rightfully belongs to the boy, a portal will open within the clock's face."

"A portal that leads to his Neverland?"

Chief Hiawatha nodded.

Journal entry no. 8

We needed a plan to steal the clock with four faces from Hook's cabin. I do not know about you, but I find that plans are best come by whilst pacing and slashing at imaginary pirate foes. I felt the gaze of the Lost Boys upon me as I blocked and parried. Meanwhile, Tink danced the part of Juliet in the ballet of *Romeo and Juliet,* as this helps *her* think. Mercifully, she long ago gave up asking me to dance the part of her Romeo. During her dance, she spun across my path, and I was forced to freeze mid-swipe.

"I have an idea!" she said, spinning to a stop. I slid my sword back into my belt. "Well then, let's have it."

"Hook's first mate, Smee," she said quietly, taking off her ballet shoes. "We must kidnap him."

"Why *that* chubby pirate?" I asked.

"He's the only one who's allowed to go in and out of Hook's cabin unchallenged. My spies inform me that he even has his own set of keys."

"You think he can be convinced to join us?" said Nibs.

"Of course not," Tink admonished him. "That round pirate is bad through and through. But if we kidnap him, I can turn

Peter into his doppelgänger. Then, using Smee's keys, he can enter Hook's cabin and find the clock he seeks. Well?" she asked me, "what do you think of my plan?"

I placed my fisted hands on my hips and cock-a-doodle-dooed.

We soon discovered that opportunities to kidnap Smee were few and far between. Tiger Lily was tasked with spying on him, and she reported that the only time he was alone was when he visited the ship's latrine. "He insists on being alone when he uses it," she said. "So he can read *The Pirate Times* in peace."

I should explain that when pirates go to the toilet, they hang their bottoms over the stern of their ship. On pirate ships this is known as the poop rail, and it explains why you never find mermaids swimming below that location – at least none with any self-esteem. "If we're going to abduct Smee from the poop rail, we shall need a boat," I said.

"We still have the one we used to escape Hook's ship the other day," said Nibs.

"Good. We will row out to the ship's stern, where I will fly up and knock Smee unconscious. I will need a rope to carry him down to the waiting boat."

"We have plenty of rope, Peter," said Tootles.

I placed my hand on my chin in a thoughtful way. "I will also need to borrow your umbrella, Tootles."

"Why? Are you expecting rain?" he asked.

"Not rain, but something far worse."

The penny dropped (in much the same way as the poop might) and everyone grimaced.

As soon as night fell, the Lost Boys and I set out in the lifeboat for Hook's galleon. It was a windless night and, with the exception of the splish of our oars, the water in the lagoon was flat. As we drew nearer the ship's stern, the splish of our oars was accompanied by the occasional splash of... well, I'm sure you can work out what, reader.

Once we'd reached the stern, I tied the rope about my waist, opened the umbrella, and flew up close to the ship so as not to be spotted by look-outs. Tink's spies had confirmed that Smee likes to sit on the poop rail at 11.15pm. From the position of the two moons, I judged the time to be 11.14pm when I arrived below the poop rail. I summoned my courage and peered around the umbrella's edge. A dark shadow moved over the rail above me. If Tootles's umbrella was to be spared, I had absolutely had no time to lose. I dropped it, flew up, and knocked Smee unconscious with a blow from the hilt of my sword. I tied the rope to the poop rail, threw Smee over my shoulder, and climbed back down the rope to the waiting boat. "Bind his hands and feet, boys! And be quick about it!" I whispered.

Journal entry no. 9

Smee was still unconscious when we got back to the lagoon. Tink knelt down beside him, examining him from the 'tip' of his flattened nose to the heels of his brown boots. "You aren't going to be a handsome boy for a time, Peter," she said.

"He isn't even going to be a boy," said Tootles.

"I will be. It's just an illusion."

Tink stood up and held her wand towards me. "Ready?" she asked.

I raised my chin. "Smee me," I said gamely, doing my best to look comfortable with my suggestion. Once Tink had cast her spell, I beheld the open-mouthed gazes on the faces of all present. I ran a hand down my nose. It was no longer short and slightly upturned, but large and flat and seemingly intent on taking over my entire face.

Tink stepped forward to examine her handiwork. "If the inhabitants of the Neverland had mothers, you could fool Smee's," she said. "But try not to speak, as you still sound like yourself."

"Alright."

Tink looked a little woozy, as though she'd been drinking

fairy brandy. "You had best get going, Peter," she yawned. "Keeping you like this is a drain on my energy. When I fall asleep, which I must eventually, the spell will be broken and you will be revealed as your true self." A moment later, an apparently fat, short-sighted pirate was flying at speed towards Hook's galleon.

I swooped low and skirted the still dark water. A look-out was up in the crow's nest. If you've never seen a crow's nest, it's a wicker basket large enough to hold a skinny pirate. The skinny pirate was facing east, so I approached from the west and landed silently upon the deck. I climbed some steps that led up to Hook's cabin, and took the key from my pocket. The old key turned in the lock with a *clink*. As the door creaked open into Hook's cabin, my ears were assaulted by the sound of a thousand ticking clocks. The entrance to his cabin was dark, but towards the rear some candles lit up a platform upon which Hook's slumbering form could be seen. He was on his back, his arm dangling from the bed and his razor-sharp hook resting upon the ground. Behind and encircling him were a dozen shelves that went from floor to very high ceiling. As I crept closer, I could see the bristles of Hook's moustache moving as he breathed in and out. I climbed the final step and looked down at him, thinking it the perfect opportunity to rid our Neverland of its greatest villain. I felt for my sword… but it wasn't there! I found only Smee's pistol. I reconsidered Hook's immediate fate and whispered, "Killing one's greatest foe while he slumbers would be bad form, and it would make me no better than he." I crept past the bed to the shelves of clocks beyond, scanning them for a clock with four faces. I saw it, six shelves above me: a clock with four sides, a face on each, like a miniature of Big Ben in London. I was about to float up to retrieve it when a sleepy voice said, "Smee?" I turned to see Hook sitting up on his side, head in palm and black curls about his face and shoulders. "I'm glad you're here, Smee," he said sleepily.

I lowered my voice as best I could. "Evenin', Cap'n,' I said.

Hook yawned. "Is that a frog in your throat, Smee?"

"Aye, Cap'n," I said. "The little blighter's been there all evenin'."

Hook retrieved a pistol from under his pillow. "Come closer, Smee," he said, cocking the pistol, "and let me blast the blighter where it lurks."

I shook my head and lowered my voice as best I could under the circumstances. "There's no need to waste a shot from your pistol, Cap'n."

Hook waved his pistol about his head. "If you're sure. Tell me, Smee, what are you doing in my cabin at this hour?"

"I couldn't sleep, Cap'n. And when I can't sleep, I like to, ah… wind your clocks."

"I never knew that about you, Smee. But then again, I've never awoken and caught you in the act before."

"Right you are, Cap'n. Now go back to sleep. Big day tomorrow."

"Big day tomorrow, you say, Smee?"

"Biggest of days."

Hook lay back down. "I'll take you at your word. Smee?"

"Yes, Cap'n?"

"Since you're here, would you mind combing your old Captain's hair like you used to?"

"*What?*" I croaked.

"I know I told you never to speak of it, but once more couldn't hurt. You remember how quickly I used to nod off? I still have the brush; it's in the bottom drawer of my chest."

Reader, I would prefer to skip the scene where, as part of this important covert mission, I was left with little choice but to brush Hook's hair until he fell asleep. And so I will jump to the part where the dread pirate in question was snoring soundly...

By the time Hook was snoring, my chubby fingers had grown longer and thinner, and I knew that Tink's spell must be wearing off. I tossed aside the comb, flew up to the sixth shelf, and grabbed the clock with four faces.

Outside I flew straight and true for the highest peak in the Neverland. By the time I arrived, I was myself again. I placed the knee-high clock upon the ground, and admired the views of the Neverland around me. To the east, the sun's first rays cast their light upon deep valleys, while to the south they reflected off seas of blue, and to the north they lit forests of green where animals of both fact and fiction have always roamed. I shall leave what I beheld in the west to your own imagination. I reached into my pocket and took out Kenneth's toy knight. "And now I must bid you farewell, my Neverland, and embark on a journey to another. But fear not, for I shall return soon enough with the evidence I need to prove that Kenneth lives on."

"You do know that talking aloud to yourself is a sign of insanity, don't you?" said Tink from behind me.

I looked over my shoulder at her. "I didn't see you there."

"Obviously not."

"What are you doing here, Tink? Aren't you exhausted? I thought you'd be sleeping."

"I've been sleeping, and now I've come to instruct you in the ways of the clock." Tink knelt and opened two of its faces: the one that faced east and the one that faced west, thereby creating a passage between the two. I knelt beside her and peered through to the other side – to a world where the light of an afternoon was far brighter than that of the sleepy morning in my own Neverland.

"You have the toy knight that belongs to the nether boy?" Tink asked.

I nodded.

"Then place it inside, as Chief Hiawatha told you."

I did as she instructed, then stuck my hand all the way through the clock and wriggled my fingers about. "My hand is in Kenneth's Neverland?" I asked.

"If that toy belongs to him."

"It does."

"If what you say is true, then once you've passed through to the other side, the toy will guide you to its owner."

"The entrance is much smaller than I imagined it to be. You know of a way to make it larger?"

Tink shook her head knowingly. "I must make you smaller."

"How much smaller?"

Tink replied by bringing her thumb and forefinger close together.

If truth be told, I didn't much like being bumblebee-sized, and I wondered how they manage to remain so upbeat while collecting pollen. Thankfully, I wasn't so small for long, and once through to the other side, felt myself extending like a telescope. Within seconds I was my old self again, and soaring over Kenneth's Neverland in the sunlight of a bright afternoon.

This Neverland was very different from my own, its landscape more in tune with the English countryside than the tropical isle of my own Neverland. As far as the eye could see, it looked deserted of people. I took Kenneth's toy knight from my pocket, flew up to just below the clouds, and held it above my head. "Light the way to your earthly owner!" I commanded. A light shone from the knight that disappeared over the horizon. I flew at the speed of sound in that direction, and cock-a-doodle-dooed as my sonic booms echoed across the green meadows below.

I saw something that caused me to slow from hundreds of miles per hour to a standstill in a second: it was a fire-breathing dragon as tall as Tink's oak tree! Galloping towards this fearsome beast was a knight dressed in silver armour and riding a black stallion. The dragon opened its wings and breathed fire down upon the knight, whose horse reared up and threw him to the ground. The knight rolled from the path of the fire, and the ground was left scorched and smoking. I flew into the dragon's line of sight and drew my sword. I had hoped to distract it, and it worked: it roared at me and its breath brought with it fire to roast me. I flew up

257

out of its path, and then down upon the dragon where I slashed at its scaly chest. Meanwhile, the knight had climbed back on his horse and was holding a lance. He held it up to get my attention and beckoned to me. I flew in his direction, the dragon's fiery breath nipping at my heels. As the dragon spun about, the knight shot forwards upon his horse, caught the beast unawares, and buried his lance deep in its chest. The dragon roared and threw its head from side to side, then breathed its last and slumped to the ground. "Well fought, sir knight!" I called from high above.

The knight climbed down from his horse and took off his helmet, and I could see he was a boy no taller than I. "Well fought yourself, sir!" he said.

I floated down and landed beside him. "Only too glad to come to the aid of a fellow hero. I've little doubt that the beast had it coming?"

The knight strode to the body of the beast and kicked it. "You have no idea. This monster has been killing the good citizens of Camelot for many a year. And now, thanks to your timely distraction and my trusty lance, they can once again sleep easy in their beds." He kicked the dragon one more time, I supposed for luck, then turned to me. "And now, flying boy dressed in the leaves of the forest, what might I do for you in return?"

"A timely question. You could point me in the direction of Kenneth."

The knight looked puzzled, as though some unfathomable mystery had been laid before him. "*Kenneth*?" he murmured.

"Yes. I do not know his other names. I know only that his Christian name is Kenneth, and that he hails from a town called London in the real world."

"*Kenneth*?" murmured the knight again, as though his faculties had deserted him. His eyes opened wide as though a penny had dropped and raised a pair of shutters. "What a small land it must be, for *I* am *Sir* Kenneth."

"The land is indeed small," I said, smiling.

"Why do you look at me with such knowing eyes?" he asked. "Surely, I cannot be the Kenneth you seek? I have been *Sir* Kenneth for as long as I can remember."

I stepped forward and placed a hand on the confounded knight's shoulder. "And how far back *can* you remember?"

Sir Kenneth licked his dry lips. "Truth be told," he said, "now you mention it, I cannot remember as far back as I imagined I might."

"Come with me," I said, leading him to a tree that had been felled by the dragon's death throes.

We sat side by side on the tree, and with his gaze fixed firmly upon the ground he said, "You think *I* am the Kenneth you seek?"

"I grow more certain of it with every moment that passes."

"And who might you be?" he asked.

I told him that I was Peter Pan, and of that there could be no doubt. I took the toy knight from my pocket and placed it in his hand. He felt it for a moment, like a blind boy reading Braille, and then looked down at it. "I *know* this toy," he said.

"That's because it's yours… it's the knight you gave to your friend John. You remember him?"

"*John?*"

"That's right. Brother to Wendy and…"

"… *Michael?*"

I smiled. "Your earthly past is coming back to you! I can see it in your eyes."

Kenneth stood up suddenly, as though startled, and peered closely at the toy in his hand. "Tell me, Peter, do I have something of John's?"

"Yes!" I said, standing and clapping him on the back.

He looked around uncertainly. "And has he come to collect it?" he asked.

"No, he couldn't come. Leaving the earthly realm would have been impossible as he has grown too heavy of heart. But as you rightly say, you have something of his that, should I return it to him, will relieve him of his sorrow."

He looked at me, such a serious look, and said, "Is it a toy soldier?"

"Yes."

"Then we must find it so you can return it to him without delay."

Journal entry no. 10

Sir Kenneth was on his white charger and galloping at great speed towards Camelot. I flew above him, occasionally shooting on ahead and then doubling back to fly alongside him. Before long the walls of that fabled city appeared and spanned the horizon from east to west as far as the eye could see. He rose up in his saddle and coaxed his horse to greater speeds, then pulled on the reins and brought the horse to a thundering halt. He shielded his eyes from the sun and called up to me. "Peter!" he cried. "It would be best if you did not fly into Camelot, but rode on the back of my horse."

I swooped down towards him. "But why?"

"The good people of Camelot have never seen a flying boy of the forest. It may give them cause for alarm. They are kind but simple folk, and therefore they are frightened of the unknown rather than awed by it, as they should be."

"Agreed! I will trust your judgement," I said, landing behind him on his horse.

Upon our approach, the drawbridge was lowered and hundreds of townsfolk spilled out for news of the dragon. Sir Kenneth sat proud and straight in his saddle. "It has been slain!" he said. "The dragon can harm you no more!" The townspeople cheered him. "Enjoy this time of peace!" Sir

Kenneth went on, "but be ever mindful that a new threat may come one day to replace the dragon." The crowd fell silent. "But fear not!" cried Sir Kenneth, "for whatever foes are thrown against us, they will be vanquished just as the dragon has been! This, my friends, is my solemn pledge to you all!"

We rode through the streets of Camelot to raised hats and cheers, and arrived at the tower where Sir Kenneth lives. We climbed its many steps, and at its top entered his private chamber: a luxurious room with arrow slits cut into its thick stone walls. Between these slits were hung tapestries depicting great battles where Sir Kenneth could be seen in the thick of the action. All about the room were shelves with medieval weapons: axes, crossbows, maces and lances. Sir Kenneth went to a bowl and splashed water on his muddy face. I scanned the room for the toy soldier I'd come to find, but I could see no toys. The truth is this: Sir Kenneth's toys were *everywhere*. In the Neverland, toys are the real thing.

"It's a fine collection of weaponry, is it not, Peter?" he asked.

I picked up a long sword and swung it skilfully. "The best I have ever seen!"

He cast his gaze about his chamber. "I don't recall ever seeing John's soldier. If I had, I would have remembered him. What if it isn't here?"

"It is here. You brought it. I know you did."

Sir Kenneth's gaze found his bed – a four-poster with a canopy, the kind of bed a king would be happy to sleep in. He cast his gaze beneath it, and furrowed his brow. "You've remembered something?" I asked hopefully.

"Could it be…?" he murmured. Sir Kenneth shook his head.

262

"I don't suppose it's inside that…"

"That what?"

"That *box of kisses*," he said, disdainfully.

"Box of kisses?" This mention of a box of kisses rang a bell in my own mind, and its sound sent a shudder through me. "What's inside it?" I asked uneasily. "Not *actual* kisses, surely?"

Sir Kenneth shrugged. "I have always felt it contained *sentiment,* which is why I have never opened it."

I held up a palm. "Say no more. I know better than anyone how sentiment has no part to play in the life of a hero." I approached the bed, knelt down, and pulled out a small wooden box. On its top the word *Kisses* had been engraved. I took it in both hands and shook it gently, as though it might contain an explosive. It did not explode, but rattled. I turned towards Sir Kenneth and extended the box towards him. "Take it and open it," I said.

Sir Kenneth's arms stayed at his sides. "You open it if you must," he said with scorn.

"But this box of kisses is not mine to open."

"You mean you have one too?"

I shook my head. "Of *course* I don't. But if I did have one, which I don't, I would not hesitate to open it. Call yourself a brave knight?"

"That's easy to say when it's not your box." He was right, of course. Sir Kenneth steeled himself. "Hand it over," he said bravely.

A moment later, the lid's box had been tossed to the ground, and Sir Kenneth stared down into it. I say stared, but his eyes were closed and he was muttering something like a prayer under his breath. I peered into the box and smiled, for among the objects within was John's toy soldier. "We've found it!" I whispered.

Sir Kenneth opened his eyes and lifted his chin high, as though knights were impervious to such things as sentiment. But then he looked inside the box again and his eyes grew misty with sorrow. He drew a deep breath, reached into the box, and took out a photograph of two grown-ups.

"Are they your parents?" I asked.

"Yes, I remember now," he said quietly. In the photograph his parents were smiling and waving at him. "Why did they abandon me, Peter?" he asked.

"They didn't."

"Then I abandoned them?"

I squeezed his shoulder and nodded. "But the choice… it was no longer yours to make."

Sir Kenneth furrowed his brow. "Where are my parents?" he asked.

"In the real world, where you left them."

Sir Kenneth's eyes opened wide, as though he'd spotted something of great importance. "Of course! Great Ormond Street. I must get back there. Mother and Father will be worried about me."

"No, they won't. Not anymore."

Sir Kenneth shuddered as he came to the same false conclusion as his parents. "Am I *dead*, Peter?"

I shook my head so hard I might easily have pulled a neck muscle. "Answer me this: do dead children slay dragons?"

"It sounds unlikely. So where *are* we?"

"In the Neverland."

Sir Kenneth looked about him. "Is the Neverland real?"

"It's as real as anywhere else," I confirmed.

"But my parents *think* I'm dead?"

I nodded. "They are lacking in imagination, so what else were they to conclude?"

"They must have grieved for their only son. And yet I had forgotten them. I don't deserve to be missed."

"Maybe so. But you remember them now."

"Yes, but only because you convinced me to open my box of kisses."

"You would have opened it in time. You didn't *want* to forget them. Otherwise why bring these things here?" I reached in and took out John's toy soldier. "And that goes for your good friends the Darlings. You *wanted* to remember them."

"They grieve for me too?"

"Yes, and their gloom is of the most serious kind."

"How serious?"

"So serious that I fear they may grow up before their time."

"Would that really be such a bad thing?"

"The worst. Don't you know? To grow up too soon is the greatest tragedy that can befall anyone. If it happens to the Darlings they will no longer be able to fly, and should that happen they will never be able to visit the Neverland and fulfil their oaths to you."

"Oaths?"

"Yes. To say goodbye."

Sir Kenneth nodded. "I remember now." He took John's soldier from the box and handed it to me. "Then you must take this to them, and without delay."

Journal entry no. 11

With John's toy soldier in my possession, I returned to my own Neverland, but moved swiftly through it on my way to the Darlings.

I arrived in the real world, and found it to be much colder than when last I visited. For this reason their bedroom window was closed. I pressed my nose against the frosty pane and, but for the pink glow that came from the little night lights beside their beds, it was black as pitch inside. I tapped on the window, and tapped again as a chill wind nipped at my sides. I was relieved to see movement within and, moments later, the window was opened. I flew gratefully inside.

"You'll catch your death of cold!" said Wendy, rubbing her shoulders in her night dress. "Have you no coat?" she added, closing the window.

"The sun keeps the Neverland warm all year round."

"Here the sun neglects us every winter," she said.

"You came back!" whispered Michael. "I knew you would. See, John. I told you Peter would come back."

I looked at John, who sat up in bed and rubbed at his eyes.

"Why ever would you doubt it?" I said.

"You said you'd be back tomorrow, Peter," said Wendy.

"And here I am."

"Yes, but it's been two months since your last visit."

Michael rolled his eyes. "John said you were never coming back because you stole Kenneth's knight."

"Stole?" I raised my eyebrows.

"Yes," said John. "What else would you call it? But you're here now, so I presume you've come to give it back." He extended a hand towards me.

I shook my head. "That is not why I'm here."

"See, Wendy. I told you your *friend* was nothing but a common thief," said John.

"Oh, Peter," said Wendy. "What have you to say to that?"

"That I have brought you something to replace it."

"You *can't* replace something like that," said John tearfully. "Not ever. It belonged to my best friend, and I shall never see him again."

"I'll wager that *this* will replace it," I said, extending my hand and uncurling my fingers to reveal his soldier.

John climbed out of bed and took it from my hand. "But it *can't* be the soldier I gave to Kenneth," he said, and moved to his night light to examine it.

"Well?" said Wendy.

John gazed at her over his shoulder, his mouth fallen open and his eyes filled with wonder. "It is! It's the soldier I gave to Kenneth."

"And you're sure?" said Wendy.

John nodded. "It has two tiny scratches on its chest from that time when Kenneth and I hurled stones at each other's army." His gaze jumped to me. "The hospital searched everywhere for it. They were *certain* it was lost. So where did you find it?"

Michael took a step towards his brother, and smiled the smile of the knowing. "Isn't it obvious, John? Kenneth must have given it to him."

"He is *Sir* Kenneth now, and he is the bravest knight in Camelot."

"Honestly?" said Michael.

I crossed my heart. "We slew a dragon together." Michael's mouth opened as if to speak, but he made no sound.

The same could not be said for John, who asked, "I'm not saying I believe you. But *if* it were true, if Kenneth is a knight in Camelot, why would he want to know us?"

"I will not lie. When at first I found him he had no memory of his life here, but that is always the way with new arrivals to the Neverland. But those who *wish* to remember in time, are permitted a box of keepsakes. We found Sir Kenneth's box, and your toy soldier had been given pride of place inside it."

John looked down at the soldier in his hand. "He didn't want to forget us, then?" he said quietly.

"No. And once his memories were restored, it became his fondest wish that I return the soldier to you."

"Why?" asked Wendy.

"So that you would be unburdened of your heavy hearts, learn to fly, and travel to the Neverland to fulfil your oaths to him."

"To say goodbye?" asked John.

"To say goodbye," I repeated.

"Does this mean that you're going to teach us to fly now, Peter?" asked Michael, finding his voice again. I bowed low and smiled.

The twelve pages that followed here explained everything a person (of sufficient imagination) needs to know in order to fly unaided, but on Tink's advice I have erased those twelve pages. She has been checking my diary, and when she read them she enquired if I'd lost my mind. "Never easy to tell. But why do you ask?" I enquired back.

"Because you can't write down secrets like that where people in the real world can read them."

I folded my arms. "And why not?"

"Because the skies of the real world will end up filled with flying people."

I chewed on a nail. "If you've a point to make, fairy, then make it quickly," I said.

"Perhaps the clue can be found in the word *real*."

I chewed my nail some more. "Flying's real," I said.

"In the Neverland, perhaps. But in the real world they need contraptions with wings and motors to overcome the laws of gravity. There are *physics* in the real world, Peter, and they must be respected."

"Why?"

"I think you'll find that's the whole point of the *real* world."

And so, reader, it is with a heavy heart that we must rejoin the Darlings some thirty minutes later, as that is how long it takes to teach a novice in the real world to ignore the laws of physics and fly. And that novice was called Michael Darling. "Yippee! Look at me, Wendy! John, look! I'm really flying!"

Wendy silently clapped her little brother. "You really believe that I'll be able to do that?"

"It is not for me to believe, Wendy. It is for you. And then nothing can prevent it."

John shook his head slowly. "Nothing but *gravity*," he murmured.

"Simply ignore gravity. And ignore John. Just as Michael is," I told Wendy.

John folded his arms. "Yes, go on then Wendy. Simply ignore gravity as Michael is."

"But I'm not so young as Michael, Peter," said Wendy. "Please explain how to ignore gravity one more time?"

You will know the drill by now... and so we must rejoin the story two pages later (as two pages was what it took to sum up the previous twelve).

"I'm doing it!" cried Wendy.

"Call that flying?" said Michael as he darted about the room.

"If not flying, then what would you call it?" she asked him.

"You're floating," said Michael.

Wendy looked at me imploringly. "You've done the difficult part," I said. "Now all you have to do is *will* yourself to move in the direction you want to go."

She looked up into the top left-hand corner of the room and shot backwards in the opposite direction. I caught her before she flew out of the window. "What happened then?" she asked, strangely content to be held by me.

I put her down. "You may have been looking where you wanted to go, but you must have been thinking about me."

"You know, I believe I was. I was thinking how much I didn't want to let you down."

"That's just it. In order to fly, you mustn't *think* at all. Do you think to walk in a direction?"

"No, of course not."

"It's the same with flying."

Wendy thought about that, and then flew into the corner of the room she wanted to reach. She floated about to face me. "I see what you mean..." And then off she flew in pursuit of

Michael, and the pair chased each other's pyjama tails like children on a funfair ride.

John had been watching his siblings from the corner of his eye. I flew the two metres to his bed and set down at the end of it. "Now it's your turn," I said.

John shook his head. "I can't."

"Nonsense. You were listening to every word I taught them."

"It doesn't matter."

"And what's more, you can see them doing it with your own eyes. Look!"

John jumped off his bed and threw his arms wide. "Just because I can see them doing it doesn't mean I can too!"

"Of course it does," said Michael from the ceiling.

"That's rubbish," said John. "I can watch a surgeon do an operation, but that doesn't mean I can operate myself, does it!"

"That isn't true. You could carry out an operation quite easily," I said.

"Maybe so, but I'd kill my patient."

I leaned closer to him. "What have I told you all about getting bogged down in tiny details?"

"*Killing* the patient is a tiny detail? What land are you *from*?" asked John.

"The Neverland! A place where nobody has ever needed an

operation."

John went red in his face. "Oh, you… you... you…"

"Me thrice *what*?"

"You think you have an answer to everything."

"I do. And if I don't, then Tink will find me an answer."

Wendy landed gracefully beside me. "Who's Tink?"

"A fairy and a loyal friend."

"She sounds wonderful! And she's a real fairy?"

"As real as any other."

"Can we meet her?" said Michael from the ceiling.

"Yes. Of course. But first your brother must learn to fly."

"Why must I? Why don't you just go without me?"

I looked at John. "Kenneth is more your friend than Wendy or Michael's. Is he not your *best* friend?"

"Rub it in, why don't you?"

"It's true, John," said Wendy. "Don't look at Peter like that. He only wants to help."

"Why? What's in this for him?"

I felt the gaze of all three upon me. "I believe that your coming to the Neverland will result in a great adventure for us all."

John huffed. "Adventures involve danger. How much danger can there be in a place called the Neverland that's filled with little fairies?"

I stepped towards him, my voice little more than a whisper. "Not just fairies… there are cold-blooded pirates and savage Indians, and a crocodile so enormous it would not fit inside this room. What's more, after dark, the things that go bump in the night come looking for terrible mischief, and are themselves frightened away come morning by the creatures that stalk children in their dreams."

John gulped.

I lowered my voice further. "Would you like to hear the greatest part of the adventure?"

Behind me Wendy said, "Yes, Peter."

I turned to face her. "No child from the real world has ever set foot in the Neverland. Not a single one since the very beginning of time." I turned slowly on the spot and pointed from one Darling to another. "That means you three shall be the *first* to make the crossing." I drew my sword with a flourish and stepped towards John.

"What are you going to do with that? Cut me?" he said.

"Not *you,* but your doubts about being able to fly!"

What followed here was a page that explained how to cut away any doubts about defying gravity. And so, reader, we now rejoin the story just as John's feet left the ground for the first time…

"This… this… this …!"

I placed my fisted hands on my hips and enquired, "This is what?"

"Impossible!" said John, smiling despite himself and rising up to bump his head on the ceiling.

Journal entry no. 12

I suppose the journey to the Neverland could be a little scary the first time. The first big hurdle to overcome (I discovered) was this realisation of John's: "We must be flying as high as the dome of St. Paul's Cathedral!" This truth caused much shrieking and covering of eyes – and that was just me – at which point John said a fruity word that made Wendy blush and Michael cover his ears. This word, I have been reliably informed by Tink, has no place in this diary.

Up we flew, higher still, for that is the direction you must fly in to get to the Neverland, and it wasn't long before we entered something that John called the earth's outer atmosphere. From here the planet Earth can be seen as a ball of blue and white. You might imagine that Michael, being the youngest, would have been the most scared, but the opposite was true: his imagination told him that the higher he travelled the more magical and safer things became. Which of course is true.

What gave John the most concern in the outer atmosphere is best summed up by what he said when he arrived: "There is no air for us to breathe in the earth's outer atmosphere! We're all going to die!" He repeated this fiction thirteen times, and only stopped when Michael puffed out his cheeks and blew a raspberry in his face. "See! There's plenty of air to breathe!"

"How is this possible?" said John between gapes.

I flew back to him. "As I taught you, once unlocked, the power of your imagination can make anything possible."

Next came outer space: a void of darkness where the nearest stars are so far away they appear impossible to reach. For a time, my companions were filled with awe as they flew towards billions of stars. John even gave Michael and Wendy the thumbs up, as if to say travelling to the Neverland had been all his idea and what a brilliant idea it had been. But the trouble with those who live in the real world is this: they grow bored quickly, and feelings of awe are replaced by yawns and the desire for something new. And so it was with my companions, whose awe-filled expressions changed to those that said they'd rather be *anywhere* than flying through space towards a galaxy of stars that came no closer. I suppose that's why what happened next caught them unawares. I speak of the secret black hole that is the shortcut to the Neverland. The Neverland lies beyond any star that is visible to the human eye, and so a shortcut is needed to arrive there in a single evening. When at first you fly into the secret black hole, all the stars in the heavens appear to have been snuffed out, and you are blinded by darkness. Soon after that, the quickening begins, and it feels as though you've entered a tunnel where all the stars in the galaxy rush by at astronomical speed. I know to keep my eyes closed during the quickening. This explains why, when I shot out the other side of the black hole over the Neverland, I was able to fly straight and true. And also why my companions fell like shrieking stones into the mermaid's lagoon.

I set down on a rock at the edge of a lagoon beside a mermaid called Miss Roe. "Hello, Peter," she said, flip-flopping her tail against the rock upon which she was sunbathing.

"A good morning to you, Miss Roe," I said.

She gazed out to where my companions were splashing about in the lagoon. "Friends of yours?" she asked.

I nodded. "Indeed. They have just arrived from the real world."

"That doesn't really excuse the dreadful din they're making."

I folded my arms. "Forgive them."

"Why?"

"Because it is the first time that anyone has ever made the crossing from the real world to the Neverland."

"Maybe so, but if they carry on making that *din* they're going to attract the attention of the crocodile. Peter?"

"Yes?"

"Can they swim?"

"Who knows? It never came up." I took a step to the edge of the rock, and placed a hand over my eyes to shield them from the sunlight. "They look to be doing something similar to swimming," I said.

"Splashing about in no particular direction is nothing like swimming. Take it from someone who knows."

"No particular direction? A problem easily rectified," I said, sticking two fingers in my mouth and whistling. They stopped splashing about in no particular direction for a moment, and then began splashing towards the rock upon which I now sat beside Miss Roe.

I have thought long and hard about the word that best sums up how the Darlings looked when they finally climbed out of the water onto the rock. The one I finally chose was this: bedraggled. Panting, they lay on their backs for some time, and John was the first to speak. "He's trying to kill us!" he said, between gasps.

"You said you wanted an adventure," I reminded him.

"Oh, Peter. What if we'd drowned?" said Wendy.

"You can't drown. Not in the Neverland."

"How can you be so sure?" asked Wendy.

"Because nobody ever has."

John struggled up onto his elbows and looked at me. "You think we can breathe? Underwater?"

"You managed to breathe in outer space, didn't you? Correct me if I'm wrong, but isn't there even *less* air in outer space than underwater?" My logic must have been sound, because John nodded and lay back down.

Wendy sat up. "I had no idea the Neverland would be so beautiful!"

"Yes!" said Michael. "It looks just as I imagine Treasure Island to look." He turned and looked at me. "And are there really pirates here?" he said, noticing Miss Roe. At this juncture, it should be recorded for posterity that the spotting of Miss Roe was not Michael Darling's finest hour. He scrambled to his feet as though his pants were set alight and said, "Wendy, John, look! It's a big smelly fish with a pretty face and red hair!"

Wendy and John stood just as quickly, and all three gaped at Miss Roe. The scales on Miss Roe's golden tail bristled. "The flies in the Neverland are as big as fists and carry twice the punch," she accurately informed them.

"Really?" said Michael, gazing about. "What should we do?"

"Close your mouths," said Miss Roe. Three mouths snapped shut.

Wendy was the first to find her manners. She stepped forward and curtseyed. "I'm Wendy Darling," she said, "and I've always wanted to meet a mermaid." Her brothers did the same (with bows that appeared suspiciously like my own) and, once the introductions were done, Wendy insisted they lie beside Miss Roe and sunbathe until their clothes were dry. "I won't have Michael catching his death of cold," she said.

They had not been sunbathing long when Tink arrived. "So here you all are!" she shrieked, appearing in a sudden puff of smoke. So sudden and dramatic was Tink's appearance that everyone present jumped to their feet (including Miss Roe, who has no feet, and a moment later she'd fallen in the lagoon).

"Who *is* this?" asked Wendy.

I was going to tell her who *this* was when *this* spoke for herself. "*I* am Tinker Bell. And who is *this*?" said Tink, looking Wendy up and down.

I gave Wendy a moment to answer, but her expression led me to believe that meeting a fairy for the first time, and discovering her to be so rude, had robbed her of the power of speech.

"Wendy *darling* isn't at all what I was expecting," said Tink.

"You took the words from my mouth," said Wendy.

"How dare you insult me at a time like this?" said Tink.

"Is this a bad time? I had no idea," replied Wendy politely.

"Then you can't have much of an idea about anything, as this is the very worst time," said Tink, clasping her cheeks.

"What's the matter with the fairy lady?" yelped Michael.

Tink fluttered her pretty wings. "Thank you for asking, young man." The young man blushed, and Tink leaned forward so they were eye to eye. "You see," she said, "while Peter was off frolicking in the real world with all you little *darlings*, the pirates attacked the Indian settlement."

Michael clasped his cheeks now. "They did?"

"Yes. They attacked them in the dead of night and took them by surprise. By now they must have wiped out half their number."

"Tink!" I said. "Is that true?"

"Please tell your friend Peter that it is true. And that *that* isn't all."

Michael looked at me. "It is true and that's not all," he said.

"There's more?" I asked.

"Tell Peter that when someone says *that's not all,* it generally implies there's more, yes."

"Tink!" I said.

She straightened up and looked at me. "Hook discovered that one of his clocks was missing, and convinced himself the Indians were responsible."

"But why? I took it."

"It seems that Hook has been looking for an excuse to attack the Indians after dark," said Tink.

"He needed an excuse?" said John.

I thumped my fist into my palm. "It is *the* unwritten rule of the land that both sides agree on a time *and* a place before a battle can commence."

"Hook's broken this rule?" asked Michael.

"So it seems," I said. "For how else was he to win an outright victory against such a brave foe?"

"Why did you steal his clock, Peter?" asked Wendy.

"It was not Hook's clock. He stole it, and I needed it. It contains powerful magic, magic that allowed me to cross into Kenneth's Neverland."

"So this attack on the Indians is our fault," said John.

I glanced at all three Darlings in turn. "Do not trouble yourselves. Only Hook and his bad form are at fault here."

"It's only a matter of time before he slaughters all my kin," came Tiger Lily's tired voice. We looked up to see Tiger Lily standing on a rock above us. Her face was smeared with dirt, and she looked exhausted from battle. "I have run out of arrows," she said, a tear rolling down her cheek.

"You poor beautiful girl!" cried Wendy, reaching up with both arms as though to hug her.

"Where is Chief Hiawatha? Is he safe?" I asked Tiger Lily.

"He's holed up with the other survivors at Moat Creek. But for how long? Hook has them surrounded and hopelessly outnumbered."

"Then we must go to their rescue!"

"*We?*" said Tink. "I trust you don't mean us and these earthly *darlings*."

"Don't you like us?" asked Michael.

Tink glared at Wendy, then smiled sweetly at Michael and said, "You are nice enough, little man., but Peter should never have brought you here. The Neverland is no place for children of the real world."

"Why not?" asked John.

"Haven't you been listening? It's too dangerous," said Tink.

"It's dangerous in the real world, too," John informed her. "Very dangerous. There are wars and fighting there too."

"Maybe so, but none that are fought by *children*," said Tink, folding her arms.

"They're not in the real world now. They're in the

Neverland," I said.

Tink glanced at Wendy again, and fluttered her wings impatiently. "And?" she asked.

"And the Neverland *is* imagination. So there are no limits here, and they can become whatever they want," I said.

"With a little help from me, you mean?"

"Please, Tink," said Tiger Lily. "Do whatever you have to to help my people survive."

Wendy stepped forward. "I want to help. Truly I do."

"Me too," said Michael.

"And me," said John.

"Cock-a-doodle-doo!" I crowed. I took to the air and flew around them so fast as to make them dizzy. I tapped Michael on his shoulder and said, "Which great warrior would you like to become?"

Michael thought for a moment, and then his face lit up. "I learned about Perseus in school recently. Did you know he had winged boots that meant he could fly?"

"He did?" I said.

"Yes! And a golden shield that reflected the gorgon's stare back at her. It turned her to stone. Might I have a shield that can turn *anyone* who stares into it to stone?"

"You shall have your shield! And you will become the Perseus of your imagination! Make it so, Tink."

Tink stamped her foot.

"Impertinent fairy! Make it so or I shall never again call you friend."

Tink poked her tongue out at me, then transformed into a ball of light that darted about Michael's shoulders and sprinkled fairy dust upon them. The dust was absorbed by Michael's imagination, and together they transformed him into the Perseus he'd imagined during his classes. Once Tink had finished, Michael was wearing a bronze breast plate and bronze boots with white feathered wings, and strapped to his arm was a golden shield that could turn any enemy who saw their reflection in it to stone. Michael smiled and took flight on the air of his winged boots. "Do be careful, Michael!" Wendy called up to him.

Next, Tink turned her attention to John. She flew about his shoulders sprinkling her fairy dust. John's eyes lit up. "I shall be the Duke of Wellington!" he said. "The greatest military strategist who ever lived!"

"Are you sure?" I asked.

"Yes, of course. If we're to save the Indians we're going to need the tactical brilliance of a great general."

"Then make it so, Tink!" John was suddenly on a tall black horse, dressed in the gold braided uniform of a general. He drew a long thin sword from a scabbard at the horse's side, and both horse and rider took to the air. I turned to Wendy. "And what will you become?"

Wendy shook her head. "I'm sorry, Peter. I have no heroes of violence as Michael and John do."

"You must *think*, Wendy," I said.

"I suppose I could become Florence Nightingale."

"What weapons did she wield?" I asked.

"She had no weapons. Just bandages and antiseptic. She was a nurse."

"We have no need of bandages in the Neverland."

Wendy looked appalled. "But why ever not?"

"Because in the Neverland, non-fatal wounds heal themselves quickly. There must be someone you've always wanted to be?"

Wendy sat down and thought for a moment. "I want to be the best mother a child ever had one day."

I knelt down beside her. "Then you shall become Mother Nature, and protect the children of Tiger Lily's people."

Wendy smiled at me, and so sweet was her smile that it stole my breath away.

"Yes!" cried Tiger Lily. "Turn Wendy into Mother Nature, and let her protect the children of my people."

Wendy nodded, closed her eyes, and said, "Yes, Peter. Please, make me Mother Nature."

Tink sprinkled her dust on Wendy, and all at once she was dressed in a dark green toga. The toga was made from all the things of the forest that possess life-giving and healing qualities. Wendy opened her eyes and smiled up at her brothers. "I *am* Mother Nature," she said with certainty.

"What powers do you have?" asked Michael.

Wendy held out her hands, and produced a gust of wind that sent Michael laughing and tumbling head over heels. "I imagine I can make thunder and lightning, too!" she said, flying up to join her brothers.

Journal entry no. 13

A little later, we were joined by the Lost Boys. We lay on a high ridge that looked down upon the creek where the Indians had retreated. Tootles, Nibs and Slightly were at the end of our line beside the Darlings in their new guises as heroes. "Are you really Mother Nature?" Tootles whispered to Wendy, who lay beside him.

"Yes. For the time being, anyway."

"Will you be *my* Mother Nature?" pressed Tootles hopefully.

"If you'd like me to be," said Wendy.

Tootles looked very serious. "I speak for all the Lost Boys when I say we'd like that very much."

Nibs inched forwards so he could see past Tootles to Wendy. "It's true," he said. "Tootles does speak for all of us. You see, not one amongst us has ever had a mother. Let alone a Mother Nature."

"Is that why you stare at me so?" asked Wendy.

The Lost Boys nodded.

Tink tutted. "Don't I look after you all?"

The Lost Boys shook their heads.

"That's gratitude for you," snapped Tink. She fluttered her long eyelashes at me and said, "*You* don't look upon me as being a mother, do you, Peter?"

"Of course not, Tink."

Tink smiled and stuck her tongue out at Wendy.

"Would you please stop this bickering!" commanded Tiger Lily.

"Tiger Lily is right. We must concentrate on the adventure at hand," I said.

John was studying the creek below us through a telescope. "It's very quiet," he observed. "The pirates must be waiting till dusk to finish what they started last night."

I scrambled to my feet and drew my sword. "The sun is about to set, so we attack now." I looked to John in his guise as the Duke of Wellington and saluted. "What is your plan, great general?"
John leapt up into the saddle of his horse. "Wendy and Michael, you will distract Hook's men from their left side. Wendy, send powerful winds down upon them, and Michael, when they look to see what has caused these winds, fly down and use your shield to turn any pirate foolish enough to look up into stone."

"It sounds an awfully important job," said Michael.
I saluted both. "And one that you and Wendy are more than up to."

"Peter," said John, "you and the Lost Boys will attack the

advancing pirates from the rear."

"An excellent plan, General. And where will you be?"

"I will stand as a barrier between the pirates and the surviving Indians. If that's alright with you?"

"I defer to your superior knowledge of the battlefield," I said, bowing. "And now we put your plan into action."

The first thing Wendy did was to swoop low over the Indian survivors. She saw many petrified children in the arms of their mothers, and her instincts to protect these children overwhelmed her. Wendy conjured winds so powerful that their like had never been felt in the Neverland before. The pirates were forced to bend double and place their hands over their eyes to shield them from the debris that flew at them. Any pirate who squinted up, curious to see the source of those terrible winds, beheld Michael swooping down upon them, and any who saw their own reflections in his shield were turned instantly to stone. The pirates who witnessed this turned and fled into the avenging blades of Peter Pan and the Lost Boys.

While this was going on, Hook and a handful of his most trusted lieutenants had advanced upon the last surviving Indians. Hook, motivated by blood-lust and villainy, and riding a black steed, soon encountered the only person who now stood between him and victory over the Indians: the Duke of Wellington on his horse. "You will not get past me!" cried John.

"What have we here?" sneered Hook from his saddle. "A little *boy* dressed up like a general?"

"I am the Duke of Wellington, the greatest strategist in the history of warfare!"

"Never heard of you," said Hook.

"Let that be your undoing," said John, his horse rearing up on its hind legs.

"I don't know who you think you are, *boy*, but you do not even belong in this world. Which is why I'm going to slice you in two and send both parts back to where they came from!" Hook galloped forwards. Sword smashed upon hook, and hook upon sword, until John, overpowered by his grown-up foe, tumbled from his mount. Hook climbed down off his horse and stood over his quarry. "Prepare to meet thy doom, *boy*." John raised his sword to deflect the hook that now plunged towards his heart. He tried to stand, but each time he was thrown back down. Hook caught John's sword, which flew from his grasp and left his heart exposed. It was then that another warrior on a horse thundered down upon them both: a knight in silver armour and holding a lance.

"What's this?" said Hook. "Are we to be deluged by interlopers who have no place in our Neverland? Come and taste the deadliest steel in any land, if you dare, little knight!" The little knight *did* dare, and then some. On he came, riding faster and faster, lance held strong and true before him. Seeing that his bluff had been called, Hook thought better of being turned into a pirate shish kebab, and ran for his miserable life.

The knight climbed from his mount and offered his hand to John, who took it without hesitation. He stood up and tried to see the person beyond the eye slits in the knight's helmet. John saw only a pair of dark eyes, gazing back at him, unblinking. The knight lifted off his helmet and cast it to the ground. Two boys stood facing one another, young men who had been the very best of friends until separated by… by what, reader? By what grown-ups lacking in imagination have labelled *death*? John was the first to smile, but only by a fraction. Kenneth extended a hand for him to shake. John ignored it, and instead stepped forwards and threw his arms around his best friend. At first Kenneth froze. As you must doubtless be aware, hugs between boys are not necessarily the done thing.

"I thought I'd never see you again!" said John, with a smile so big that his face struggled to contain it. "And just look at you! You've become the brave knight of legend that you always wanted to be."

Kenneth shook his head. "At this moment it means nothing. I'm just your friend."

John glanced down at the splendid, gold braided uniform he was wearing. "And neither am I the Duke of Wellington." Both boys laughed and shook hands with gusto.

I had been hovering just above them, and now I set myself down. "Our reunion would never have been possible without Peter," said Sir Kenneth.

John offered me his hand. "I'm sorry for doubting you, Peter," he said. I shook his hand warmly.

Wendy and Michael landed beside us. "Kenneth!" cried Wendy. "Is it really you?" She threw her arms around him.

"Hello, Kenneth," said Michael, with no little awe in his voice.

"And hello to you too, young Michael Darling!" said

Kenneth.

"Your armour's amazing," said Michael. "Are you completely safe inside it?"

"Not completely, but I wouldn't recommend taking on a fire-breathing dragon without it."

"How did you get here?" marvelled Wendy. "I thought we'd have to visit another Neverland to find you."

"I am curious to hear the answer to that myself," I said.

Kenneth went to the saddlebag on his horse, opened it and lifted out the clock with four faces. "I discovered this in my land, and sensed there were people beyond it in peril. People I care about. So you see, I had to come."

Journal entry no. 14

After Chief Hiawatha had emerged from the undergrowth and thanked us for saving his people, and Sir Kenneth and I had pointed out that it was all in a day's play for us, Wendy, Michael and I flew to my underground hideout. John and Sir Kenneth raced each other over land on their horses, while the Lost Boys followed on foot. When I arrived back, I drew a finishing line in the sand for John and Sir Kenneth.

The two friends soon came thundering around a rock in the cove and across the finishing line. "A photo finish!" I cried.

Wendy gazed out over the golden beach to the bluest of seas beyond. "Is this really where you live, Peter?" she asked.

I breathed in deeply and filled my lungs with warm sea air. "Yes. Do you like it, Wendy?"

"Very much," she replied. "But where are your things? Do you sleep on the ground?" The Lost Boys had arrived by this time, and all three laughed at her as though she were their real mother.

"No, Wendy," I said. "The entrance to my home is hereabouts."

"Entrance?" said Wendy. "But all I see are trees."

"Could it be that the entrance lies within one?" I said.

"You live inside a *tree*?" asked Wendy.

"Not inside but underneath," I said, glancing at a spot on the ground between two trees. Wendy ran to the spot and examined one of the trees, while Michael ran his fingers over the trunk of the other. He looked across at his sister. "The entrance *must* be in your tree, Wendy," he said.

"I was about to say the same to you, little brother."

"You *both* need to look harder," said Kenneth.

"Oh, we do, do we, clever clogs?" said Wendy. "Over to you," she said, standing aside and beckoning Michael to join her.

Sir Kenneth stood between the two trees and stroked his chin thoughtfully. John joined him and tapped on one of the trees, while Sir Kenneth looked up into its branches. "Would you fly up there and bring me the stick that rests on that branch, old friend?" he asked John.

"I'd be delighted!" replied John, flying up to retrieve the stick. He landed and handed it to Sir Kenneth, who held it diagonally before him. The gnarled stick was over twice his height. Sir Kenneth planted one end of the stick firmly in the ground at his feet.

"Nothing's happening," said Wendy, sounding rather pleased.

Sir Kenneth smiled, lifted the stick onto a horizontal plane, and stepped back so that one end of it went into a groove in the bark of one tree, and the other end did the same in the other. "Open sesame!" I cried, as the sand beneath Sir Kenneth's feet fell inwards as though through an egg timer. Moments later, he was standing at the top of the stairs that led into my underground den.

"Bravo!" cried John, clapping his friend.

Wendy saw that I was looking skyward and that my lips were moving. "Who are you talking to?" she asked.

"I was thanking my lucky stars that Sir Kenneth is not a pirate. If he were, they might have discovered the entrance too, and murdered me while I slept."

"May I be the first to see it?" asked Wendy, making her way to the sand-covered stairs.

I bowed low and beckoned her towards the entrance. "Sir Kenneth, please step aside and allow Wendy Darling to descend into my home."

Sir Kenneth stepped off the top step, and Wendy went down into my den as though it were her own. We all crouched by the entrance to await her verdict.

"It's nice and cosy," came her voice.

"I am glad you find it so," I called down.

"Although, it's obviously a place where a *boy* lives," she said.

The Lost Boys patted my back. "All the better for it!" I said.

"That explains why it needs a woman's touch," came Wendy's reply.

We all shook our heads. "I'd rather you touched nothing," I called down.

"Just a little spring-clean. I promise not to disturb anything," came her busy-sounding voice.

I turned to Tink, who had just fluttered down and joined us. "Tell me, fairy, is it springtime?"

Tink wrinkled up her nose. "Why ever would you ask such a thing? You know it's always summer in the Neverland. What's going on?"

"It's Wendy," said Tootles. "She says it's time that Peter's den had a spring-clean."

Tink clenched her fists, and made to descend the steps. I grabbed hold of her arm. "She's only trying to help. I trust her," I said.

"Oh, you do? Well, be it on your head when she's done *spring-cleaning* and you can't find anything you need."

While Wendy spring-cleaned in perpetual summer, the rest of us played on the beach. We built sand knights and soldiers, and John and Kenneth captained their armies. The battle commenced in earnest, and we hurled sticks at the two opposing sand armies. Before long, all but one sand figure remained – a soldier, which meant John's army had been victorious. I saw how Sir Kenneth had held back towards the end. He had let his friend win. *The very epitome of good form*! I thought.

It was not long after this battle was over and Wendy had re-joined us, that Sir Kenneth said something that caused the hearts of the Darlings to sink. "The time has come for me to return to my own Neverland. Therefore, we must say our goodbyes."

"Must you go so soon?" said Michael.

Sir Kenneth nodded. "The people of Camelot rely on me to protect them."

"What should I tell your mother and father?" said John quietly. "They miss you and grieve for you so much."

Sir Kenneth placed a hand on his shoulder. "Tell them they needn't be sad, that you've seen me, and that I live on, and could not be happier. And be sure to tell them that I love them."

"But what if they don't believe me?" said John.

"They will *want* to believe, and so in time they will come to believe."

"Neverland has made you very wise," said John.

"If it has, it can only mean one thing: that wisdom comes from facing and overcoming our fears."

"More than that," I said, "it comes from looking upon every fear we encounter as nothing more than a new adventure that must be undertaken." I looked at the Darlings, who appeared melancholy despite the wisdom I had shared. "Buck up," I said. "The time has come for you all to fulfil your oaths."

Wendy was the first to hug Sir Kenneth goodbye, followed by Michael, and then by John, whose hug was the most heartfelt of all. Sir Kenneth went to his saddle bag and lifted out the clock with four faces. He set it upon the ground and opened the entrance and the exit. He turned to his friends. "I shall value your friendship always, and never forget you."

"Nor we you," said Wendy, as she was the only one who could find her voice.

"Farewell!" said Sir Kenneth, whereupon horse and rider shrank and galloped through the clock's entrance. The Darlings stared down at the exit, but Sir Kenneth did not reappear. He was already back in his own Neverland. A heavy silence followed, soon broken by Wendy. "I have something to show you, Peter," she said.

"What is it?" I asked. Wendy smiled her sweetest smile, got up and walked down the steps into my underground den. I followed her without thinking, and let that be a warning to all who follow without thinking.

Once below, Wendy went to my bed and retrieved something from beneath it. "Look what I've found," she beamed.

"What is it?"

"It's a little wooden box, Peter."

"You found a *box*?"

"Yes. A box of kisses. Why do you step away from me?"

"Because you are mistaken. That can't be mine. I have no such box."

"Everyone needs kisses, Peter."

"Not I."

"Why not you?" asked Wendy, looking at my lips.

"Need it be said? I am a great hero."

"Sir Kenneth is a great hero, yet he had a box of kisses. So why not you?"

"That's different."

"Why is it?"

"I should have thought it obvious. Sir Kenneth has parents in the real world… people who would miss him." I closed my eyes and turned my head away. "I have no parents, Wendy."

"No parents? Then where did you come from?"

"As with all things in the Neverland, I was born of my own imagination."

When next Wendy spoke, I felt her breath on my ear. "I think you *must* have had parents, and that all you need do is *remember.*" Although chilled to the bone, I felt beads of perspiration on my forehead. *"What's the matter, Peter? You've turned dreadfully pale."*

I opened my eyes. "I *can't.*"

"You can't what?"

"Remember."

"Peter?"

I did not answer her.

"Have you ever seen a single baby in the Neverland?"

"Of course not. The Neverland is much too dangerous for

babies."

"Well, then, haven't you just answered the question?"

"If you've a point to make then make it quickly."

"My point is this: you *must* have been a baby once. And that means you must have been born in the real word, to parents who would have grieved when you went away. You suddenly look so pale and unwell! Turn your back, and I shall put the box back where I found it."

"No! That which is found cannot be unfound. I will open my box. And whatever happens next will just have to be looked upon as all things must."

"And how is that?"

"As an adventure, Wendy."

"Oh, Peter! Your parents would be so proud," she said, handing the box to me.

Journal entry no. 15

I don't remember very much about the journey back to the real world with the Darlings. While not in actual shock, I may have been in a state like it. My ears were ringing, my head felt fuzzy, and my heart was beating too quickly. All had been caused by a single realisation: that I, Peter Pan, *must* have had parents of my own once. Wendy said she'd found the names of my mother and father inside the box. "Leave it in my capable hands, and I will find them for you," she said.

The Darlings had been sitting on their beds when Wendy said it, and John explained that, when it came to finding things, Wendy's hands were by far the most capable. Michael agreed with his brother, and Wendy said I should return in one week's time. "By then I will have found a way to sneak out and visit the public records office," she said. John explained that the public records office was where they kept the records of everyone who has ever lived. I told them I had been alive for a great many years, and that it would not surprise me if the records didn't go back that far.

"Don't be silly," said Wendy. "They've been keeping records since the time of William the Conqueror, and he lived a thousand years ago. I don't think you're as old as all that, Peter."

As I recall, those words were the last that the Darlings and I exchanged before I returned to the Neverland. The week that followed is vague. I recollect being late finding the Lost Boys on four of the seven days, and that on the other three I forgot to find them altogether. Tiger Lily found them, but not until after lunch, by which time they were much vexed. But their vexation was nothing compared to Tink's. What a mood that fairy was in all week long! She had taken to dive-bombing Hook's galleon, and was twice nearly blown to bits by its cannons. "You are a reckless fairy whose luck must soon run out if she's not careful," I warned her.

Tootles raised his hand.

"Yes, Tootles?" I said.

"I seem to remember that in the real world they have something called *anger management.*"

"What does that mean?" asked Tink.

"I think it means they teach angry fairies like you how not to get blown to bits by cannons," said Tootles.

"What nonsense!" scoffed Tink. "First of all, they don't have fairies in the real world, and secondly you came here as a small boy. So you couldn't possibly remember something that specific."

"If Wendy does find your parents," said Nibs, "does that mean you'll return to the real world for good?"

Tink folded her arms and looked away from us. "It could mean exactly that," she said quietly.

I shook my head. "She can't *find* them. Not the *actual* them.

Wendy is only looking for a piece of paper. One where a record of my parents is written."

"What kind of record, Peter?" asked Slightly.

"Who could say? Where they lived, or if they had any other children."

"Or when they died, and where they're buried," said Tink hopefully.

"Yes, Tink, exactly. Where they're buried."

Journal entry no. 16

The night I returned to the real world to see Wendy was a peculiar one. First of all, the stars had shifted their viewing positions in the heavens slightly. It was as though they had rearranged themselves to get a better view of something. I hoped it had nothing to do with me, but whenever I glanced in their direction they flickered strangely, as though they they'd been caught in the act of spying. The winds, too, seemed a little out of sorts, and for the entire journey from the Neverland they blew from behind as though trying to hasten me. Even the Darlings's house as I approached it seemed to lean forwards, as if pushing the window closer. I flew through it and discovered the Darlings sitting cross-legged on the floor playing cards.

The children immediately jumped up, and at once my hand was being shaken and my back patted. They stepped aside to reveal a suit of clothes placed on John's bed – a dark suit that lay beside a white shirt and red tie.

"What's this?" I asked.

"It's John's best suit," said Wendy, squeezing my shoulder.

"It's for you to borrow," said John.

"But why?" I asked.

"Because I've found her. I've found your mother, and come first light I'm taking you to see her."

"You've found my mother?" I whispered.

"Yes," said Michael. "And it's respectful to wear a suit when going to visit one's mother for the first time." I had hidden in cemeteries many times, watching young men in their Sunday best visiting the departed.

"Wearing such a garment is a sign of respect?" I asked.

"Yes, Peter," said Wendy. "Now go across the landing into the bathroom with John and he'll help you dress."

"Come on," said John. "I'll help you put on your tie."

We had to be quiet so as not to wake the parents, and when we returned Wendy gasped and placed a hand over her mouth. "What is it?" I asked.

"John's suit fits you so well! You look so handsome, Peter."

At dawn's first light we left through the window and floated to the ground. Wendy stepped off the kerb and took the lead. "We're in the real world now," she said, "and so we're going to behave like real people."

"Meaning?" I asked.

"Meaning we're going to catch a bus."

It was a Sunday morning, and therefore the bus was not packed with grown-ups on their way to make a crust, and before long it pulled up outside the gates of a cemetery.

The gates to the cemetery were open, and we walked through

them onto a path surrounded by well-kept lawns. Bluebells grew by the side of this path, and I remembered how people in the real world liked to carry flowers to leave on the graves of the departed. Wendy must be a mind-reader. "Why don't you pick some bluebells for your mother?"

"If you think it a good idea."

"I do."

I picked the bluebells and we continued along the path. Before long I saw a row of gravestones and stepped off the path toward them. Wendy took hold of my arm. "We're not going over there," she said.

"Then where?"

Wendy looked to the path's end, where a grand white building nestled amongst tall trees. When we reached this building, Wendy looked up at its many windows as though she wanted to pick one. She turned to me, centred my tie and said, "Now remember your manners."

"My manners? But why?"

Wendy smiled. "Your mother isn't dead. She lives here, Peter."

I looked up at the building. "You are mistaken. My mother would surely have taken leave of the real world long ago."

"No, Peter. Your mother is very old – one hundred and nine years old, to be exact. Your father departed this world many years ago. I'm sorry, but your mother is still here." Wendy floated up towards the window and reached a hand down to me. "Are you coming?"

I caught her up and looked through the window. Inside, an old woman sat in an armchair beside a bed. She was dressed very smartly, and her cheeks were powdered a bright lilac. She clutched the top of a cane, and she smiled at its brass top as though it made her happy.

"The window's latch is open, Peter. And she's expecting us," said Wendy.

"She is?"

"Yes. I met with her yesterday and told her to expect a very important visitor."

I pressed my nose to the window. "Is that why she looks so smart?"

"It is."

"Wendy?"

"Yes?"

"Am I the important visitor?"

Wendy smiled at me and nodded.

"Are you sure? I know I am important in the Neverland, but in the real world I am just a phantom, one who visits people in their dreams."

"Not so us lucky Darlings. You came to visit while we were awake, and now you must do the same for your mother. Her name is Lily, and she told me that not a single day has passed when she hasn't thought about you. And that's why she considers you a *very* important visitor." Wendy looked through the window. "Shall we?"

I opened the window and flew inside with Wendy. We landed in the room in front of my mother. She gazed over her cane at me with eyes of the lightest blue that went slowly from top of my head to the tips of my toes. "*Peter!*" she said suddenly.

I nodded and bowed. "Wendy says you are my mother."

Tears welled in her eyes, and she replied with quick nod that said *I am your mother and of that there is no doubt.* Then, with considerable effort, she huddled over the top of her cane and pushed herself to her feet. Once standing, she allowed her cane to clatter to the floor. Slowly, as though balancing on a tight rope, she opened her arms wide.

"Go on, Peter," said Wendy. "Go and embrace your mother."

I took a single step forwards and studied her face. I clasped my hands to my own and pulled the skin back so that my eyes must have been slits. I looked at my mother, and without asking she did the same, rolling back the loose folds of skin until it was pulled taut over her cheekbones. "Yes, I *have* seen you before. I remember now," I said. With a great effort of will, my mother took a step and wrapped her arms around me. I discovered that my mother was stronger than she looked. Much stronger. She clung tightly to my arms and looked into my eyes. "You used to come and visit me in my dreams, Peter. And you looked *exactly* the age you do now."

"I remember," I said uncertainly. "I'm sorry that I forgot to visit you, Mother. I brought you some bluebells."

My mother took the flowers and smiled. "Thank you. Children do forget, but scarcely a day has gone by when I haven't thought about you."

"How did you lose me?"

"You were poorly, and a hundred years ago doctors weren't so good with their medicines as they are today. Where have you been all these long years?"

"The Neverland."

"And you never thought to grow up?"

"Never. Tink would never forgive me if I did."

"Tink?"

"She's a friend."

"Tinker *Bell*?"

"Yes. How did you know?"

My mother asked Wendy to go to her dresser and open the bottom drawer. "You'll see a small wooden box. Bring it to me," she said, her eyes shining with happiness. Wendy opened the box's lid, and my mother reached in and pulled out a brooch. It was a small silver Tink. "I used to wear this brooch when you were a baby… you were fascinated by it and always reached for it."

"Oh my goodness, look at this," said Wendy, taking another object from the box. It was a little red Indian carved from wood. "It's Tiger Lily," she said. "And… oh, look!" she breathed, tilting the box so I could see inside. "There's a pirate with a hook, a pirate's ship, *and* an alligator."

"They were your favourite playthings, Peter," said my mother.

"Why did you keep them?"

"When you visited me in my dreams, you told me to look after them. You said you would come back for them some day." With a shaky hand my mother picked each of the toys out of the box and placed them inside the pockets of John's jacket. "It makes my heart glad that you remember them, Peter."

"Remember them? I have been with them every day since I went away."

My mother was going to say something else but was silenced by the tinkling ball of light that flew in through the window. Tink hovered close to my shoulder and tinkled furiously.

"What is *that*?" asked my mother.

"It's Tinker Bell. Tink, show yourself to my mother." Tink moved to my other shoulder. "It's okay, I give you permission."

My mother placed the back of her hand to her mouth and tears welled in her eyes.

"There is no need to be upset. Fairies aren't supposed to show themselves in the real world," I said.

"Why ever not?" gulped my mother.

"They aren't supposed to exist. Obstinate fairy! Show yourself to my mother!" Tink appeared as her human-fairy self, and looked every bit like the silver brooch my mother had kept.

"Mother meet Tink. Tink, meet my mother."

My mother extended a very shaky hand towards her. Tink glanced at it and raised her chin as though she would not shake it. "Are you going to stay here with your mother?" she asked me.

"Of course not, foolish fairy. I'm only visiting."

"So, you'll be returning with me to the Neverland?"

"Of course."

"Alright, then." Tink shook my mother's hand and did a fairy curtsey. "You should know that your son is a great hero in the Neverland," she said.

My mother nodded. "He used to tell me so when he visited me in my dreams."

"Then you'll also know that your son isn't exactly known for his humility."

"I had wondered," she replied.

Tink's expression changed, and she looked at me imploringly.

"What's the matter?" I asked.

"It's Hook. I've never known him so angry as he is over what happened at Indian Creek. He's on the warpath, Peter. He's searching the lagoon, and it's only a matter of time before he finds the Lost Boys."

My mother reached out and cupped the side of my face in her palm. "It sounds as though you're needed, my dear lost Peter. I'm so proud of you."

I placed a hand over my mother's, and smiled reassuringly. Withdrawing my hand, I removed John's suit and tie to reveal my own suit of clothes beneath it. "Please don't be sad, Mother. I promise to come back and see you." I took the toys she had given me from the pockets of John's jacket and, as I handed them to Tink for safe-keeping, my mother watched me intently in case I should drop one.

"I am very old, Peter," she said. "So when you return I may not be here." I placed both my hands on her shoulders. "You must not be afraid, Mother. To leave the real world, even as a grown-up, will be an awfully big adventure."

Tink transformed into a ball of light, flew to the window, and tinkled furiously. "I am coming," I said.

Wendy grabbed my arm. "You will come back and visit us, won't you? John and Michael would be awfully sad if you didn't."

"Won't you be sad, Wendy?"

"Of course I will, you beautiful foolish boy. I shall be the saddest of all!" she said, kissing my cheek.

I placed my hand on the spot. "We shall see," I said. "And now I must go and find the Lost Boys before Hook does!" I flew out of the window, came back, waved one last time, then fixed my gaze on the third star on the left, and flew straight on till morning.

The end

Thank you for reading! If you enjoyed these diaries you might also enjoy the latest novel by the same author *The Scratchling Trinity*. The opening pages of which follow here …

Book description: *The Scratchling Trinity*

No one knew the importance of the Scratchling-born, until now.

When orphan called Eric Kettle scratches a desperate cry for help into a wall in 1840, little does he know that it's about to be answered by luckless Max Hastings in 2016. Both Max and Eric are soon to discover that they're Scratchling-born, and that along with the Ellie Swanson, a no-nonsense Scratchling veteran, they are destined to form the Scratchling Trinity. With an evil headmaster, a flying boat, two vengeful giants and a clutch of ghostly helpers along the way, they are off on an incredible adventure!

One
Max Hastings

London, England, 2016

Max Hastings was leaning low over the handlebars of his bike, and pedalling like he'd flipped out. The distance from his school to his home was two and a half kilometres, and Max *had* to smash his personal best time. The reason was written on a scroll of parchment, held closed by a black ribbon and jutting from his blazer pocket like a piston powering him towards a new school-to-home record. He sped up his drive, leapt off his bicycle and sprinted, arms flailing, towards the front door. Once through it, he darted into the living room, unclipped the strap on his bicycle helmet, and cast the helmet onto the couch. Max was twelve years old, of average build if a little on the chunky side, with a shock of white-blond hair that grew every which way except the way Max would have liked. Max drew the scroll from his pocket, gunslinger style, straightened his back, and announced his extraordinary news to his parents: 'I've finally *won* something!'

Mr Hastings looked at Max over the top of his newspaper. 'There must be some mistake,' he said.

'That's what I thought when Miss Hale announced the name of the re-cip-ient.'

Mrs Hastings, who was holding Max's one-year-old sister Maxine, put the baby down in her walker. 'Congratulations, Max! So what have you won?'

Max gazed at the rolled-up parchment in his hand. 'It's a grand prize,

Mum. They picked *my name* out of a hat during the last assembly of term.'

'You've broken your duck, then?' said his astonished father. 'If memory serves me correctly, you've never won anything in your life. Not even when you went through that annoying competitions phase.'

'I know, Dad. I was there.'

'So *what* have you won, exactly?' asked Mrs Hastings.

'No idea.'

'Well, then, I suggest you untie that ribbon and find out.'

Max glanced from the parchment to his mother and back again. Mrs Hastings placed her hands on her hips. 'Whatever is the matter with you?'

'It's just so ...'

'So what?' said his father.

'Official-looking.'

'Which must bode well for the prize,' said Mr Hastings, putting down his newspaper. 'Give it here, son. I'll open it.'

Max shook his head. 'I'll do it.' He untied the ribbon and unfurled the parchment. His lips moved slowly as he read it, and his brow furrowed.

'Well?' pressed his mother.

His father leaned forwards in his armchair. 'What are you the recipient *of?*'

'Of a life-time membership ...' murmured Max.

'A life-time membership of *what?*' said his mother testily.

Max read the words slowly. 'The Ancient Order of Wall Scratchings.'

'Of *what?*' said Mr Hastings.

'Of *wall* scratchings,' repeated his mother helpfully.

'But what does that even mean?' mumbled Max, his eyes glued to the parchment for some clue.

'Oh, for pity's sake, give it to me,' said his mother, sliding it from his hand.

Mrs Hastings scanned the parchment. 'Oh, my goodness. Max has been invited to a private viewing of their wall scratchings tomorrow, at Mansion House!'

Mr Hastings cleared his throat. 'What? The place where the Lord Mayor of London lives?'

'Yes!'

'There must be some mistake,' asserted Mr Hastings.

Mrs Hastings shook her head. 'No mistake. The Ancient Order of Wall Scratchings, Mansion House, City of London, London.'

Max sighed. 'Trust me to win a grand *booby* prize. Tomorrow's *Saturday,* not to mention the first day of the Christmas holidays. I'm not going.'

'Not going?' echoed Mrs Hastings.

316

'Why would I? Since when was I interested in *wall scratchings*? I don't even know what they are!'

'They're scratchings on walls, presumably,' said Mr Hastings, happy to apply his keen insight to the problem at hand.

'Well, whatever they are,' said Mrs Hastings, glancing at the parchment in her hand, 'it says here that they have the world's largest collection of them.'

'Not helping, Mum,' said Max. He went to the dining table and opened his laptop, muttering absently to himself as he typed *the ancient order of wall scratchings* into the search engine. He sat back in his seat and breathed a sigh of relief. 'Just as I thought. There's no such place. It doesn't even exist! ... What are you doing?' Max asked his mother.

'There's a phone number on here. I'm calling them.'

'But—' said Max.

'But nothing. I intend to get to the bottom of these ... these *scratchings*.' She tapped her foot impatiently as the phone rang at the other end of the line.

A woman with a cut-glass English accent answered. 'Thank you for calling the Ancient Order of Wall Scratchings. How may I help you?'

'My name is Mrs Hastings, and my son Max has just won a free membership to your organisation.'

'Hearty congratulations!' said the woman.

'Be that as it may, there's no mention of you on the internet. No mention whatsoever.'

The woman drew a deep breath. 'Ours is an ancient organisation, Mrs Hastings. As such we frown upon all modern conventions.'

'Alright. But your address appears to be the very same as the Lord Mayor of London's.'

'That's right.'

'And the Lord Mayor?'

'What about him?'

'He's happy to share his residence with your organisation?'

'The Ancient Order of Wall Scratchings has been located at this spot for over a thousand years, Mrs Hastings. Since the year 1065, to be exact. The first Lord Mayor didn't move in until some seven hundred years later, in 1752.'

'*And?*'

'And since then we've had no complaints from any Lord Mayor in office.'

A man's voice came on the line. 'Max is going to benefit greatly from his membership, Mrs Hastings,' he asserted.

'*Max is going to benefit greatly from his membership,*' repeated Mrs

Hastings, as though in a trance.

'And he'll meet a great many important people.'

'*And he'll meet a great many important people,*' echoed Mrs Hastings.

'People,' the voice went on, 'who will be able to help him in his chosen career.'

'He wants to test video games for a living,' murmured Mrs Hastings.

'*Help him in his chosen career,*' said the man, raising his voice.

'*Help him in his chosen career,*' repeated Mrs Hastings obediently.

'Tell Max he's welcome to bring a friend tomorrow. Goodbye.'

'Goodbye!' said Mrs Hastings, putting down the phone. She turned to Max. 'You're welcome to take a friend tomorrow,' she said, grinning terrifically from ear to ear.

Max scratched absently at his left cheekbone, just below his eye, where there was a birthmark that looked as though someone had signed their initials in black ink. 'O-kay. Are you alright, Mum?'

'Never better,' she replied. Mrs Hastings's smile then did the seemingly impossible and grew wider still. Max had never realised his mother had so many teeth.

Two
Eric Kettle

Yorkshire, England, December 1st, 1840

Inside a carriage drawn by two horses, a frail boy sat shivering beside a giant of a man. The man was expressionless and granite-faced, and indeed any onlooker might have thought him cut from granite. The only clue to his being flesh-and-blood was the smile that curled his lips whenever the carriage hit a pothole and the boy yelped. The man took up most of a bench designed for three adults, squashing his young companion against the carriage door like an item of worthless baggage. The boy's name was Eric Kettle, and Eric looked so fragile that he might break in two every time the carriage lurched over a bump in the road – of which there were a great many, and many more potholes besides. Despite these hardships, Eric's saucer-like brown eyes gazed with extraordinary hope from a face gaunt with hunger.

It was gone midnight when the carriage came to a halt at its destination: the St Bart's School for Boys. The school was a crumbling mansion that rose from the Yorkshire countryside like a vampire's abandoned lair. The carriage door was opened by the driver, who was hidden by an entire closet's worth of coats, scarves and gloves. The brute heaved himself out of his seat. 'Fall in behind, sir,' he grumbled at his young ward. Eric followed as quickly as his shivering legs would allow. He hugged himself for warmth, and stumbled towards the promise of heat beyond the door that now opened for them. Once through the door, Eric wondered if it hadn't actually been warmer outside.

They'd been admitted by a pale and hungry-looking boy swaddled in a threadbare coat several sizes too large. He was carrying a paraffin lamp, and, without uttering a single word, he illuminated their path across a cavernous entrance hall and up a sweeping staircase. Two flights up, he lit the way down a long corridor before finally stopping outside a door, on which a gold plaque read: *Headmaster. Augustus Mann.* Augustus took a key from his pocket and unlocked the door. He turned to the boy carrying the lamp, now hastily lighting a candle by its flame, and snatched the lamp from his grasp. The boy scurried off on bow legs, and Eric watched the candle light until it disappeared from sight at the end of a corridor. 'Fall in, sir!' came the gruff voice of Augustus Mann, from inside the study.

The headmaster placed the lamp on a desk piled high with books, and pointed to a spot on the wooden floor before the desk marked with an X in chalk. 'Stand there, arms at your sides, chin held high. That's it. And stop your shivering.'

'I'll try, sir, but it's just so …'

'Say the word *cold,* and as God is my witness, I'll thrash you where you stand. Perhaps you think that I should light a fire for you? Waste good wood? Is that what you think?'

'No, sir.'

'Speak up when I address you!'

'No, sir!'

'No what?'

'No, I don't think you should waste good wood on me, sir.'

'Spoilt! That's what you've been. Spoilt to the core.'

Eric shook his head. 'They work us very hard at the orphanage, sir.'

The headmaster sat down and opened a folder on his desk. 'It says here that your father went off to seek his fortune the day after you were born. Wherever he went, he must have liked it there.'

Eric smiled. 'Do you think so? Why do you say so, sir?'

'Liked it more than he liked *you,* anyway.' Eric's smile vanished as the headmaster grunted and went on, 'I see your mother went looking for him soon after, and whether or not she found him, nobody knows. Never seen nor heard from again. But whatever she *did* find, she must have preferred it to you.' The headmaster observed Eric through narrowed eyes. 'What is it about you that so vexes others, *boy*?'

Eric's gaze dropped to the ground. 'I'm sure I don't know, sir.'

'After so many years in an orphanage, I dare say you thought your ship had come in, with your name chosen from a hat to receive a scholarship to attend a fine Yorkshire school of good repute. Thought you'd get yourself a proper education, eh? Those abominable do-gooders, passing their laws that say the likes of *me* must look with charitable eyes upon the likes of *you.* The paltry compensation I will receive for your keep will barely cover my costs.'

'I'm very sorry, sir.'

'You will be. The fact is, you are worth more to me *dead* than you are alive – a fact that doesn't bode at all well for you,' said the headmaster, rising from his chair and turning to face a collection of canes hanging on the wall. He stroked his grey moustache thoughtfully, smiled, and then reached for one.

'Please,' implored Eric. 'I don't know why my parents left me. I did nothing wrong. I was just a baby, and that's the God's truth, sir.'

The headmaster turned and swiped the cane back and forth to gauge its suitability. 'I would strongly advise you not to take the Lord's name in vain. Not in this establishment, *sir*, or God help me ...'

As Augustus Mann made his way around his desk towards him, Eric closed his eyes and willed himself back at the orphanage. It didn't work, although the heavy blow that struck his face might almost have launched him back there. Eric's legs gave way beneath him, and he collapsed to the ground, groaning and clutching a cheek that felt savaged by a thousand bee stings. Augustus Mann loomed over him, cane in hand. 'Down at the first lash? Pathetic! That is what you are, pathetic. Is it any wonder your parents left you?' The headmaster yawned, ambled back around his desk, placed the cane back on its hook and walked towards the door. 'You can spend the night there on the floor, like the dog you undoubtedly are. Although I can assure you that your life expectancy is considerably shorter than a dog's. A truth I intend to take *considerable* comfort from,' he yawned. Augustus Mann stepped through the door, closing it and locking it behind him.

Eric dragged himself into a corner, where he huddled miserably for warmth, trying to remember a legend he'd heard some years before at the orphanage: *If a child of kind heart and noble mind is ever in mortal danger, all he needs do is scratch a message of help into a stone wall, and help will find him.* Eric fumbled down his side for one of the safety pins that kept his clothes from falling apart, and with it he scratched the following words in tiny letters into the wall: *If ever a boy was in mortal danger, it's me. Please, if anyone's there, help me!*

Thank you for reading! If you enjoyed this sample, *The Scratchling Trinity* is available from Amazon.

Made in the USA
Middletown, DE
04 September 2017